ALL THE BEST THINGS

LINDA SHANTZ

eBook edition ISBN: 978-1-990436-13-0

Paperback ISBN: 978-1-990436-14-7

Hardcover ISBN: ISBN 978-1-990436-16-1

For my brothers

CHAPTER ONE

IF SOMEONE HAD CHOSEN to write a novel about her, this is not the storyline they would have gone with, but Emilie loved her life. It wasn't perfect, but what was?

She loved being the last to leave the physiotherapy clinic where she worked, shutting down her computer after updating her patient notes; turning off the lights, locking the clinic door behind her. She loved her trusty Honda Civic, hopping in it for the short drive home. She loved the eclectic playlist she sang along with, and she loved her brother-in-law for putting it together for her. He had the best taste. In music and in women, because he had, of course, married her sister.

She loved the farm she shared with them, where she got to indulge in her passion — retraining retired racehorses for new careers — and they got to indulge in theirs, breeding and training those Thoroughbreds for the races.

She loved her dog, the happy black Lab she'd adopted Christmas Eve, Holly, bouncing enthusiastically in welcome when released from her kennel, ready to go for their evening romp. As long as Emilie didn't mention food. If she did, Holly dove back into her kennel, no matter how badly she had to go, waiting till Emilie served up a treat, if not her dinner.

She loved this time of night. It wasn't her favourite — that would always be dawn — but there was something magical about the spectrum of orange deepening to indigo as it curved away from the horizon after the sun had dropped below it. The gentle music of the cicadas and frogs provided a soothing soundtrack.

The novelist would no doubt have written in a love interest, but while her own attempts at actual plotlines had come up short, a man proved to be unnecessary for her to feel fulfilled. She had enough. The good job, the satisfying hobby, great family and friends, and Holly the Labrador. If Mr. Right came along tomorrow, she wouldn't chase him away, but she wasn't waiting for him. She was living her life, with or without him.

She wandered around the farm with Holly. Some of the horses were tucked into their stalls, others wispy shadows in the fields behind white stud rails. She didn't even mind the mosquitoes. Okay, she did. They were aggravating. Holly, with her lustrous black double coat, didn't seem to care.

The June days were warm enough that most of the horses lived outside this time of year and came in for the hottest hours of the day. The exceptions were the layups and her project horses, all of which lived in the training barn, and she switched on the lights to the tune of their hopeful nickers. Night check had been done by the farm manager two hours ago, but Emilie's nightly walkabout was extra assurance that all was well on the property.

She peeked into the stalls of the occupants whose heads didn't immediately appear over the gate yokes, the attentiveness of those who did due to the realistic assumption their vigilance would be rewarded with a peppermint. The others dozed, her arrival not enough to rouse them.

This one was on stall rest, a post-operative case following knee surgery to remove chips. That one was waiting for the vet to give the go-ahead before starting back into light work as part of rehabilitation for tendonitis. Her project ponies waited expectantly. None of them would ever miss out on their late-night treat.

First was Excursion, an older gelding born and raised on the farm, retired this spring after a solid career. She'd started working with him three weeks ago and had a riding lesson with him set up for Friday. She hadn't taken a lesson in years. Time in the saddle when she'd been in school had meant helping gallop at the racetrack or teaching horses like Excursion the very basic-basics, nothing advanced — just enough to help them find their next job. She was excited. And terrified. It was going to be great.

Next was Miss Talk About It, a five-year-old mare she'd taken on for New Chapter, the local Thoroughbred retirement group. Volunteering for New Chapter had been Emilie's pet project for a few years. Last fall when their parents had moved back to Montreal, her sister Liv had agreed that Emilie should make a stall or two available for overflow from New Chapter's home base farm. Miss Talk About It was the first. Someone was coming tomorrow to try her. If that was her person, another horse waited to fill the stall.

The dark face of one of the racetrack layups appeared, attracted by the crunch of peppermints. He craned his neck over the stall gate hopefully. Trop was a three-year-old colt who had yet to run a race and her sister Liv had sent him home for a little holiday when she'd decided he'd benefit from the removal of his troublesome manly bits. He was a brat, always ready with a quick nip, and his inability to focus on training at the track had earned him next week's appointment with the vet.

Emilie grinned as he dove for the peppermint, keeping her

palm flat and her fingers safe. "Your cuteness is a problem." She swept his generous forelock to the side to take in the ever-present mischief in his big dark eyes.

She flipped off the bright fluorescents and left the barn, a yard light high on a hydro pole flooding the immediate area. Holly snuffled along the edges of the laneway as she walked out of its domain. The two mares in the big pasture to Emilie's right, near a small barn that housed the farm office, raised their heads at the motion of woman and dog, and the smaller, darker one rumbled a greeting. Chiquenaude, the horse Emilie credited with bringing Liv and Nate together. That was as much of an accomplishment as the wins and earnings the mare had accumulated at the track. Now Chique was officially a brood-mare, in foal with her first baby, due the end of January.

Passing the house she shared with Liv and Nate, Emilie headed to the rear of the property along the lane adjacent to the training track. It was dark here, nothing artificial to illuminate her path, but the lack of light pollution made it the perfect place to stop and throw her head back. She stared up at the expanse of the sky. It always made her feel like a child again, counting the brighter, steadier planets amid the endless tiny, flickering pinpricks of the stars. It might make a girl feel lonely and small. But it didn't. Instead, it felt like a hug; a reminder things were fine exactly how they were. She breathed in and threw her arms wide... then swatted at a mosquito. Holly ran back to her from whatever scent she'd been engrossed in and Emily propelled herself forward again, the Lab a prancing, companionable presence at her side.

How could she complain about her life? About this magnificent sky, this beautiful farm, those wonderful horses, her amazing family. They even, finally, had a great farm manager who everyone adored. For once, everything felt settled.

The stallion barn was quiet, but she walked through just to

be sure. Just Lucky, who topped the sire ranks in Canada right now, napped in his deep bed of straw, all curled up with his nose resting on the golden cushion. So cute when he was sleeping, but he was a rascal when he was awake — just like his son, Trop. Next door, Starway, no slouch in the breeding shed himself, stood with hip hitched, one hind leg cocked, resting but aware. Both had hay and water, so she left them to it.

Kerrie's cottage was dark, the farm manager probably asleep. She'd have all the horses fed before the staff arrived at seven in the morning so she went to bed religiously at ten, except on those occasions she joined in on the fun of a bonfire or barbecue with the staff. Kerrie had initiated those events; just part of the above and beyond that made her such a perfect addition to the farm.

The main house was also dark when Emilie returned, save for a light in the kitchen. Nate and Liv would be fast asleep by now too, because they were up even earlier than Kerrie to head into the racetrack. Emilie passed through her apartment to the door that opened into the main part of the house because, even though the apartment had a kitchenette, Nate was a better cook than she was, and when their schedules didn't allow her to join him and Liv for dinner, Nate usually left her something in the fridge. She was always hungry after she and Holly walked, the short-term benefit of the snack-size yogurt she'd scarfed down at work a few hours ago long since gone.

Holly bounded ahead of her, disappearing around the corner to the indistinct murmur of a voice. Clearly the kitchen wasn't empty.

"Hey, Nate. What are you still doing up?"

Her brother-in-law sat at the breakfast nook, flipping absently through something on his phone with one hand while he scratched Holly behind the ears with the other. He lifted his head, smiling, his blue eyes tired, and dropped his phone on the table to run fingers through his blond hair as he yawned.

"On the phone to Calgary," he said.

As soon as Emilie dipped into Holly's food container, the Lab abandoned him, diving into her stainless steel bowl before Emilie even set it on the stone tile of the kitchen floor.

"Everything all right?" Emilie asked as she opened the fridge and spotted the leftover salad and salmon waiting for her. She set it on the counter and opened the cutlery drawer. Should she heat the salmon, or just dive right in?

"Oh yeah," he assured her. "Time difference is all. I was talking to Tim."

She felt his eyes on her when he tacked on that last bit, waiting for a reaction. She wasn't going to give him one.

When Nate had started working on the farm almost six years ago now — where had the time gone? — Emilie's playful crush had turned into an easy friendship. As soon as everyone learned he had a younger brother, they'd all decided she and Tim were meant to be. She'd let herself believe it, for a while. Why not? If he was as good-looking and kind as Nate, she was in.

Except he wasn't. Sure, he was seriously attractive — more so, even, than Nate. He had a body any girl would swoon over, thanks to being a professional hockey player. But the rest of it? The whole nice guy thing? Nope. All the looks in the world didn't make up for what he lacked.

Even after he'd given her the cold shoulder at Liv and Nate's wedding, she'd thought there might be a chance when, for some reason, he'd friended her on Facebook on Christmas Day. And for some reason, Emilie had accepted. She was convinced it was because of Holly, who she'd introduced to Nate and Liv while FaceTiming them when they were in Calgary with Nate's family for the holiday. Tim had appeared on-screen reluctantly to say a no-doubt coerced hello, but the smiling Labrador had brought out something resembling warmth, so that must've weakened her. They'd started a cute back-and-forth correspondence through Messenger. It had been fun, for a few months.

Then he'd ghosted her.

So his circumstances had changed when he'd been sent back to the minors after a stint playing for the Flames — Calgary's NHL hockey team. But nothing? Really? Not a peep. She was sure he hadn't lost his ability to use technology.

So, that was done. She was all for second chances, but she'd given him that. A third one would just make her look like a fool. No, thank you.

She didn't hate him. She didn't feel enough of anything for him to invest in that kind of grudge. The best thing about all of it was that he was thousands of miles away. These days, he barely even entered her thoughts.

"And how is Tim?" she asked, crossing her arms and leaning back against the counter.

Nate put his usual ready smile on hold. "The injury's got him down. I know the season's over, but he's pretty dedicated. He's not dealing so great with not being able to train."

She'd felt bad, really she had, when Tim had hurt his knee in a game with the farm team, necessitating surgery to repair the torn ACL. It had to suck, working that hard and hoping to get another chance at the big time, only for that to happen. Knees were tricky. She saw similar cases all the time at the clinic. Healing right took a lot of patience.

"Like brother, like brother?" she quipped.

Nate's lips twisted in a wry grin. "Smartass."

Last summer Nate, a jockey, had been the injured one, the back trauma he'd suffered in a spill at the historic Saratoga Racetrack earning him his own surgery and subsequent time off and rehab. Somehow he'd worked through it and now, here he was, happily married to her sister and back riding at the top of his game, recently adding the richest race on the planet, the Dubai World Cup, to his list of career achievements. At least he'd become an adult.

Which included not teasing Emilie about Tim anymore, something she was grateful for. He had to know they'd stopped talking, didn't he? Or maybe he was just too wrapped up in his own life as a newlywed and leading rider to concern himself with hers.

"You want anything?" She took the water jug from the fridge and poured herself a glass, then, after setting glass and plate on the table, sat across from him.

"Nah. I need to get to bed." He slid to the end of the bench behind the kitchen nook and stood, phone in his hand, then paused in the doorway. "I invited him to come out for a bit. The change of scenery will do him good."

"You *what?*" The reaction she'd so effortlessly avoided after the initial mention of Tim's name charged back in.

"I figure he can stay in my old apartment, seeing as it's empty at the moment." Nate's tone stayed casual, but his eyes continued to gauge her carefully.

Really, what could she say? *Why didn't you ask me first? This is my home too. No, he can't come. Or if he does, tell him to bring a bodyguard, because I can't promise I won't try to kill him.* Jerk. Tim, and his brother too.

"See you tomorrow Em."

As soon as Nate slipped away, Emilie dumped the rest of her water down the drain and found a bottle of wine, from which she poured herself a generous portion.

So she was wrong about Tim. She did hate him.

CHAPTER TWO

THE KITCHEN HAD ALWAYS LOOKED like this — at least for the duration of his memory. The walls were sunny yellow, the appliances the avocado green of a bygone era. Mom liked bright colours, but even she wasn't terribly fond of that green. Word was the ugly fridge and stove had come with the house, so they were old. Old appliances lasted forever, however, and Dad was cheap. No — "budget-conscious" wasn't that it? Tim couldn't grouse about that, though. That thriftiness had given him and Nate hockey camp growing up, and Phil whatever kind of summer recreation they sent smart kids to.

Either way, modern stainless would never be seen in their home as long as those old appliances did the job. They'd probably outlive the Miller family.

This was probably also the only house left in the universe that had an actual, old-school, phone, the curved handle fitting neatly into the cradle as he replaced it; a dially wheel thing instead of buttons. Is that something he could put down as a job skill if the whole pro hockey gig didn't pan out? *Knows how to use a rotary phone.* He'd just leave out the part about talking on the phone being his least favourite thing to do. He didn't really like talking at all. When he did, he usually got himself into something he wanted no part of.

Like what he might have just agreed to. How had Nate convinced him it would be a good idea to go to Toronto for the summer? He'd made the fancy horse farm he lived on sound like Club Med, with its running trails, lap pool and brand new weight and exercise room. But the real zinger had been a loaded comment Nate dropped into the conversation.

"Trust me. Even though it was under duress, moving out of that basement was the best thing that ever happened to me." In other words — saying it without saying it — *you need to grow up. Get out of your parents' house.* Nate might as well have been right there in front of him, poking him annoyingly in the chest. It stung because it was true.

He nudged Rita with his toe, the fluffy Golden Retriever rolling onto her back, tongue lolling as he rubbed her belly. Dexter, the big male, sulked with head on paws, wedged between a kitchen chair and the counter cupboards. Tim's injury had put a stop to their runs together. Dad still took the dogs out, but Dex loved those runs as much as Tim did.

Absent-mindedly fingering one of the small incisions on his knee, he stared at the crutches leaning against the wall. Those would be fun on a plane. Maybe his physiotherapist would say it was a bad idea. Give him an excuse to say no. *Right.* She'd been trying to prod him out of his rut. *You don't really need those anymore. I know you won't overdo it.* That was a safe bet, given his refusal to push it, even when she'd assured him the knee could take it.

He missed Nate, though. Even before their oldest brother, Phil, had died — and that had been horrible — he'd felt he'd already lost a brother. Nate was the one he'd been closest to; the one who'd picked on him, and stuck up for him. He'd never been friends with Phil — there was just that little bit too much of an age difference — but he felt like he'd been friends with Nate. They were more than just brothers. But then Nate had left, and the fact it was Phil's fault didn't bring Phil and Tim any closer. No one had asked him to take sides, but he'd been on Nate's side all the way; not that it was worth anything, because Nate was thousands of miles away. They'd only seen each other three times since the day Phil had married Nate's ex-girlfriend. Who could blame Nate for bolting after that?

But now Phil was dead, and Nate had a new life. One Tim had only visited — once last summer after Nate had gotten hurt in a riding accident; once last winter, when he'd gone to Nate's wedding in Florida. Neither had been a time to catch up; to reclaim some of what he'd cherished. The only time they'd had together, just the two of them, was when Nate had come back to Calgary for Phil and Cindy's funeral. Before Nate's accident. Before the beach wedding. This time would be a proper visit, and he wanted that.

There was a complication, though.

Emilie.

It wasn't as if he could avoid her. But he didn't know how to make up for what he'd done.

Their written chats had been clever, lighthearted. Casual. That day in March — the one when they'd told him he was being sent back down to the minors after finally getting called up to Calgary's NHL team before Christmas — he just couldn't be the way he had been with her; the way she expected him to be. She wouldn't want to be exposed to the version of him that was devastated by the news. He'd already chased her away once with his churlish front at the wedding. They'd built this careful, fun thing online and neither of them had crossed into talking about serious stuff. They weren't friends like that, not yet. He wasn't ready for them to be.

Some days he thought he should just take the chance, tell her he'd been upset, but he always talked himself out of it. She wouldn't want to hear it; be reminded of that guy on the beach. First impressions always carried weight. The more time he let pass without responding, the more it seemed better to let it be. He needed to focus on his game so that next season he was back in the NHL. There wasn't room for anything more. Then when he'd wrecked his knee, he'd given up on the idea entirely because everything — his career, his whole future — was a mess.

If he went to Ontario, he was going to have to face her.

It could be his chance to smooth things over — but how could he articulate the thought process behind his behaviour? He knew it was bad, and she was so normal. She'd never understand a brain like his. Emilie was everything he wasn't. Forward. Cheerful. Friendly. Realistically, he had no shot at redemption — which would make living near her uncomfortable. As if he wasn't nearly always uncomfortable, one way or another, except when he was on the ice, the one place he couldn't be until his knee healed. His only hope was to apologize, like he should have done long ago — and no matter how much harder it would be in person, if that's what it was going to take, he'd do it.

Mom swept into the room, dressed like she was going out, and the two Goldens clattered to their feet to investigate the bustle. Tuesday night, choir practice. Just one of the many things she did to keep herself busy, now that her sons were older, or gone. Tim was the only one left to notice not one of them involved her husband.

"How's your brother?" she asked, smiling. Nate always made her smile, whether he was in front of her or not.

"You know. All happy and sh —" He cut the word short but grinned unapologetically.

Mom scowled at him, but didn't reprimand him for the near-slip. Nate swore more than he did, so how could she?

"He invited me out for a few weeks," he said, leaving out the part about how he'd more or less agreed, just to see how she reacted. He and Nate hadn't actually nailed down a duration. If he went, he'd play it by ear. It would all depend on how quickly he healed; how soon he could be back on skates. As soon as he could lace up and hit the ice, he'd come home.

"That's a wonderful idea." Mom beamed. The fact she didn't look surprised made Tim bet she and Nate had already talked about it. They talked all the time. Definitely more than she and Tim did, and they lived in the same house. "Are you going to go?"

"I'll think about it. See what my PT says at tomorrow's appointment."

She grabbed her keys from a hook near the stairwell that led to the side door. "I think it would be good for you."

"But —"

She stopped and gave him a stern look. "But what?"

But what about you and Dad? he wanted to say. *What if, without me around, the last son at home, you decide you don't need to be together anymore?* He shook his head. "Nothing. Have a nice time at choir practice."

He wasn't sure it was a good idea to leave Mom and Dad right now, but what could he say? He couldn't confront them. Nate didn't know. How could he? Tim was sure Mom hadn't let on anything was awry and Nate would never guess. He was all blissed out with his successful life in Ontario. Good for him.

Mom's smile returned. She lifted her purse from the hook next to where the keys had been, and soon he heard her footsteps descending the six steps, followed by the click open, then shut, of the door. The two Goldens waved their tails as they supervised her departure.

He stood, reaching for the crutches, pausing to look out the window as Mom's sedan roared to life; watching as she backed it out the driveway. Pivoting on his good leg, he stepped and swung his way out of the kitchen and down the hall. If he went to Ontario, shouldn't he wait till he was convinced he didn't need these things anymore? Till he could do proper exercises and not feel like so much of a cripple?

But if he went, crutches and all, Nate would help him. Which meant he should go — because that was the most important thing. He had to be ready by the time training camp started. Because if he wasn't... what was he going to do?

He went to his room, which wasn't really his room, but navigating the basement stairs with the sticks multiple times a day had seemed reason enough for his mother to convince him to camp out upstairs while he healed. It was really the guest room, a strange hybrid of the space he'd once shared as a kid with Nate. The room next to it that had been Phil's was now a combination of Dad's office and Mom's sewing room — not that they were ever in there at the same time.

His and Nate's hockey trophies sat on a shelf. Phil had played house league so Dad had probably deemed anything he might have accumulated insignificant. Had Phil taken them, when he'd moved out, or were they downstairs in a box somewhere? There were framed photos of Nate's first win in the big horse race they'd watched on TV two years ago, the Queen's Plate. The bed was a double, outfitted in mismatched linens. Some of their old books filled a shelf: fantasy and sci fi and old textbooks. None of it made him nostalgic. The hockey stuff represented something he'd been groomed for his whole life. A duty to his father. A duty he was currently failing at.

Maybe his presence was interfering with Mom and Dad focusing on their relationship and it was best to give them space to sort it out. But it scared him to think without him around they might find they no longer had anything in common.

He slumped onto the bed, stacking pillows against the headboard and under the crook of his knees, then grabbed the thick fantasy novel from the bedside table, finding his spot. He wanted to lose himself in the pages; forget about what the injury might mean for his career. And about his parents. And about how he'd made Emilie hate him when he really, really liked her. Not that anyone knew that but him.

The heroine in the book made him think of her. She was strong, and brave, and beautiful, shooting arrows from the back of her horse. And she was totally going to go for the tall, swarthy sellsword, helping him see the error of his ways and turning him into a good guy. There was a reason they called this stuff fantasy.

He should just stay home. Because guys like him, who made it to twenty-three with no idea how to talk to girls his age, did not end up with women like Emilie Lachance.

The ping of his phone pulled him out of his morose thoughts and he grabbed it and activated the screen. The text notification was from Nate, telling him to check his email. When he did, he found a ticket for a direct flight, YYC to YYZ — Calgary to Toronto. First class.

An all-expenses paid trip to Club Med King City, Ontario.

He stared at it for what had to be a full minute before replying to the text. *Thank you. You shouldn't have.*

But Nate had. Backing out now would be pretty rude.

It was a big farm, wasn't it? Nate said Tim could have his old apartment, which wasn't even close to the house where Nate and Liv and Emilie lived. And Emilie was a busy person. She was always at work or riding horses or volunteering for charities. She would want nothing to do with him, and he would stay out of her way. Nate's best friend Will, who used to live just down the street from them here in Calgary, was in Toronto now and around a lot because he was dating a neighbour, Liv's best friend Faye. And Tim had hung out with Faye's older brother, Dean, at the wedding. He was a cool guy. So there would be plenty of people he knew.

People who weren't Emilie.

CHAPTER THREE

The rain drummed a steady beat on the steel roof of the indoor arena, making it impossible to hear anything else, the soft footfalls of the chestnut mare circling around her lost in the din. Emilie was glad she wasn't galloping at the track today, spending the morning sweltering in a rain suit, getting covered in mud. She got to play here, where it was dry. The forecast for tomorrow — Saturday, when she would go into Woodbine and help — was sunny.

Miss Talk About It was learning how to jog in a nice, relaxed arc on the end of the woven cotton line. Baby race-horses rarely got more than a mild introduction to longeing when they were started — sometimes they were merely chased around briefly in a round pen, just to get used to the feel of a saddle on their back, a girth under their belly. Emilie usually began from scratch to reintroduce the skill. It wasn't her favourite way to pass time — who enjoyed standing on the end of a rope watching a horse go round and round? But it was in the required skill set for a show horse, so she taught it.

The trial ride with a potential adopter had gone okay, but

Emilie didn't think the woman was "the one." Miss Talk was just a little greener than the woman wanted, so the mare would probably be around a while longer. With that daisy-cutter, ground-eating trot, someone would snatch her up for the hunter ring soon enough.

It was quieter in the barn; the ceiling dampening the sounds from outside and accentuating the ones within — the rustle of hay, the nostril-clearing snorts of horses, the even clip of Miss Talk's shoes on the concrete floor as she ambled in next to Emilie. The mare was good enough in crossties now — another skill most racehorses didn't learn — for Emilie to feel confident she'd stand while the polos came off and her feet were picked. Outside the wide door at the other end, rain no longer gushed, petering to a drizzle. By the time she and the mare walked outside it had completely stopped, sunlight reflecting off the puddles left behind. She scanned the sky for a rainbow.

She turned Miss Talk out in one of the smaller grassy paddocks near the barn and the mare immediately rolled, because that was what any self-respecting horse did when presented with perfect mud conditions. Excursion, next up, had likewise indulged. It had to be therapeutic. She'd heard some old Standardbred trainer's wives' tale that horses did that when they hurt somewhere, like it acted as a poultice or some-thing. If that was the case, Excursion hurt all over, which she seriously doubted because he received regular massage therapy and chiropractic, and Emilie was learning bodywork herself, transferring her knowledge of human anatomy to the horses. Maybe one day, after practicing enough on the horses, she'd be able to give up working on humans in favour of them. She didn't mind people, but given the choice, she'd pick this. Except, of course, she had yet to have a human show up for an appointment covered in mud.

"You are a little piggy," she told the gelding as she curried away the already dry grey layer on his bay coat, crusted extra-thick at his withers. The dried lumps in his mane made him look like he had dreadlocks. Thank goodness it was short.

The rumble of a motorcycle engine disrupted the usual farm sounds, coming closer before it cut abruptly. Emilie cursed under her breath. *Great. She's early, and I need an extra ten minutes to get this guy clean.* She should have predicted Excursion's state. It wasn't as if slathering himself like this was new.

She attacked the clumps in his mane with extra vigor, twisting and bending them with her fingers so the dirt broke up into dust — covering his neck, the sleeves of her sunshirt, and the mat under their feet — then worked a hairbrush carefully through the tangled parts. There was no hurrying this; it wouldn't speed the process up. Finally, after she dipped her brush in the short bucket of water next to the grooming kit and ran the bristles from the roots to the ends, the mane was lying in a straight line again. Excursion shook his head, tickled by the water dribbling on his neck, and Emilie sighed as his mane now looked like a disrupted keyboard. Oh well. It was clean, anyway. She finished currying quickly and grabbed her brushes, flicking away the dislodged dirt.

The click of boots on concrete approaching sounded like a gunslinger in an old western, the gentle echo ringing through the stable. The zippers of the chaps the woman wore were probably responsible for that, though Emilie wouldn't have been surprised to see spurs. It would suit the look, even if the big rowels she imagined likely weren't appropriate gear for either a motorcycle rider or an eventing coach. The woman's top half was clad in a leather jacket, open to show a white shirt underneath. Golden-brown hair was pulled into a braid, and as the coach's head shifted side to side, taking in the stalls, Emilie caught the flip of the end of the plait, almost at the woman's waist.

She dropped her brushes into the tote and wiped her palms on her dusty grey breeches before smiling and offering a hand. "Jodi?" she guessed.

The woman's palm was warm and felt damp, probably just because her own was dried out by the dirt-removal process.

"And you must be Emilie."

Emilie thought she detected traces of a British accent, but it might just have been Jodi's diction. It made her self-conscious about her own. When she was in the barn, she left the professional tone she used at the clinic behind and fell into something more relaxed with the farm help. It got even worse at the track.

"And this is?" Jodi held a hand out to the bay gelding waiting in the crossties.

"Excursion," Emilie said. "Possibly the only horse around who managed to escape my brother-in-law's penchant for finding nicknames for everyone."

Excursion dipped his muzzle into Jodi's palm and Emilie breathed a sigh of relief when the gelding didn't make it glaringly obvious he regularly received treats.

She ducked to his off side and retrieved her brushes. "I'm sorry for being a little behind. I intended to be on him by the time you got here. He was just a little muddier than I expected. Which I should have anticipated after the rain we got yesterday." She was rambling. Nerves! Excitement and apprehension faced off in her brain now that the instructor was here.

"That's all right. I know I'm early. Lovely farm."

"Thank you," Emilie said, settling back into the rhythm of grooming. She ran a rub rag over the gelding's coat to bring out the shine, then quickly secured boots on his front legs. Faster than polos, but also justified because the ring outside was probably going to be sloppy. "So how long have you and Nicole known each other?" Nicole galloped for Liv at the track — she was one of those hybrids who lived in both the racehorse and show horse worlds.

Jodi chuckled. "Since Pony Club!"

"I always wished I'd been in Pony Club. Is it too late?" Emilie grinned, setting a clean white saddle pad on Excursion's back before placing the saddle on top. Once she'd buckled the girth, she grabbed her helmet and slipped on the bridle.

"You're fast," Jodi commented.

"That's one thing you learn at the track. How to go fast. Both on the ground and on a horse! Slowpokes don't last long on the backstretch."

"Is that what this guy was?" Jodi asked.

"Oh no. He could run. He was a hopeful one year for the Queen's Plate — four years ago now, I guess? It was just time for him to retire. He got some time off this spring before I started working with him. He's been easy. He's got a good brain. I've just never taken a horse beyond the very basics, you know? I could use some help."

"The people who think they don't need help are usually the ones who need it the most."

Emilie slid her a look, her lips crimping on one side. *It's like that, is it?* But probably true — and with more than just riding horses.

"I think we'll be okay to go outside after all," she said, initiating the walk toward the end of the barn. "I thought we might have to use the indoor."

She stepped onto the mounting block and Excursion showed off, standing like a champ for her. Miss Talk About It was proving to be more of a challenge with that particular exercise. The transition from the racetrack's "leg up and go" to "stand nicely by this box" was taking a while with her.

The ring wasn't as messy as she expected. It had been

freshly harrowed yesterday — Emilie would bring the farm manager, Kerrie, some butter tarts later as a thank you for that. Everything looked impressive, and she and the gelding were acceptably turned out, save for her breeches being slightly grimier than she would have liked. At least she hadn't worn a dark colour. The thing was, she wasn't sure she could live up to appearances, so the nerves came back.

After a leisurely warmup, Jodi made her work, and the nerves fluttered away because she didn't have time for them. She was glad Excursion was fit, even though she wasn't sure she was herself, quickly breaking into a sweat. Half an hour into the lesson she knew she was going to hurt tomorrow. Forget that. She was going to hurt in an hour.

But it was amazing. Jodi offered basic things that made big differences, Excursion becoming light and responsive as he began to find his balance — because she was finding her own. *Relax. Breathe. Shoulders back* (darn the way galloping had made her lazy). *Hands forward. Elbows in. Shorten your reins. More. Good. And, walk.*

"That was brilliant," Emilie breathed at the end, then draped herself over the gelding's neck, not sure she'd be able to sit up again. "You're the best, buddy."

She exhaled, and Excursion did too, a big happy snort that reverberated through his body. She'd never shared Liv's passion for competition. Never envied Liv her days in the hunter and jumper rings when she'd ridden for their grandfather. Never been tempted to join her when she'd transitioned into eventing after they'd moved to Ontario. Never felt the draw of anything more than galloping and breezing horses at the track. But right now, she got it.

What if she kept Excursion around at least for long enough to do a show? Maybe she'd hate it. Or maybe she'd love it and jump — literally — into a whole new thing.

"I like him," Jodi praised. "What are your plans for him?"

"He's a project horse. I just need to put a bit of polish on him to sell him." She hated to admit it, but the little girl in her was already heartbroken at the idea of letting him go.

"Do you have jumps?" Jodi asked.

"Somewhere. There are a few poles and standards in the indoor arena, but there used to be enough for a full course. I'll ask my sister." Excursion sauntered on a loose rein, Emilie enjoying the way his loose walk made her hips roll like they'd never rolled before. She was like jello. She turned him into the middle of the ring and brought him to a halt. "Thank you so much. Same time next week?"

Just like that, she was hooked.

She untacked Excursion in a radiant glow and gave him a bath, her legs shaking the entire time. Even watching him roll when she turned him back out, still wet, didn't dampen her spirits. Though she questioned her ability to get on anything else right now, she was so inspired she gave Miss Talk a short ride while Jodi's tips were still in her head, and it didn't go as badly as she'd thought it might — though a long, hot shower was in her immediate future.

The backstretch had a schedule; it had a beginning and an end. Mornings at the farm were different. Hours disappeared. Glancing at the time as she finished up, wiping and putting away the tack, she was shocked at how late it was. Walking as fast as her wobbly legs would allow, she headed back to the house for that shower.

Her phone rang, just as she slipped on her housecoat after peeling off her sweaty riding clothes. She groaned. Better check who she was ignoring before silencing it.

Nate. She groaned, then picked up. "Hi Nate."

"So," he said, dragging it out, which immediately made her regret answering.

"Out with it. I'm just about to hop into the shower."

"You're coming to the races, right?" he asked.

"I am," she said with caution.

"Great. So you won't mind picking Tim up at the airport and bringing him over."

"What? No, Nate. Just... no."

"C'mon, Em. You know I'm stuck in the room, and Liv's waiting on the vet."

"The vet? Why what's wrong?"

"Nothing serious," Nate said. "Cam cut himself. It's a long way from his heart, but he needs stitches."

"So, that won't take long," she said.

"C'mon, Em. It would be a huge help."

"Tim's a big boy. He can get a cab. It's not that far."

"That's not very sisterly, Em."

"He's not my brother!" she snapped. If Nate hadn't known how she'd felt about this whole Tim coming to stay thing, he did now.

"You know I wouldn't ask you if I had other options," he said.

"Like Dean? Or Will? Or your agent?" What was an agent for, after all? The guy didn't have to work that hard to get a rider like Nate mounts.

"You're mad at me for this, aren't you? For inviting him."

She pressed her forehead against the wall and resisted the temptation to bump it repeatedly. "Okay fine. I'll do it. Can I go now?"

"You're the best, Em."

"I know." *But I will make you pay for this, dear brother-in-law.*

CHAPTER FOUR

IT WAS SO crowded in the terminal, there was no avoiding people. He should be over this. When he'd travelled for games, the crowds had never bothered him. He'd felt he had a purpose then, though; that on some minor scale, he was somebody. But he wasn't here in Toronto to play for the Flames against the Leafs. That was how he'd always pictured his return to this city: Nate and Liv coming to watch him in a game, cheering him on.

Was it just last summer he'd been in this airport for the first time? It had been a late flight, and Liv had met him and his parents, dropped them off at the hotel and taken them down to the hospital to see Nate before his surgery the next day. So much had changed for her and Nate since then. They'd powered through a massive rough patch and were living their happily ever after. If they could overcome much bigger challenges, shouldn't that inspire him to take advantage of this trip? To show Emilie... what? Show her who he really was? He wasn't sure he knew himself.

He waited for his bag at the luggage claim, hating that he'd had to check one but between the crutches and the unknown length of his stay, a single carry-on piece hadn't been practical. An airport worker took pity on him and found him a cart even when he insisted he didn't need it — he could sling both bags over his shoulder and still manoeuvre on crutches. He thanked the man, but ditched the cart before he got out into the waiting throng.

Which, in hindsight, was stupid. The cart would have given him a shield; helped him get through the mob by clearing a path. He was vulnerable on crutches and he got more stares than sympathy as he struggled to make his way. A woman eager to meet an arrival jostled him in her excitement, then a kid nearly tripped him up, making him slam the bags perched on his shoulder into a guy twice his size who gave him a nasty glare. Whoever thought Canadians were nice hadn't been in the Toronto airport. He wanted to escape, uneasiness creeping through him from the inside out.

Nate had promised Liv would meet him. He liked Liv. They'd never exchanged more than a few words, but they shared something just the same. Not just a love for his brother. It was an identity. *Extreme introverts-R-us.* He didn't feel like he had to be anyone but himself around her.

He searched the crowd for her face, slowly navigating through the sea of bodies, careful to avoid any more collisions. If he were waiting for someone, he wouldn't be standing in the thick of things, so he made his way to where the crowd thinned out. He didn't see her. Amid all these waiting people there was no one waiting for him. Gradually the mass broke up, and still, nothing. He leaned on the crutches, shoulders aching from the weight of the bags, his good leg cramping and tired, his knee sore and stiff.

Finally he found a seat by the windows and parked himself where he hoped he could easily see Liv come in — or be seen by her. He pulled his phone from where he'd stashed it in the side pocket of one of the bags, checking the screen in case he'd missed a text. He hadn't heard the phone go off, but sometimes it was flakey and didn't audibly alert him. Obviously Liv was late. Nate was always telling one story or another — he could probably write a book called *Things That Go Wrong With Horses* so it wouldn't really be a surprise if something had come up to delay her. They were beautiful animals, but the more Nate told him, the more he realized how fragile they were.

Oh. *Idiot.* He'd forgotten to take the phone off airplane mode. As soon as he did, a voicemail notification came through — from hours ago, when he'd still been in the air.

Hey, kid. Liv's going to be a bit late, sorry. The message went on to relate a new story for the book, the result of which was, Liv was waiting for the vet. She'd been in vet school when she and Nate had first met. Maybe she should have stayed. Seemed like that degree might have come in handy.

He'd never even thought to ask Nate for Liv's number, naïvely assuming everything would go smoothly. He should have known better. Nate didn't respond right away to the text response he fired off. His brother was normally good about replying, so he must be working, riding in a race. It was quarter to one and Tim tried to remember what time the first one went off, feeling totally inept.

Nate had said the racetrack wasn't very far from the airport. He wondered if he could walk there. *Sure.* The guy on crutches. He pictured himself, pushing a cart with his two bags piled on it, crutches propped between them. Would someone stop him before he got off the airport grounds for stealing a cart? He'd probably look like a homeless person. He might be better dressed, but it would still appear suspect. Pulling up the maps app quashed the thought entirely. An hour and a half on foot? How could that be? But he wasn't familiar enough with the roads to know if there was a shorter route.

So, he was probably in for a long wait. Even though it was tempting to try to find a bottle of water and a snack — he was starving — he'd better stay put, just in case. Retrieving his book from where he'd zipped it safely inside his carry-on, he settled down to read, resting his phone on his thigh so he wouldn't miss it if someone tried to contact him.

"Tim."

The voice jolted him and his head snapped up so abruptly he fumbled the book, his phone tumbling to the floor. Instead of reaching for it, he stared. Because that voice didn't belong to Liv.

Emilie Lachance stood there, the dress she wore not as fancy as what she'd had on at the wedding — but the indignant expression on her face was more or less the same as the one she'd given him that afternoon. Her dark hair was down, straight and skimming her shoulders; her arms crossed over her chest, shoes matching her outfit — which he noticed because he was sure he'd caught her toes tapping with impatience.

"Oh. Hi. Sorry." He stashed the book then reached for his crutches, pushing himself to his feet. Or foot. His good leg protested more than the bad one.

"Crutches? Are you kidding me?" Her hands were on her hips now, dark brows knotted. "Nate didn't tell me you were still on crutches."

"Sorry for being such a bother." He scowled at her; he couldn't help it. Then he knocked the bag closest to her out of her reach with the end of one crutch before she could grab it. "Just lead the way."

She gaped at him, remaining rooted in the same spot as he scooped up first the carry-on, then the duffel, layering them on his left side again and regretting this most recent of his life choices. He should have known coming here would be a disaster. Optimism didn't come naturally to him; he should have remembered that and stayed home where he belonged.

"Is that your phone?" Emilie asked, spotting it before he remembered he'd dropped it.

He slumped his shoulders, and the bags slipped to the floor. "I've got it. It's fine."

But she was faster than he was, probably because both her knees functioned properly and she wasn't encumbered by crutches. Even though his arms were longer, she snatched it from where it lay just before he reached it, his fingers brushing her arm. He retracted his hand like he'd been burnt.

They both straightened, her dark blue eyes simmering, but she dropped her gaze first.

"Here." She slapped the phone into his palm.

"Thanks," he muttered, staring at it like it had betrayed him before tucking it into his back pocket.

"Will you give me one of those bags?" she asked, exasperation in her voice.

"I said I'm fine." He arranged them on his shoulders once more and shot her a glare. "Can we go, please?"

She didn't move for a moment, her hands back on her hips. Then she sighed and spun on her heel with a toss of her hair, her deep brown locks swinging with her hips. It mesmerized him. All of her did.

CHAPTER FIVE

SHE WANTED to ask him why he was being so miserable, but she knew why. He had a right to be. The truth of it was, she was the one who was being difficult. Could she have been any ruder?

That didn't stop her from power-walking to where she'd left the car, the skirt of her dress swishing with each stride, stopping only to stick the ticket in the machine to pay. She wasn't worried about Tim keeping up. He was doing just fine on those crutches, even with the load he carried. Stubborn jerk, for not letting her carry a bag. She unlocked the Civic with a beep of the keys and lifted the hatch, waiting while he dumped his load.

She felt guilty — really she did — watching him fold himself into the passenger seat, crutches stashed behind it, but it wasn't as if he'd let her do anything, so she started the car and once he'd clicked the seatbelt into place, began the round and round drive of getting out of the many-tiered garage. Once off the airport property the track was only five minutes away, but it took at least that long to reach the public roads. With a flick of her wrist, she turned the stereo volume up just enough to preclude conversation. Not that he'd made any attempt to initiate any.

"I should drop you off at the gate. You're probably tired." See, she wasn't totally obnoxious.

"Don't worry about it," he said, his voice low and quiet. "I can manage."

That was it. She was done trying to be accommodating. "Suit yourself."

A warm breeze fluttered the flags at the entrance, and with the sun at its hottest for the day, she was glad to get under the covered walkway that led toward the grandstand. She realized people were watching — not her; at least no more than a woman in a dress got ogled at the racetrack — but Tim, like they were trying to figure out who he was, as if he must be a celebrity they didn't recognize.

It was his flawless physique; she was sure. He looked like an athlete, and not a casual one. Not just some guy who was buff because he spent all day at the gym. His face would seem familiar but that was because of his resemblance to Nate. She knew that. They didn't. The crutches just added to the puzzle as they scrounged their memories for someone in the news who had suffered an injury.

It wasn't unusual for sports celebrities to attend the races on the big days. The goalie of the Stanley Cup-winning team — a Toronto native — would be at the Queen's Plate breakfast this year to assist with the draw, and an Olympic gold medalist was supposed to give the riders up call on the day of the big race. On an ordinary Friday afternoon, however, she could see their consternation. *Who is that guy?*

Who, indeed? She cast Tim a sideways glance, her lips pursed, but his eyes were focused resolutely on the ground, as if he expected to see potholes that would swallow him up.

Maybe, given her less than welcoming behaviour, that's what he was hoping for.

The telltale aroma of horse intermingled with cheap after-shave wafting from the punters who lined the rail of the saddling enclosure. It took a moment for her eyes to adjust after being out in the sunlight, then she quickly pulled up the race entries on her phone so she knew where to find Dean's horse. Number two. She pressed past the bodies, Tim silent a step behind her, and elbowed her way to the front. Tim was tall enough to look over her shoulder so she'd leave him to that.

Nate was riding Dean's horse, and he leaned against the wall of the stall as Dean adjusted the red and white blinkers on his tall grey charge. Nate grinned and raised his whip, and Emilie stuck her tongue out at him.

"You made it!" Nate called.

Emilie felt eyes around them turn her way, though Nate's were acknowledging Tim's presence. She refused to look behind herself, dropping her gaze to her phone while totally aware of Tim moving slightly closer; of the slight shift of air as he raised his hand to his brother, too self-conscious to speak.

The groom left the stall with Dean's horse to walk around, and Nate shifted his attention to the trainer for his instructions. As soon as Dean legged him up onto the grey's back, Emilie turned, ready to make the dash for the escalator to beat the crush of bodies that would soon funnel that way. She skidded to a halt, finding herself staring at the buttons of Tim's burgundy dress shirt and sucked in a breath, overcoming the urge to rest her hand on his chest, wondering just how it would feel as her senses flashed back to the solidness of his arm when she'd wound her fingers around his biceps for the dance on the beach. *Gah. No.*

"We'll go upstairs and watch, if that's okay," she said in a rush of words, ducking to the side to slip past.

"Cool." Tim nodded and looked genuinely interested as he followed.

"Emilie! Wait up!" Dean dodged racegoers to catch up with them, holding the door open to let her and Tim through before he followed them onto the escalator.

Thank goodness. Dean saves the day. Mediator. Liaison. Chaperone? *Nope, not going there.*

"So, is your horse going to win?" Emilie asked, stretching a hand to the railing — and taking an extra step up and away from Tim.

"I like him in here," Dean responded.

Emilie controlled her smile. Dean always liked his horses' chances, even when he probably shouldn't.

Dean (*bless his heart*) started chatting with Tim, asking him all the questions Emilie had neglected to. *Hey, Tim, great to see you. How was the flight? How's the knee? How long are you staying?* Leading the way to the second floor seating, she could hear Tim's soft voice as he answered. Not that she was listening.

Making sure Dean was in the middle, she watched the horses come onto the track with their pony escorts, jogging until they were in front of the grandstand, the announcer introducing them one by one. When Dean lifted his binoculars to study the grey, conversation paused.

"He looks good, Dean," Emilie said as the post parade finished and Nate took the horse away to warm up.

"What's his name?" Tim asked.

"Quest For All," Dean answered. "He hasn't won a race yet, but he's been close a couple of times. Maybe this is his day."

It was, apparently. With Emilie and Dean on their feet screaming, the three-year-old gelding came on in a rush to stick his nose in front at the wire. Tim perched on the edge of his seat, following the horses as they galloped out with an actual grin on his face. She almost didn't recognize him.

"Come down for the picture, both of you," Dean insisted.

"Really?" Tim's face lit up, and he scrambled to his feet, propping the crutches under his arms.

"Of course." Dean nudged Emilie. "Onward!"

She kept glancing over her shoulder as she skipped down the stairs. It was weird seeing Tim look... happy.

"That was for you, kid!" Nate grinned as the groom led Quest For All into the winner's circle for the photograph. When Tim grinned back at him they looked even more alike.

Once Nate hopped off, Dean thumping him on the back, Tim edged forward. Emilie hovered, worried she was going to have to rescue him from something stupid. Quest For All was excited after his win, pushing against his handler. All she needed was for Tim and his crutches to get run over — but apparently he had enough sense to see the possibility of that himself, stepping out of the way before the gelding barged past.

"You staying to watch our race, Dean?" Emilie asked when Nate left for the scales with his saddle. It came out more like a plea.

"I need to check on the horse," he said, apologetic but oblivious to her plight. "Good luck! See you around, Tim."

Of course. Dean was that kind of trainer. "Thanks Dean. Catch you later." She eyed Tim. "You holding up okay?"

He looked surprised she'd asked. She couldn't say she blamed him.

"Yeah. Thanks." And with that, the mask settled back into place.

It was a relief to see Liv waiting in the paddock for their filly Justakiss to arrive. Emilie had led Tim through the shortcut under the grandstand, but with the tense silence between them it was like an endless expedition through the bowels of a mountain. Just a little better-lit, maybe.

"Sorry I couldn't meet you," Liv said, exchanging a cautious embrace with Tim. Her sister wasn't a big hugger, and Emilie would bet Tim shared her aversion.

"What was the problem?" Emilie asked.

"Cam. He sliced his nostril on something and Jake had to come throw sutures in it. Now, if he doesn't tear them out, maybe the whole exercise won't have been a waste of time."

"Could you have done that? You were in vet school, right?"

Emilie gawked when Tim spoke unprompted. So was it just her he didn't want to talk to? Well. That should work out perfectly.

Liv's laugh was quiet. "I suppose, in theory, yes. In practice, having the sedation and local anesthetic on hand so I could do it would get me ruled off the track."

Tim elected to stay on the outside of the paddock when Emilie went with Liv to the saddling stall. He was safer out there, especially with the crutches. Kiss was a nervous filly, and this was her first race. She trembled, bug-eyed, as Liv went through the motions of securing Nate's saddle.

"Brave girl," Emilie crooned. "You're all grown up now."

Tim watched the activity intently, almost studiously. He certainly didn't appear bored. That was something. When they reached the seats to watch the race, he remained silent — which should have let her focus on the race, but his presence was still a distraction.

Nate did his job, giving the green filly a good first experience. She didn't win. The upside of Kiss not giving Nate his second victory of the day? Emilie didn't have to deal with anyone suggesting Tim was some kind of good luck charm.

"She did really well though, right?" Tim said, following Liv to the trackside apron after the race.

"She did," Liv confirmed. "She held it together, which is no small feat for a filly like her, and she put in an honest effort. You two going to hang out here? I'm going back to the barn after I talk to Nate."

"Uh —" Emilie needed an answer, fast. She glanced at Tim. She wasn't his babysitter, but she couldn't abandon him either.

"Do you want to come to the backstretch and see the horses?" Liv asked him.

Emilie held her breath, waiting for his response.

"Can I?" Tim said.

She let the air slip slowly through her lips, hoping her relief wasn't obvious. This time, surprisingly, her sister had saved the day. Liv wasn't usually one to rescue anyone from awkward social situations because she was normally too busy fending for herself.

"Of course," Liv said. "You'd better come with me, though. That way Emilie doesn't have to sneak you past security."

"Security?" Tim looked baffled.

Liv just smiled at him. "Let's go. You don't need anything from Em's car?"

He shook his head, looking just as happy as Emilie that they wouldn't be stuck with each other again. But as Liv and Nate discussed the filly's performance, the groom leading Justakiss back to the barn, Emilie felt a pang she couldn't identify at first.

Anger, she realized. He was happy to leave because she was horrible company. She huffed and left him to wait for Liv, deciding to stay for the next race. Nate was riding again.

"What'd you do with my brother?" Nate asked suspiciously when he saw her at the paddock on her own.

Emilie narrowed her eyes. "Unloaded him on your wife."

"You sound, I don't know, snippy, Em. What's up?"

His roguish grin made her simmer. "You're needed else-where," she snapped. "Go make some more money."

When he laughed, it just made her more furious. It was as if he thought she was overreacting. She wasn't. Was she?

As she watched the horses warm up — a field of eight low-level claimers — she studied the ones who might make the best future riding horses instead of assessing who she thought might win the race. She loved watching them run, but had never developed that eye that let her pick out a winner. This was why Liv was at the track and she stayed mostly on the farm.

Nate didn't win the race. Emilie wasn't even sure where his horse finished. She looked up the mare's record, seeing a decline in her performance, and wondered if the owner would be receptive to retiring her to New Chapter. The mare was a nice mover, looked like she was still sound — she'd just lost her desire to compete. She'd ask Nate for his thoughts.

A text notification from Liv flashed onto her phone screen. *Bring Nate back to the barn? His last mount was just scratched. I have the car.*

Emilie answered. *Why don't you come over here?* When she knew full well Liv liked to avoid playing jockey's wife after the races. *People might talk. Me, him, we have a history, you know.*

All that got her was a laughing emoji.

Her crush had always been openly good-humoured with Nate — it had been fun to be the counterpoint to her sister's resistance in the early years. She didn't go in for the whole damaged guy thing, which Nate had too obviously been when he showed up on the farm for an interview. Almost six years ago, now. Time did fly. The damaged label didn't apply to Tim, as far as she knew, but the whole grumpy and distant persona was a hard *no* for her.

Enduring the cracks from the riders killing time before the next race, she waited for Nate outside the jock's room. She knew all of them; had essentially grown up with some of them and dated others. Nothing had ever come of any of it. She wasn't sad about that; she just wondered sometimes about herself. Was she doing something to land herself in the friend zone? Or worse yet, the sister zone? Had that been Tim's concern? They weren't actually related because of Nate and Liv, but maybe he thought it was weird. Not that it excused him for being such a grouch. Was she just too picky, holding out for impossible standards? It just seemed wrong that Faye and Liv, who had both fought so hard against love, had it, while she remained alone.

You're happy, remember? Tim's arrival had her all "what could have been," and that persistent thought was just as annoying as the intrusion of his presence in her world.

Nate appeared, bag slung casually over his shoulder. He looked good in those chinos — or were they khakis? Was there a difference? His dress shirt did a good job of matching the arresting warmth of his blue, blue eyes. It wouldn't have mattered what kind of face those eyes were in. They made women stop and stare — but the face didn't hurt. When he smiled like that it was pretty hard not to forgive him for what he was putting her through, at least for a minute.

"Thanks for picking up Tim," he said.

"Emilie's Taxi, at your service," she said, dipping her chin as she swept an arm across her body with a shallow curtsey.

"I ordered a limo," he deadpanned.

She gave his shoulder a shove. "You'd better tip well, that's all I'm saying."

"I'll buy us dinner, how's that?"

She grinned. "Works for me. Your brother is your responsibility from here on though, okay?"

Nate snorted. "Did I ask you to babysit him?"

"Just being clear."

Liv had their big horse, Just Jay, grazing on the lawn near where Tim sat at the picnic table with a bottle of water. What a good girl, Liv, getting him a cool drink. Her sister was notoriously absent-minded about such things. Conversely, she was ashamed of herself for not asking. Except he'd squashed every attempt she'd made to be nice. That had to let her off the hook.

Nate went over to Liv and Jay, offering the horse a peppermint before he leaned in and kissed Liv. It was brief, but he hovered a breath from her mouth before stepping away, and it made Emilie twitch, her breath catching. She glanced automatically at Tim. *Why?* Why did she have to do that? He ducked his head.

"C'mon Big Horse," Liv said, giving a tug on the lead shank. Jay snatched one last mouthful then followed her into the barn. Nate went too and Emilie scurried after him because she was not standing out here not-talking with Tim.

"How's our girl?" Nate found another peppermint for Kiss, now in her stall and decked out in clean, white stable bandages. He blew in her nostrils after she daintily accepted the candy.

"None the worse for wear," Liv said. "Jo said she'd hang around so we can get Tim home. You must be dead on your feet." Her eyebrows lifted slightly, but Tim, who had followed them in, only shrugged in response.

"Em's making me buy dinner, but we can pick up pizza or something," Nate said.

"Let's get going, then," Liv said. Her gaze swept from Emilie's face, to Tim's and landed on Nate. "You two should catch up."

Emilie caught the glint in her sister's eyes.

"We'll take the Porsche." And Liv held out her hand, palm up, fingers rolling.

The look on Nate's face was priceless. It wasn't anger.

More like dismay, but there was no way he was going to deny his beloved's request. He sighed and relinquished the keys.

"Here you go, Nate!" Emilie tossed him the fob for her now-aged Honda Civic with glee, and he snapped them out of the air. This was a good place to start, making him pay for this Tim thing.

"See you at home," Liv called over her shoulder, already on the way to the sleek sports car.

Emilie gave a little wave — and a little side-eye to Tim, the interloper — before catching up. "Can I drive?" she asked.

Liv shot her a look. "I don't know about that."

"Liv. Come on."

"No!"

"You're mean," she said, but Liv just grinned as she ducked behind the wheel, slipping on her sunglasses. Nate took his time backing the Civic out of the way. He wasn't going down easy.

"What's with you?" Liv asked after turning the key, the engine purring to life. "You're in a mood. This isn't just because Tim's here, is it?"

Emilie avoided Liv's eyes and stared out the window. She wasn't interested in getting into her stupidly fluctuating emotions right now, so time to redirect. "I had my first lesson with Jodi this morning! You should have seen Excursion. He was great. Even if I won't be able to walk tomorrow. This dressage stuff isn't for wimps."

Liv laughed. "No, it's not."

"I've got the best idea for a new fundraiser for New Chapter." She plunged further away from the topic of Tim. "A celebrity horse show with available horses! We'll get you, and Nate, and some of the other jockeys and pair them up with horses. We could host it at the farm. Sell tickets to make money, have food trucks, and showcase the breed."

"I claim Excursion then." Liv gave Emilie a sideways grin.

"He's not part of the New Chapter program, he's ours. Besides, we'd have to draw horses, of course. No playing favourites. What do you think?"

"I think that's a legitimately good idea," Liv said.

"Of course it is. I always have great ideas."

Nate, on the other hand, did not. Because bringing Tim out had definitely been a bad one.

CHAPTER SIX

For the first time since he'd left the house in Calgary, Tim relaxed. This was a more familiar scene: Nate behind the wheel, the two of them headed to get pizza, even if the memories it stirred were from years ago now. And as much as he wished they were in Nate's nifty car instead of Emilie's beater, it had been pretty funny to see Liv commandeer the Porsche.

"I'm glad you're here," Nate said as they drove off, the smile on his face helping unknot the tension Tim had carried with him all day. "Are you tired?"

"Kind of a stupid question, don't you think?" Tim's lips twisted. "I'm starving, that's for sure. I hope you remember what toppings I like."

"Guess you'll have to wait and see," Nate said, his smile getting wider. "Everything go okay today?"

He hesitated. What did he say to that? He wanted to pour out all the things he'd brought along. All his apprehension — about leaving, about coming. He needed to tell Nate about Mom and Dad, and he wanted to share the confusion and frustration he was feeling about Emilie but it was simpler right now to focus on the positive.

"Yeah," he finally replied. "It was pretty cool seeing you ride, and to get to be in the win picture. Dean's nice. And I like the horses."

Nate slid him a look, like the pause had given away that there was a lot more going on in his head than he was letting on. There would be time for all of that. And he was tired. He couldn't really complain about Emilie. She had picked him up under duress.

He stayed in the car when Nate went to pick up the pizza, leaning against the headrest and closing his eyes, and was on the brink of falling asleep when the sound of the car door opening brought him back. The smell of the food made his stomach rumble. Nate passed the boxes over to him and Tim set them in his lap, lifting the lid of the top box a crack and peeking in. He inhaled and sighed. Nate didn't comment when he pushed the box the rest of the way open and peeled off a slice. It had cooled just enough to not burn the roof of his mouth when he crammed it in.

He mumbled through his mouthful of crust and cheese and toppings. "Sorry. Rude."

"Only if you don't pass me one," Nate said.

Tim set his half-eaten slice on the dash on top of a napkin printed with the pizza joint's logo. If it hadn't been so dusty he wouldn't have bothered, but if this car was any indication, Emilie was kind of a pig. He fished out a slice for Nate and passed it over. Nate devoured the whole thing before waving Tim off when offered a second slice. That didn't stop Tim from helping himself.

The cheese and the carbs were probably going to put him right back to sleep. And so they did. He didn't wake until, begrudgingly accepting the return of consciousness, he regained a sense of where he was. Nate was heading up a long driveway lined with beautiful maples in full summer dress. The sun was low enough to be a big orange fireball filtered by the canopy of leaves. It was breathtaking. Tim rolled down the window and inhaled the country air.

Nate pulled up in front of a house that seemed enormous compared to their home in Calgary. His brother was out and all the way around to Tim's side, and Tim still stared.

"It's not Casa Loma," Nate said after he'd swung the door open, reaching for the pizza.

"Casa Loma?" Tim's brow furrowed as he passed Nate the boxes and climbed from the car before collecting his crutches.

"We'll have to fit in some sightseeing while you're here. Haven't been there yet myself, but it's one of those things you're supposed to see in the big city of Toronto."

There were half a dozen steps up to the front door, and Nate waited at the top as Tim made his way, step by slow step. The large front door was unlocked and opened into a vestibule, a second French door with pretty bevelled glass windows preventing a black Lab from greeting them. Her nose pressed to a pane as she wagged her tail so powerfully her whole body swayed, excited whimpers accompanying her dance. When Nate opened the door with his free hand, pizza boxes balanced on the other, the Lab tumbled in and bounced first to Nate then to Tim. Before he had a chance to lean over and give her the attention she looked like she'd die without, her nose went into overdrive, sniffing him from kneecaps to feet and back again. Finally she paused long enough for him to run a hand over her pretty head.

"Hi, how are you?" he asked, a grin taking over his face.

"That's Holly," Nate said.

The introduction was unnecessary. Tim felt as if he'd met

the Lab because Emilie always talked about her. Or had. Back when they'd messaged. Before he'd disappeared on her.

"This way," Nate directed, and the Lab doubled as escort while Tim caught a peek of the sunken living room, towering ceilings slanting toward sliding doors that opened to a patio beyond.

"You live here?" he said, voice hushed. Nate shrugged with a look that suggested he wasn't yet convinced himself and kept walking.

Tim jarred to a halt in the doorway, planting the rubber ends of the crutches on the line where hardwood changed to slate tile, and gawked again, barely noticing Emilie ripping pieces of paper towel to supplement the napkins and Liv taking glasses from a cupboard and setting them on the counter. The kitchen was gorgeous. Spacious, with granite counter tops; flashy stainless appliances, warm white cabinets. Holly circled Nate with a hopeful expression as he set the pizza on the table of a cozy breakfast nook, long benches on either side.

Emilie placed the folded paper towels next to the boxes and flipped open the one on top. Nate went to Liv and kissed her. Again. At least Emilie was more concerned about the pizza this time.

She'd changed from the dress she'd worn into khaki green cargo shorts and he had to force his eyes from the v-neck of her loose white t-shirt. Her hair was pulled back in a high ponytail, leaving her long neck bare as it fell to the side while she peered at the pizza.

"You guys started without us?" she said, frowning as she sat. "And what is this, veggie?" But she shrugged, removed a slice, and bit in. Why was everyone eating his pizza?

"What do you want to drink, Tim? We can get whatever you like the next time we're at a grocery store but for now there might be some kind of pop, and there's beer, or wine..." Liv's voice drifted off as she peered into the fridge.

"Water would be great," he said. He hadn't moved from the doorway.

"Sit down, you poor kid." Nate grabbed a glass and filled it with ice from the fancy fridge then set it on the table.

Tim tossed Emilie a doubtful glance as he slid onto the bench across from her, staying near the end. Nate took away his crutches, and he followed them like someone had just stolen his getaway car until a wet nose nudged his hand.

"Hello, Holly. I'm happy to see you, too, pretty girl," he crooned gently, giving her a more thorough head-rub than he'd been able to at the front door. He was grateful to have something to focus on, feeling awkward again.

Emilie's face softened, the corners of her mouth crimping. It was just in passing though, because when Tim removed his hands from the disappointed Labrador to slide the top pizza box off its mate — maybe just a little possessively — her eyes narrowed.

"Is that for your benefit?" she said, opening the second box — the one with meat. "You're... not... vegetarian, are you?"

He nodded, removing a piece, then took a careful sip of water, swallowing. The arc of her raised eyebrow captivated him. It had a nice shape, dark and not artificially thin, and it framed the dark blue eye beneath it.

She choked on a laugh. "Is that even legal? For a hockey player? A hockey player from Alberta, no less? Aren't you legally required to eat beef?"

He was used to the flak; it was never ending from the guys on the team when they found out he didn't eat meat. He couldn't be bothered defending himself with his teammates, so he sure wasn't going to engage Emilie in a discussion about it.

One day, he'd be a role model for kids. He'd prove you didn't have to eat meat to be a professional athlete.

"This is pretty good pizza for a chain," he said instead, and caught Liv's subtle smile. He didn't know what that was about, and right now he was too tired to care. The fact that Calgary was two hours behind Toronto meant nothing. It felt like midnight as far as his body and brain were concerned.

"Maybe we should get you set up so you can go to bed, Tim," Liv said. "Just as well you got a head start on the pizza."

She was officially his favourite sister-in-law for that. It didn't matter that now she was his only sister-in-law.

Nate nodded in agreement and asked, "Can I borrow your trusty vehicle a little longer, Em? Tim's stuff is still in the back of it. I'll drive him down to the apartment."

Emilie's mouth was full, and she nodded as she chewed, but her expression slowly changed. She swallowed, and the corners of her mouth dropped. "That's not going to work, is it?"

"What do you mean?" Nate asked.

"The apartment. Those stairs. His crutches." She punched the words out.

Liv's gaze shifted to Nate. "Good point."

Emilie released a breath, her shoulders dropping like she was deflating. "He'll have to take my apartment. I'll grab my stuff and I can stay over the barn."

Tim didn't know whether to be impressed by her generosity, or embarrassed he'd caused trouble — again.

"This just gets better and better," she muttered as she wiped her fingers on a paper towel and brushed past, Holly on her heels.

So, the latter, then.

"I'll get your bags, Tim," Nate said, his brother's departure considerably less aggrieved than Emilie's.

He was glad when he was finally alone. He wandered

around her space, trying to see what he could learn about her by the furnishings and what hung on the walls; the contents of the small refrigerator, the books on her shelves.

The books drew him most, a love of reading the one small thing he knew they had in common. There were non-fiction horse books and thick textbooks. Anatomy books for both humans and equines — more than one for each. Other random texts that must've been for electives. And a boatload of paperback novels: romance, fantasy, fantasy romance. The romance made him uncomfortable; the fantasy made him happy, like he'd found friends in a foreign land.

He could hide away in here if he had to. And so far, it was feeling like that might be the best plan.

CHAPTER SEVEN

THE ALARM SANG her to consciousness, and she rolled over with a grunt, almost falling off the edge of the bed like she'd misjudged it. Her body was one big ache. When she stretched for her phone, a searing pain shot up her neck. The bedside table was in the wrong spot. The lamp, too. Was she still asleep, and this was a dream? Then it dawned on her. This wasn't her bed. This wasn't her room.

Her phone kept playing its cheery alarm tune, and she pushed herself into a sitting position, moaning. How had Nate slept on this mattress all those years? It was terrible. And this dressage stuff hurt too much. Her thighs screamed, and she'd thought she had good core muscles from galloping, but apparently she'd found a bunch of new ones she didn't use. Maybe she should stick to galloping on the weekends and doing only as much as her casual hunter background let her do with the off-track projects. Jodi had praised her after the lesson on Excursion for "managing not to screw him up." That was praise, wasn't it? It could be enough.

Anyone who'd ridden a horse was familiar with DOMS —

delayed onset muscle soreness. By the time they'd gathered for dinner last night it had begun seeking out every under-used part of her. If she'd been feeling less stabby it might have occurred to her to have a nice, hot Epsom salts bath to give her poor muscles some relief. Then she realized the bathroom in Nate's apartment only had a shower — no tub.

She still thought of it as Nate's apartment, this space above the office barn where he'd lived from the time he'd been hired to help on the farm and start yearlings six years ago until this spring when, upon returning from a winter in Florida, he'd moved in with Liv to the newly renovated version of the house Liv and Emilie had called home since their move from Quebec. An upgrade, for sure. That bed should be burned. She wouldn't feel half this wrecked if she'd slept in her own.

Tim. It was all his fault.

Holly shifted at the foot of the bed and thumped her tail against the comforter, meeting the edge of Emilie's gaze with her soulful eyes. Her neck wouldn't let her turn all the way, the jab radiating into her shoulder.

"I should have thought ahead, Holly. I should have trained you as a therapy dog so you could help me out of bed."

A hot shower was going to have to do for now. Maybe later today she'd sneak back to the house and use Nate and Liv's ensuite — and have a glass of wine — while they were away. She wasn't going to risk running into Tim by using the bathroom in her own apartment.

Holly didn't understand why it was taking her so long to negotiate the stairs from Nate's apartment down to the barn, and the horses rumbled, expecting breakfast. While she waited for Holly to sniff about and do her thing on the patch of grass between the barn and fence, she texted Liv to say she'd feed them. Then she added, *I might be late getting there. I'm not moving too fast this morning.* She'd have to stop by the house on her way to the track because she hadn't packed Advil, and would need some onboard if she was going to gallop horses this morning.

She'd be fine once she was on the first one and doing something. Endorphins would kick in and help mask the soreness, but a bit of anti-inflammatory help would bridge the gap enough for her to survive the leg up into the saddle. She had to navigate the stairs back up to Nate's apartment first though. It seemed a little pointless to shower before getting on horses, but she needed what relief she could get.

Leaving Holly in her crate in the house's kitchen, because the Lab was still young enough to find trouble if left out when no one was home, she went in search of ibuprofen. She had some in her apartment, but she was not going in there with Tim asleep in her bed. Her beautiful, comfortable bed. There had to be some in the powder room. No such luck. She stared at the staircase to the next level a hard moment before beginning the slow climb, grasping the railing for support. Her legs laughed at her with each step.

The two bedrooms on this level had been hers and Liv's, and she checked the cabinet in the bathroom they'd shared. It was guaranteed that two women of a certain age would have a stash of Advil — it was compulsory for management of a certain monthly issue — but again, she came up empty. Had Liv gone on a cleaning spree in here? Or, unforgivably, run out? Only six more steps to the top level. She could do it.

She shuffled through Nate and Liv's room to the ensuite and looked with longing at the big tub in the corner of the spacious bathroom before focusing on her mission. *Bingo.* Extra-strength Liqui-gels, just what the doctor ordered. Then a small amber vial caught her eye. She peered at the label. Muscle relaxants, dated around the time Nate had hurt his back last summer. They'd barely been touched. This would be way better than an anti-inflammatory.

She tucked the capsule into the pocket of her jeans and trekked down to the main floor. After filling her travel mug with the last of the coffee from the carafe and unplugging the machine, she grabbed her water bottle from the fridge, put the capsule on her tongue and took a swig to wash it down.

"See you later, Holly!"

Her weekends were backward to most working people. She got up earlier on Saturday and Sunday for this foray into Woodbine than she did on weekdays. It gave their two exercise riders each a day off without leaving Liv short-handed, and Emilie liked to have a reason to keep a toe in things. She was just one set of eyes looking out for horses who were getting to a place in their careers that they might be at risk. She and some of the other representatives from New Chapter did their best to intercede and advocate for them. It wasn't so bad this time of year, at the height of the season, but as the months wore on and they got closer and closer to the end of the meet, it became increasingly important.

By the time she was halfway there, she could feel the effect of the medication, easing her pain, giving her neck a tiny bit more mobility. Taking a sip of her coffee, she sighed. She might actually be able to climb out of her car without assistance once she got to the track.

But then... *oh*. Why couldn't she feel her fingers?

The security guard looked at her strangely as she fumbled with her badge, nearly dropping it before he scanned it. What was his problem? With all the half-sober people who went through this gate on a Saturday morning, why was he looking at her like she was one of them? She was sober. She just felt... oh... a little... numb.

Parking far from the other cars in the small lot at the east end because she didn't trust herself not to hit one, she concentrated hard to be sure she locked the Civic, then cradled her water bottle and coffee mug to her chest for the walk to Barn Five, grateful it was dark, because she did not feel right.

The shedrow was bright — too bright — and Nate saw her first.

"Hey Em. Um, you okay?"

She gave him an exaggerated nod, though she'd tried to control it. "I just... borrowed one of your... no, sorry, I won't give it back. I took one of the muscle relaxants from your medicine cabinet because I was so sore." Her words sounded amplified, even to her. "So sore," she repeated, "from my dressage lesson yesterday. And that bed. Why did you never say anything about that bed?" She couldn't understand why he was gaping at her like that.

"And you drove here?" Then he started laughing.

"This is not helping your case any, mister," she mumbled. Even in her semi-incapacitated state, she could tell he had no idea what she meant.

"Come on. You'd better not get on any horses this morning. I tried one of those things after I hurt my back — you know, the thing those pills were prescribed for? It flattened me. I should have gotten rid of them. But then again, how could I anticipate that my sweet sister-in-law would find them and take one for DOMS?" And he started laughing all over again, guiding her toward the office.

Which was the first good idea he'd had in a while. She closed her eyes and thought about the comfy sofa in there. Nope. She wouldn't be any help to anyone this morning.

The overhead light was on, and there was already someone on the couch. She squinted. *No...*

"What are you doing here?" Had she said that out loud?

Tim lifted his head from a book, so she was guessing, yes.

Or maybe it was the grandness of her entrance that attracted his attention. Even before Nate said, "Why don't you just sit for a bit and let it wear off?" she was diving for the free spot on the sofa, Nate trying to keep her from flopping like a tranquilized Panda.

"Okay then," Nate said. "I seem to remember it took about four hours to wear off. At least you should be sober enough to drive yourself home. Thank goodness you got here in one piece."

He muttered something to Tim that she didn't hear and left.

Tim was quiet, and she was grateful for that, closing her eyes and letting her head loll to the back of the loveseat. *Loveseat.* How ironic to find herself on a loveseat with Tim Miller.

"What are you, a drug addict?"

She didn't bother to raise her head. She'd thought she missed that dry sense of humour. It had been endearing when they'd been carrying on their little Facebook exchanges, but didn't have the same appeal at the moment.

"Go away," she mumbled. *Like back to Calgary.*

"Why did you take muscle relaxants, anyway?"

Really? He picked now to be chatty? Likely because she was at a complete disadvantage. "I had a riding lesson yesterday. I hadn't had one in years. It was hard, like a full-body workout. Muscles I don't think I knew I had were called into action and today, they hate me." She sighed and rolled her head toward him. "You're probably one of those people who think the horse does all the work and the rider just sits there."

"Me? No way. Nate is my hero. He'd crush me in a fitness test. Well... right now that might not be saying much, but, you know. Even at my fittest he'd kick my butt."

She didn't think she could hold any tension in her body

thanks to the drugs, but she felt her features soften, so some must've remained in the muscles of her face. She tried to grin but had no idea if she pulled it off. "I bet he totally would. He's a rock star."

Tim met her eyes, and the smile he gave her was nothing like Nate's easy flash of teeth. No teeth at all. But it did something to her stomach just the same.

"Sorry about the DOMS," he said, his lips falling into their usual line, but there was genuine sympathy in his eyes. "DOMS suck."

"DOMS sucks?" she suggested.

"Whatever, Professor."

"Yeah, whichever. Whatever. It does. I'm not looking forward to tomorrow." Because it was always worse on the second day. She also wasn't looking forward to sleeping in that stupid bed again. *Tim's fault. All Tim's fault.*

She didn't even try to resist dozing; there was no point. Nate was right. The best strategy was to sleep it off.

When the click of the office's screen door brought her back to consciousness she had no idea what time it was. Somehow she'd ended up lengthways, her head on the fat armrest, legs tucked where Tim had been sitting. Tim was gone, thank goodness. She sluggishly pushed herself upright.

"How do you feel?" Liv asked, tucking her hands behind her and leaning against the doorframe.

Thank goodness for that, too. She couldn't take more of Nate's ribbing right now. Her head felt like it was a hundred pounds. She pressed her palms to her cheeks. "I think I'm starting to feel my face again."

Liv laughed but before she could comment the click of the door opening again had her shuffling out of the way. Nate squeezed in.

"You okay?" he asked. "First thing I'm going to do when I

get home is flush those things so that it doesn't happen to anyone else."

"You shouldn't flush medications," Emilie muttered. "They need to be properly disposed of."

Nate grinned at Liv. "Yep, she's okay."

"A sure sign," Liv agreed.

Emilie shook her head, with some degree of control, even. This wasn't the first time she'd suffered through their teasing about her concern for the environment and it wouldn't be the last. The thought brought her overreaction to Tim's vegetarianism surging back. *Cringeworthy, Em.*

Why had she been so catty? Everyone poked fun at her for trying to be socially responsible about the environment and eating right went hand-in-hand with that. She was health-conscious about her choices — but Tim's revelation made her feel as if she'd been one-upped. He hadn't preached or lectured or in any way explained or defended his position. All he'd done was answer her question.

"We should take Tim sightseeing one day," Nate said. "You know I've lived here six years and have yet to see any of it?"

"That is sad, Miller," Liv said.

"Like you're one to talk," he retorted.

Liv grinned. "True."

"Ahem," Emilie interrupted. "Let me rephrase that for you, Nate. You should take Tim sightseeing one day. Leave me out of it."

"Aren't you Miss Sunshine," he said. "I remember well the day of my interview when your sister here passed me off onto you. You were a first-rate tour guide, Em. I bet you'd be great at showing us the city."

"That was then," Emilie said. "This is now."

"Where is Tim, anyway?" Nate asked.

"Somewhere out there. Talking to horses. It's cute," Liv said.

Tim's fascination with horses had caught Emilie off guard. Dogs, okay. Almost everyone likes dogs. She'd expected his response to be more like Will's had been; that whole arms-length, *I'll leave that to all of you, thanks* attitude. Instead, Tim seemed drawn to them.

"Let's get him licensed. I've got to go to the race office, so you can help him, right Em?" Liv looked at her.

Emilie frowned. Now her sister was roping her into the babysitting. "What, exactly, are you hiring the guy on crutches to do?"

Liv scribbled her signature on the application. "It's a formality. Do you want to have to sign him in at the East Gate every time he comes?"

I don't want to have anything to do with Tim. She sighed. "Well, he won't be the first useless person to be employed at the racetrack."

She slipped out onto the shed, happy, at least, to be more or less in command of her limbs again, and there he was, the reason she'd been deprived of her own, comfy bed. He stood in front of Reba's stall, having some kind of private conversation with her favourite filly.

Emilie sighed. It was more than cute; it was adorable. How could she be mad at that? Then she turned her head as Liv came out of the office, her neck twingeing a reminder. How? That was how.

CHAPTER EIGHT

EMILIE WAS DOING a good job of making him feel like a burden. When Liv suggested they should drive wherever they were going, Emilie pointed out it wasn't that far, so he insisted he was fine to walk. Well — she and Liv walked, and he kept pace on the crutches. When Liv went through the doors on the left of the foyer of the red brick building, Emilie directed him to the right.

"Do you have cash? It'll cost you twenty bucks," she said.

So he had to pay to be that burden? *Fantastic.* He shoved a hand in his pocket and came out with a five.

Emilie sighed and handed him a twenty.

"I'll pay you back. I have money at the house," he promised.

"Fine," she said, though she didn't sound fine at all. "Hi Mel."

The young woman behind the counter looked up, her eyes locking on him before shifting. "Hi Emilie! New recruit?"

"This is Nate's brother. Tim," Emilie explained, making it sound like she was introducing an eight-year-old.

But Mel smiled at him warmly. "Hi Tim. Are you here from Calgary?"

"Yeah," he said with a nod. Everyone knew his brother around here, and liked him. Nate was easy to like.

"Nice," she said. "I'll take that."

He slid the paper across the smooth surface between them, along with the money, but she only took the application, scribbling in the "for office use" portion. Tim stared around the room, absently taking in the wall decor — which seemed to consist of old posters — as she did whatever she was doing.

"Come on over here and we'll take your photo." Mel waved him to the side. "It's okay if you smile."

So it wasn't like a driver's licence? He did as he was told; not smiling, exactly, but trying not to look like a serial killer, because he figured the best plan was to follow instructions so they could get out of there. He didn't want to take up any more of Emilie's time.

When all was said and done, he had a badge that said "hotwalker," which apparently was the lowest of the low when it came to jobs around here. He didn't care. He thought it was cool, even though it looked like a bad joke because of his crutches. Hopefully, they'd let him walk a horse once he didn't need them. He was an athlete; that should make him qualified, right? Horses didn't scare him, and he understood about cooling down muscles and rehydrating. It might be his chance to finally feel useful.

Liv met them outside, and the three of them walked back to the barn in silence. Because they started so early in the morning, the grooms were almost finished work now, and it wasn't even eleven AM. If his hockey career fell through, could he move out here permanently and do this job for real? Nate would give him a place to live, wouldn't he? He was only half joking — Emilie might not appreciate his presence becoming permanent — but the horses were so gentle; so peaceful once their training was over. They all seemed so content. It could rub off on a guy.

The horse he had been talking to earlier had its head sticking out of the stall and was eating hay from a netted holder, and Emilie gravitated toward it. It was so pretty — a bright orange colour and looked as if someone had taken a wide brush, dipped it in white paint and dragged it crookedly down its face. Emilie became noticeably softer, more approachable, as she fussed with the horse, so he inched closer. She looked like a proud parent.

"This is Reba," she said without prompting. "Official name: She Sings. She won the Canadian Oaks not long ago; the most important race for three-year-old fillies in the country."

"Is she yours?" he asked.

She laughed, a wistful sound. "No. Well... technically she's my father's. But I usually gallop her on the weekends. Stupid DOMS."

He suppressed a chuckle, and she gave him a twisted smile back. She dug into her jeans' pocket for something and held a fist out to him. "She likes peppermints."

Reba reached for him, her neck stretching so far he was sure she was going to touch him. He didn't think she'd bite — she'd been so sweet before — but he figured he'd better stick a candy in her face just in case. She was careful when she took it, her whiskers tickling his palm as the round white disc disappeared followed by *crunch, crunch, crunch.*

He glanced at Emilie and found her watching him, so he snapped his gaze back to the filly. Her earlier mood seemed to have dissipated — and he was sure the horse got the credit for that. Reba nudged him, hard. *You're not much different from Holly, demanding attention, are you?*

"Careful, filly," Emilie said, eying his crutches. Was that worry creasing her forehead?

"I'm fine. She can't knock me over."

"You'd be surprised." She grinned.

He shuffled back just the same, and raised an eyebrow at her, controlling his mouth so he didn't give himself away. "So, you're not an addict?"

"No! I can't believe you asked that." She was trying to glare at him, but a wry smile tugged at her lips, her eyes lit with mirth instead of scorn. It was nice to get even that much from her after their rocky start.

"So what happens now?" he asked.

"We don't have anyone racing today, so everyone gets to go home. Two of the grooms will come back to feed the horses again this afternoon, then they start all over early tomorrow morning."

He felt as if he was walking a fine line with her and didn't want to misstep. Asking what she was doing next might invite the return of antagonism — he didn't want her to think he meant it might involve him, so he kept quiet. Then Liv reappeared from the office. A lucky break. He hoped she was ready to leave. Not that he didn't enjoy hanging out here. He'd sit on a bale of straw and read all afternoon if that was an option.

"So are you okay to drive home, Em or do you need me to?" Liv asked, just a hint of teasing in her voice and eyes.

Emilie covered her face with both hands and groaned. "This is going to haunt me forever, isn't it? Were you planning to go home with me?"

Liv turned to Tim. "What do you want to do? If you want to watch your brother ride this afternoon, we can stay and go back late with him. Otherwise we can head out now with Em."

"Going back to the farm is fine," he said. Being honest, he didn't need another afternoon of navigating escalators and stairs and strangers on crutches — he was going to assume there would be other chances to watch Nate once he was free of them.

"You can drive." Emilie handed Liv her keys. "Just in case there's any residual effect from my stupidity. Let's get out of here."

"Are you hungry, Tim?" Liv asked. "Should we stop for food?"

He shook his head quickly. The idea of a grocery store on a Saturday made him shudder. He'd probably end up living on yogurt and salad till he went home, but whatever.

"Can we stop for coffee? Please?" Emilie begged as they reached her Honda Civic, Liv popping the locks. "You can sit in the front, Tim. Just in case I need another nap."

"Didn't you just ask for coffee?" he said, instead of the more appropriate *thanks,* waiting while she squeezed in the back of the two-door hatchback.

"I could fall asleep between here and Starbucks, trust me."

But she stayed awake, and he was grateful for it. He listened to her and Liv talk, trying to glean what he could from their conversation. It was all about the horses, Emilie wanting to be brought up to date after missing the morning. The details fascinated him. He'd watched — while she slept off her drowsiness — but there was rarely someone to answer the questions that kept coming to him. He tried to pick up everything he could just by listening and observing — the equipment, the terminology, the training methods — in hopes of better understanding it all.

Liv pulled into a crowded Starbucks parking lot with a frown. "The line-up for the drive-through is insane."

"What do you want? I'll go in," Emilie said, a hand on either bucket seat as she leaned between them. She didn't seem to care how close her face was to his, but he was careful not to turn toward her. "You'll have to let me out, though, Tim."

He did, flipping the seat up for her. "I'll come too." Liv was already typing something into her phone. She didn't care about being left alone. But when Emilie raised an eyebrow, he thought maybe he should have waited for an invitation. "Is that all right?"

She gave a one-shouldered shrug. "Sure."

The way she'd said it, she might as well have added, *it's a free country.*

There were no empty tables, but the lineup was much shorter than the drive-through. He scanned the menu and felt his neck muscles tense, his stomach uneasy. He was always the one who never knew what to order, like he had to weigh the merits of the myriad choices before him and decide which one would perfectly suit both his mood and the needs of his body. The line was long enough he hoped he could decide before they got to the cash register.

"You can go first," he said. Maybe chivalry was dead, but his mother would tear a strip off him if he didn't adhere to the adage. If Emilie complained, like she was some ultra-feminist, he'd just tell the truth. He needed more time.

She didn't complain, though. She smiled a little, even, peering up at him before facing a guy about their age and asking for a venti double-shot latte. It rolled off her tongue with the ease of someone who had said it a million times before, and she added Liv's order for a cappuccino with the same mastery.

She gave her name and reached into her pocket.

"I'll get this," Tim said, putting a hand on her arm to stop her from paying.

She froze, looking first at his hand, then his face. "Okay. Thanks. Found your cash then, did you?"

He slid his hand back to his side abruptly. Why had he touched her? He waved a credit card.

"They would have taken that at the licensing office," she said, making a face as she stepped out of the way to make room for him.

He hadn't thought to ask. If he'd known, he wouldn't owe her twenty bucks. His eyes returned to the menu, scanning before settling on something, feeling as if everyone was waiting on him — the guy behind the cash, Emilie, the growing lineup.

"A green tea latte, please." Size, he needed to pick a size. Why didn't this place just have regular names for the portions? "Tall."

"Name?"

"Wayne." He passed the card over the reader, listening for the beep.

Emilie's lips twisted into that wry little smile she used a lot, watching him until he glanced directly at her. She turned away and walked to the end to wait for the order. When the barista called for Wayne and placed his drink on the counter, he felt that same look, but she didn't ask questions, instead requesting a tray for their three beverages and leading the way to the car. He waited while she passed Liv's cup to her through the driver's side window before she came around to slip behind the passenger seat.

"I always feel guilty getting coffee from Starbucks instead of Triple Shot," she said. He could hear her inhale the steam coming off the cup. "But, desperate times."

"We should stop there for treats," Liv suggested. "You know, in honour of Tim's arrival."

"That's as good an excuse as any," Emilie said. The prospect of treats from this place seemed to have a positive effect on her mood too. Not quite the same as the horse had.

While he could relate to the food thing, he was beginning to understand the pull of the horses, too.

The conversation dropped off for the rest of the drive, a combination of early morning and introversion, and he thought maybe Emilie had fallen asleep. He tried to catch glimpses of her in the side mirror because turning around would be too obvious. No luck. Resisting the temptation to pull his phone out because it would have felt rude, even though Liv was silent, he shifted his gaze to the unfamiliar landscape outside the window.

He had vague memories of the town Nate had driven through last night, and when Liv pulled into the parking lot of a small strip mall it clicked that he'd heard about Triple Shot. He'd met Will Callaghan's girlfriend Faye at the hospital the day of Nate's surgery last summer, then again at the wedding on the beach. He liked Faye. She was one of those people who talked, but also asked questions, forcing you to talk, which was sometimes awkward but also meant you weren't just trapped listening to the person go on and on.

A little bell on the door announced their arrival, and the three of them stepped into the shop, enveloped by the smell of fresh coffee, not unlike the Starbucks, except with it was the homey scent of baking. There was a counter display filled with a selection of goods, from cookies and tarts to the fancy French confections Will had begun making. Art decorated the walls, and two sets of patrons with white mugs and plates conversed in an area with tables and chairs.

Faye greeted him like family without making a fuss, then put together a box of baked items that had him salivating. He wasn't going to say no to the sugar cookie she offered as a taste test. Liv handed him the box once they were back in the car, and he almost said he shouldn't be trusted with it. It took all his willpower not to crack it open and at least peek in. Emilie eyed him warily, like she didn't exactly think he was dependable enough to be the custodian of the goodies. Either that or she wanted to hold it herself with no intent of showing restraint. She carried it into the house, looking covetous for a moment before setting it on the counter.

"Lunch, I guess," Liv said once they were in the kitchen. "Hmm."

"You should have said yes to the stopping for food thing, Tim," Emilie quipped. "This one relies on your brother to keep from starving."

"Exaggeration," Liv said with a scowl that quickly transformed to a grin. "But only a little one. Leftover pizza, I'm thinking."

Emilie released her dog from the plastic kennel that was tucked in the corner. The black Lab bounded out, took a few laps from her water bowl, bounced to Liv for a scratch then noticed Tim and barrelled over. He slid his knee out of the way but she screeched to a halt, sitting next to him and waiting until he indulged her. At least Emilie's dog was happy to have a visitor.

Liv threw some slices in a countertop toaster oven, but Emilie set hers on a paper towel and tossed it into the microwave. It pinged when it was done and she lifted it out carefully before tentatively taking a small bite off the end.

"Come on, Holly. Maybe by the time we're done our romp, I'll feel capable of schooling a couple of horses," she said between bites.

"The best remedy for muscle soreness is movement," Liv said. "Not stolen drugs."

Emilie stuck her tongue out at her sister as she left with the excited Labrador, so she didn't see Tim's grin.

CHAPTER NINE

So MUCH FOR never having to see Tim because he'd keep to himself and she was busy. He was showing up everywhere. This time, he was parked in the corner of Triple Shot Café with a notebook, a laptop, his phone, and that same fat book she always saw him with, everything spread out like it was his private office. He raised his head from whatever he was working on, and she lifted her hand in half a wave.

There. That was civil, right? There was no point in being overly friendly with this guy, so she didn't feel badly about not speaking. It wasn't as if he'd voiced a greeting, either — as usual. He'd really just moved his head a little, given an almost-nod, and followed her with his eyes as she crossed the shop and ducked into the back. It was a little unnerving, to be honest. Maybe he was watching to see if she was sober. She'd never live that down.

"Hi Emilie!' Sylvie Cloutier sang out, beaming as she rolled out sugar cookies on one of the stainless kitchen surfaces. "What are you doing here?"

Emilie stole a piece of dough and popped it in her mouth.

She wasn't the one working, so she wasn't breaking any rules, was she? Faye scowled at her nonetheless.

"Our internet at the farm is useless today and I want to get some work done on the New Chapter website, but I see you have a visitor," Emilie said, raising her eyebrows and narrowing her vision on Faye. "What's he doing here?"

"What you're doing, apparently, and what I used to do before I worked here," Faye said. "The two of you don't talk?"

"How did he get here?"

"Will picked him up. You could have saved him that with a bit of communication."

She had no intention of being Tim Miller's limo service. She was sacrificing enough for that man. Her hand went to her neck automatically. She was over the DOMS and her neck was much better — what good was being a physiotherapist if you couldn't help your own complaints? The resentment wasn't as easily resolved.

"Will and Nate are working on getting Tim a car," Faye added, eyeing Emilie skeptically.

"Well, that's good. We won't have to play chauffeur forever, then." Except — how long was he staying, anyway?

Sylvie finished placing the cookie shapes on a large sheet and slid it into the oven. She set a timer, then dusted off her hands and started tidying up. "I'm going to take my break, okay Faye?"

"Sure." Faye answered. "We're pretty quiet right now. Take Tim a butter tart or something though, will you? He needs to be initiated."

"Okay." Sylvie lifted a tart from a tray, setting it on a plain white plate. "You want one, Em? Or can I make you a cappuccino?"

Faye snorted. "She can make it herself. It's the least she can do in exchange for getting it for free."

Emilie grinned and made her way to the espresso machine out front. Sylvie followed with the plate but stayed with Emilie, peering around her at Tim in the corner.

"You weren't exaggerating," Sylvie whispered. "He's even better-looking than he was in the photos you showed me."

Emilie didn't bother to acknowledge Sylvie's statement of the obvious but couldn't keep herself from following her friend's gaze. *I wonder what he looks like when he smiles.*

She'd never seen him with a real smile, even in the wedding photos. She didn't know if he had perfect teeth, like Nate. Maybe it would be too much for her to handle. Could a guy be too good-looking? And did it matter how good-looking he was if his personality was unbearable?

"What are you going to do with him while he's here?" Sylvie asked, her tone still hushed as the machine hummed, the carafe filling with deep brown liquid, the crema on top the colour of the pages of an old book.

"Me?" She had to keep herself from a derisive snort. "Nothing. Nate and Liv want to go play tourist, but they don't need me for that."

"You don't like him anymore?" Sylvie asked, a little louder to be heard over the sound of Emilie steaming milk.

Emilie frowned and focused on pouring the espresso into a cup then adding the milk, creating a heart-shaped pattern in the foam. She stared at it a beat and sighed. "It didn't work out. Or didn't come to pass, more like."

"I could be his tour guide." A sly smile came over Sylvie's lips, her comment coming a little too quickly. Then she added, as if she'd realized her faux pas, "If you wouldn't mind."

"Go for it," Emilie said, lifting her cup and slurping the foam, destroying the heart design. "Good luck."

Tim was more interested in her dog than he was in women. She still felt disappointment, and a pang of jealousy — and that

Sylvie should know better than to believe her. But she refused to be possessive of Tim when she'd never been close to ever having him.

Sylvie picked up the plate and rolled her shoulders back. "Okay! I'm going in. Maybe you could introduce me?"

He didn't know if the internet was always bad at the farm, but it sure had been today. There was no way he was streaming videos there, and he'd planned to watch the replays of old games, to study them so he felt like he was doing something for his career. Will had suggested the café, and as it turned out, it was a nice quiet spot. Faye had brought him a sandwich and left him alone. Then he'd seen Emilie come in, and he hadn't managed so much as a hello.

He scribbled a box at the top of the notebook's lined page, trying to make the words come. What rhymed with "highlight?" Bright? Might? Delight? Poems didn't have to rhyme, but lyrics did. Not that he was trying to write lyrics. Was he? Nate and Mom were the musical ones in the family. Phil hadn't been able to carry a tune and Dad had to be coerced into singing "Happy Birthday." Tim loved music and could sing if he had to. And for some reason, he'd always wished he could write songs, though he didn't know what had inspired him to try it today.

Dragging his head from the memories — some good, some sad — he wondered how his parents were doing. Did his absence give them space in a good way? More freedom to work out whatever was going on between them? He'd never heard them argue; maybe a good screaming match would help. He didn't know. Thirty-five years they'd been married. How did a couple get that far and just decide to give up?

He forced his mind back to the page, but it was no good. Those words weren't coming. So far he hadn't accomplished anything online. He should get back to doing what he'd come here for.

Emilie had disappeared into the kitchen, but now she was out front, making a cappuccino, and a woman he didn't recognize, about the same age, was with her, whispering like a schoolgirl and dashing obvious looks his way. He didn't know who she was, and what he had to do with anything, other than he assumed she worked here. He repositioned the laptop and propped his book against the screen. If writing words wasn't working, he'd read them. If he looked like he was studying something, would they leave him alone?

The heroine in the story was on her horse again, chased by the villain, and he was totally visualizing Emilie crouched over the animal's neck, the mane whipping her face as they flew over rough terrain. He wanted to see her ride. He'd been disappointed when she hadn't been able to, the other morning. He'd felt bad for her, but it had been hilarious. Teasing her hadn't won him any points, though.

He'd gone out and watched the horses on the track — other girls like Emilie riding, and lots of guys. Some of them were as big as him. It was badass, the way they flew around. He wasn't sure he'd have the nerve to do it.

After cleaning the utensils and the machine, Emilie leaned back against the wall, cup in hand, closing her eyes and inhaling whatever aroma came off the beverage. The other woman was still murmuring in her ear, and Emilie slid a slow look his way. He ducked his head back to the book. How was he ever going to learn to talk to her? At least, without saying something stupid?

Oh, no... now the other woman was coming over. She was bearing a butter tart on a plate like it was the crown jewels, and maybe it was — Nate said they were amazing — but if it came with conditions or expectations, he didn't want it. Not that it looked as if he had any choice.

She was pretty, her mid-length hair held back at the nape with a clip, and she wore a t-shirt and knee-length shorts under an apron. He hadn't seen her when he'd arrived. She must've come in the back, or been here before Will dropped him off.

"Faye asked me to bring this out for you." She smiled as she set it on the table next to his laptop, then tucked a loose strand of hair behind her ear. "I'm Sylvie. Emilie's friend."

Tim glanced at Emilie, who skulked not far behind, just as she rolled her eyes and took a sip of her cappuccino. What did that mean? They weren't friends? She ambled up next to Sylvie.

"Sylvie is the daughter of Roger, our trainer. Or at least our trainer before..."

The pieces clicked into place in his brain. "Oh. Your mom was really sick, wasn't she? How's she doing?"

That was enough of an opening for Sylvie to pull out a chair and invite herself to the table. This is why he wasn't friendly. Being friendly meant people thought it was okay to do stuff like that.

"She's doing great, thanks for asking. She and my father are travelling this summer. A little 'life's too short,' you know?"

"Much to Liv's chagrin," Emilie said. It seemed, to Tim's shock, she'd decided to join them. "She was hoping he'd come back so she could ride Reba in the Queen's Plate."

Now he felt cornered, Sylvie on his left and Emilie on his right. He was stuck between these two beautiful, confident women and any abrupt escape would just reinforce Emilie's view that he was an idiot. Their proximity made his throat constrict, leaving him with less hope of producing words from it than he'd had trying to get them from his brain, to his hand, to pen and paper. Butter tart to the rescue: it might be a good time to try it. He took a large bite so all he could do was hum for a moment.

Queen's Plate. He knew what that was. The big horse race Nate had won. Twice.

"When is that?" he asked through the hand he'd raised to cover his mouth while he chewed the first half of the tart. The excitement of possibly being able to attend in person instead of watching on TV trumped his anxiety.

"Next weekend," Emilie said.

"Can I come?" he asked.

She laughed, an easy laugh that didn't make him feel like she hated him. "Of course! If you didn't bring the right outfit, though, I hate to tell you, but Nate's going to have to take you shopping. Still want to go?"

"Yeah, for sure." If he could dress up for a wedding, he could dress up for a horse race. The horse race would be way more fun.

"But you know what comes before race day, right?" Sylvie said, her face brightening.

Tim shifted to Emilie, expecting a similar look, but her face darkened almost imperceptibly. "The Plate Ball, you mean? That's work for me. I take it you're coming?" she asked Sylvie.

"Yes. My father bought tickets but they're not going to be home in time. All I need is a date."

Why was she glancing at him, her eyebrows quivering? He slouched lower in his seat, grabbing for the rest of the butter tart, and couldn't stop stealing a look at Emilie. Her mouth was in a firm line, and he thought he caught a subtle head-shake.

"Liv and Nate paid for a table, so if you think you want to come, Tim, there's a spot for you. No offence if you don't. It's just a fundraiser for the Thoroughbred aftercare group I volunteer with. We take horses that are finished racing and help find them new homes and second careers."

He nodded slowly, noncommittally, his mouth full. "Thank you," he said after he swallowed, and held Emilie's eyes. *For getting me out of that.*

Her eyes stayed locked on his for a beat, then she snatched her cup back up, bringing it to her lips and staring down into it. "Don't you have an appointment with Sam this afternoon?"

"Three o'clock," he confirmed.

"She's really good. Better work hard, because you'll want to lose the crutches by Plate Day." She tossed back the last of the cappuccino and pushed herself up. "Come on, Sylvie. You need to tell me what you're wearing to the ball and I sincerely doubt Tim wants to hear two girls talking about clothes. I want one of those cookies you made earlier, too. See you later, Tim."

"See you, Emilie," he managed. "Nice to meet you, Sylvie."

Sylvie smiled, removing the now-empty plate she'd brought him. Emilie threw another glance over her shoulder as they walked away, like she well knew she'd rescued him. He wanted to think that meant there was a chance he'd be able to open up the lines of communication between them again, if only he knew how to do that. He deserved the cold shoulder from her, even if she seemed to have a hard time maintaining it.

But even so... he always came back around to the reason he'd put that wedge between them. It had been conscious; intentional. And cowardly. What hope did he have if he couldn't be up front with her?

And even if by some miracle they ended up together, they could still turn out like his parents. It might take a few months, or a year, or ten, or thirty-five. But unless he figured out what his father never had — how to be the other half of a vivacious, generous woman when he'd never seemed wired quite right himself — they were doomed before they even started.

He pulled out the page he'd stashed, blank except for a few scribbles, and thought of all the lyrics already written that held pieces of what he felt. It was too easy to let old songs dictate their chances; to believe they were over before they'd even started. He wanted to write a new one, rebuking the labels he'd adopted in his head. Use the words to work his way out so he could convince Emilie he'd get it right this time. He picked up the pen, hovering over the paper before the ink flowed.

I let you down not once, but twice.
And I don't want to waste your time
Trying to prove to you that there is merit
In convincing you we're words that rhyme.
That you're the end of every sentence
The theme that's woven through my soul
The sustenance to get me through
When I've been living on gruel in a bowl.

Well, that sucked. He tore the paper from the notebook, shredding it and letting the pieces fall to the table.

He should probably stick to hockey.

CHAPTER TEN

SHE SHOULD HAVE JUST LET him suffer; fend for himself. Tim was an adult. He didn't need her help. But he'd looked a little panicky, and she hadn't been able to ignore it any more than she'd ignore a puppy in distress.

Had she just compared Tim Miller to a puppy? That was a warning sign. It was time to get her defences back up. She would not let him get to her again. All she had to do was figure out a way to be friendly enough not to raise the ire of Liv and Nate, but not so much Tim thought she'd forgotten what he'd done.

Inevitably, she'd run into him, which meant she needed to accept it and be better prepared. Ironic that their encounters had been off the farm so far. He seemed to have an interest in the racehorses so she could expect him to show up at the track and with the farm's rural internet he'd likely seek out Triple Shot's Wi-Fi again. She doubted he'd want to come to the Plate Ball. Dancing and socializing? No. That wouldn't be his thing. Plate Day, though? Yes. And she could deal with that.

"He's a hard one to crack, eh?" Sylvie was placing the plate in the dishwasher when Emilie tuned in again.

"Didn't I warn you?" she responded, brushing past Sylvie to add her cup to the machine, not really wanting to dwell on thoughts of Tim.

"Not exactly, no. You only said it didn't work out," Sylvie persisted. "What happened?"

Nothing. That's what happened. A big zilch. "He just takes a while to get to know, and I guess he decided when we did get to know each other a bit, it wasn't for him. So go forth and... whatever."

Sylvie crossed her arms, looking pensive. "It doesn't seem like he'd be the best candidate for the summer fling I have in mind."

Summer fling? Emilie caught herself before she laughed out loud. No, Tim wasn't a summer fling. Tim would be an investment — and not a promising one.

"Probably not," Emilie agreed. Not that she was trying to dissuade Sylvie. She wasn't. It was only logical. "When did you decide this?"

"My parents will be away for most of the summer, so I'll be on my own. And I'm going back to Montreal in the fall. I do have to face reality and finish my Masters, now that my mom is doing well. This might be my last chance."

"For love?" Emilie grinned. "Think there's a plot for a romance novel in there somewhere?"

"Are you going to start writing?" Sylvie teased.

"No way. Seems like a lot of work." She opened the plastic container holding the sugar cookies and held it out for Sylvie before taking one for herself. "So, if not Tim, who?"

Sylvie sighed, taking a bite. "When do I meet men, Emilie?"

"I can't recommend the Plate Ball for that, sorry. Faye

might have more ideas — except of course, she's practically an old married crone now."

"Excuse me?" Faye, who had obviously been listening in, said. "I am not old. I am not a crone. And I most definitely am not married."

"But you are still ridiculously in love with Will," Emilie stated.

Faye drummed her fingers against the counter, lips pursed. "Yes."

Emilie laughed. "So what's with that? Liv gave you the bouquet; you have a responsibility."

"That wasn't fair," Faye said.

"What?" Sylvie interjected. "I didn't hear about this!"

"At Liv and Nate's wedding," Emilie explained, "Liv didn't so much toss the bouquet as drive it like a killer softball pitch at Faye. And Faye caught it." Emilie tilted her head, staring down Faye. "You had choices."

"That day was all about Liv and Nate's happiness. Letting it fall to the sand would have detracted from that," Faye insisted.

"You know it's destiny, Faye," Emilie said. "Don't fight it."

"Shut up, Emilie," Faye said in her well-practiced, sarcastically sweet voice.

Emilie grinned and returned her attention to Sylvie. "I'm supposed to be asking you about what you're wearing to the ball. I want to hear from you too, Faye."

She didn't let the sound of the bell on the café's door distract her, eyes resolutely on her friends. Tim, off to his appointment. She hoped Sam wrestled those crutches away from him. It hadn't been exactly wrong that she'd peeked at his file — the PT in Calgary was a friend of both Sam and Nate's and had included her name on it, even though Emilie was adamant she wasn't working with him. The bottom line? He should already be walking without them. He was only using them as a... well... crutch. She snickered at her own ridiculous joke.

"What?" Faye asked suspiciously.

"You're both going to look fabulous," Emilie said, ignoring her, then switched topics. "We're overdue a hack, Sylvie. When are you done today?"

"Yes!" Sylvie said. "I haven't been on a horse since there was snow on the ground."

"We're in good shape here," Faye said. "If you want to take off early, you can."

Sylvie looked at Emilie. "Now?"

Emilie checked her watch. "Sure. I have just enough time before work."

She needed to clear her mind, and a trail ride was the cure for everything. She'd get that website work done another time.

***

Gone was the irritation she'd felt toward Sylvie earlier. A hack on a warm summer day was a balm to the soul. Three of them travelled single file, the woods not too buggy this time of morning: Sylvie on Excursion, because he was the sanest of the options; Jillian, one of the farm staff, on Miss Talk About It, and Emilie on Twizzle, Liv's old event mount and an ex-race-horse himself. He was the oldest horse on the farm, and still one of the spiciest. Anyone who stereotyped chestnut mares needed to meet this chestnut gelding. He'd give them a run for their money any day.

When they emerged from the trees into the clearing by the stallion barn, Twizzle's pace quickened like he was on a mission. This was the halfway point of the circuit, which for the old gelding meant it was time to speed up because they were headed home. It was the same thing every time Emilie took him for what was supposed to be a relaxing ride.

"You really are a poor role model for the younger horses, Twizzle," Emilie chastised, and Twizzle responded by giving a hard spook to the right that sent Emilie grappling for mane, the old gelding stopping just in time to save her falling to the grassy lawn below. Without missing a beat, he tried to duck his head to snatch a mouthful of grass.

"I don't think so," Emilie hissed, recovering her reins and dragging him up with legs clamped to his sides.

"Way to stick, Em."

Kerrie Evans stood on the porch of her cottage, the bright breadth of her winning smile dazzling even from a distance. It was probably what had spooked Twizzle. That and the farm manager's sudden appearance through her front door. Or maybe the small terrier-cross standing on high alert next to her. Pinhook had never once chased a horse, but he always looked as if he really, really wanted to.

Kerrie was effortlessly glamorous, even in the faded jeans and sky blue t-shirt she'd been wearing all day. Her hair was tumbled on her head in a messy bun that didn't look any different from when Emilie had seen her last, first thing this morning. Her even tan made her white hair look warm, like it was a really light blonde — which it had probably been in her younger years. If she'd been closer, Emilie would have been able to see the sprinkle of freckles over her nose and cheeks. She was a total natural beauty but also completely unassuming. Emilie had adored her on sight when she'd met her last winter and had been overjoyed when Kerrie agreed to take the job as manager. She couldn't have asked for a more perfect addition to the farm — and she didn't have to worry about Kerrie asking her out, like the last manager had.

"Let's go say hello," she said, nudging Twizzle forward.

"Confront the goblins!"

At this stage of his life, Twizzle didn't have to prove anything. He'd already established he was a clown. The spooking was an act — one he'd never pull with Liv. He'd been bold on the cross-country course, though Emilie might not have believed it if she hadn't seen it with her own eyes. While she didn't mind hacking him, she always felt he didn't take her seriously — and would probably have made a fool of her if she'd ever tried to compete with him.

Excursion walked right up to Kerrie when she came down the steps, bopping his nose against her hip, looking for treats. *So spoiled.* Miss Talk About It wasn't phased either. Twizzle hovered uncertainly, nostrils fluttering, as if he'd decided this human wasn't to be trusted — even though she fed him his breakfast every morning. Pinhook remained behind Kerrie on the top step, lying down now; head on his paws, one eye on Twizzle. They eyeballed each other like they were facing off at centre ice in a hockey game.

"I presented my idea for the celebrity challenge show to the board of directors at New Chapter," Emilie said, making sure not to let her guard down on the old chestnut lest he pull another of his moves. She watched as Excursion and Miss Talk About It convinced Kerrie to dig peppermints from her pockets.

"And?" Kerrie said.

"They loved it." Suddenly Twizzle didn't look quite as leery of the goblins. He took one step forward, then another, stretching his neck.

"It's a great idea," Jillian said. "But you have to let people who have adopted horses show too. Let the jockeys do the exhibition, sure, but then have a separate class for the graduates. That way spectators can see what everyday people have done with the horses, not just those who ride for a living."

"Even though the riding is like apples to oranges," Emilie pointed out.

"Sure, but everyone thinks Thoroughbreds are crazy, and jockeys are used to high-strung horses. By showing them ridden by normal people, it does more to showcase that they really can have good brains. I get so tired of people calling them crazy."

"Preaching to the choir, sister," Emilie said, nodding and holding up a hand — at least for as long as she dared leave only one on her reins with the aged gelding. "I'll run it past them, but it's a brilliant idea."

"I just wish I had a New Chapter graduate! The next time you'll have to include all off-track Thoroughbreds." She smiled.

"I'll need your help for this one, so you're going to be busy this time anyway." Emilie grinned and checked her watch. "We'd better keep moving. See you, Kerrie!"

The stallions were already inside, so Twizzle didn't have that for an excuse to be silly. When they were walking three-abreast down the laneway past the training track, he was finally content, wedged between the other two horses. Emilie let the reins slide out a notch, allowing herself to relax just a bit.

Then a shot of black blurred from where the lane formed a T by the house. All three horses started, and without his body-guards tightly flanking him, Twizzle was out of there with a hard one-eighty. All Emilie had time for was to tuck her arms into her body as she tumbled, landing on her butt on the hard-packed stone dust with a thud. She didn't know where Twizzle was, but Holly's face, wrinkled with concern — though still clutching the orange ball she'd been chasing — appeared above hers. *Are you okay? See my ball? Are you okay?*

I'm okay, she realized, and slowly pushed herself upright. But she'd have one spectacular bruise.

"What are you doing out?" She climbed cautiously to her feet, seeing Jillian had Twizzle, safe and sound and once again between his companions. Then she turned, slowly. Because Holly had not let herself out. And there, twenty feet away, looking sheepish, was Tim.

"Sorry," he said. And he sounded it. "Are you okay?"

He had bigger things than her tender gluteals to be sorry about. She clenched her hands into fists, glowering, feeling her neck pain return as she limped up to him. Just because she was fine didn't mean nothing hurt.

She stopped, hands on hips, seething. "I never said you could let my dog out! What if she wasn't trained? What if she ran off? What if she got kicked by a horse?"

Holly stood perpendicular to them, her tail wagging and ears flattening as she whimpered.

"I'm sorry, honey," Emilie said, leaning over. "I know, I shouldn't yell. But —" She glared at Tim.

"You told me all about the training you were doing with her." He carefully met her eyes before his darted back to Holly.

Bringing up that didn't help his case. That she now remembered she had indeed done that, back when they were messaging, just reminded her he'd left her hanging, for no good reason — so now she was mad at him for that, too.

"That doesn't guarantee she'll listen to you," she hissed.

Of course, Holly had. How dare she? *Traitor.* Except it was good she had, because the alternative... Emilie couldn't bear the thought of anything happening to her dog.

She glanced over her shoulder. "Are you okay with Twizzle, Jillian? I have to take Holly back to the house." She threw a hard look at Tim.

"I can take her back. I'm sorry I didn't ask you first if I could play with her. I just thought it would be nice." He looked adorably apologetic, raising those eyes of his from the gravel at his feet, tawny hair falling across his forehead.

Don't weaken, Emilie. But how could she not?

"Fine," she muttered. "Go. But this doesn't mean you can take her out again."

He nodded, appropriately chastised, and turned back toward the house. Emilie saw him pause, pull a second ball from his back pocket, and toss it in the air. Holly gave him her rapt attention and bounced beside him as he walked.

He walked.

"Hey!" Emilie called after him.

Tim stopped, turning forty-five degrees.

"What happened to the crutches?" She let her mouth curve into a wry smile.

One corner of his lips crimped, then he kept walking.

He had a dimple. A dimple! How could she stay mad at that?

She wandered back to Twizzle, his white-whiskered nose pressed into Excursion's withers like a worried racehorse in the post parade.

"Okay. I can do this," she said, checking to make sure the saddle hadn't slipped as she'd come off.

Gathering the reins, with Jillian on Miss Talk About It still holding the old gelding's head, she turned the stirrup toward her, grimacing as she threw her leg up to stick her toe in it. With a hop and a groan she was on, Twizzle giving a huff as she reassumed her place in the saddle.

"What can I tell you, buddy? If you hadn't ditched me, I wouldn't have had to put your old bones through that."

"So," Jillian said as they ambled back to the barn, all the excitement seeming to have taken the wind out of Twizzle's sails, the gelding now plodding like the pony he was supposed to be. "That was Tim?"

Emilie snorted, recognizing the sly smile on Jillian's face. "That was Tim. Good thing he's cute."

CHAPTER ELEVEN

HOLLY BOUNDED into the house ahead of him, Tim catching up just in time to see her hovering over her water bowl, perplexed. She still had a ball on her mouth, and a conundrum on her paws.

Need drink, but must have ball. Oh, to be a Labrador Retriever.

Nate, sitting at the kitchen table, came to her rescue, chuckling. He reached into a cupboard to pull out a treat container. Distracted for a moment by the obviously familiar sound, Holly spun to face him, and he traded cookie for ball — then hid the ball on top of the fridge. The Labrador gobbled her biscuit before messily lapping up the water.

"Emilie said you could take Holly out?" Nate asked, eyebrows raised as he slid back into his seat at the table. "She wouldn't let me play ball with the dog until I'd had a half-hour lesson," he added with a crooked grin.

Tim cast a wary look his way before shifting his eyes to Holly, who stood expectantly with tail wagging at all the exciting words being carelessly thrown around. *Out. Play. Ball.*

"No." He said it quietly to answer Nate, but Holly stilled, waiting for what might be next. "Go get your bone, girl," he suggested. She perked up again and bounced away, returning within seconds to plant herself in the middle of the kitchen floor, gnawing what looked like a nylon tibia.

Nate shook his head, lips still twisted. "I hope she didn't catch you."

Tim frowned, folding onto the bench across from Nate. He inconspicuously rolled the ball he still held from hand to hand, keeping it out of Holly's sight. "She did."

Nate's grin was full on now. "Are those clothes flame-retardant?"

Tim glared, then dropped his gaze, rubbing one hand across the table's smooth surface while squeezing the ball with the other. "It gets worse."

"How so?" Nate leaned in, hands clasped, as if he was trying to be supportive when he was far too obviously enjoying Tim's blunder.

"Holly scared her horse, and the horse threw her off," he confessed.

"Oops," Nate said, his face contorting, not looking as horrified as Tim had been when it happened. "She's all right though?"

"She says she is." Would she have admitted it if she wasn't? Probably, just to be sure he felt bad.

"Who was she riding?" Nate asked.

Like Tim had any idea. "I don't know. It was orange, kind of. With a big white band down its face."

"Twizzle. Well, that explains it. How rude." Nate was still trying to contain his laughter.

Tim winced. "I didn't mean it."

"I mean the horse, not you. That kind of action is part of

the territory with Twizzle. Don't worry. Nine times out of ten, getting dropped is not a big deal. But I bet Emilie is pissed."

Tim nodded, slowly. "More about the dog than falling off, I think."

"Yeah, well. That's to be expected too. Don't mess with her dog if you want to get on her good side."

"You could have warned me," Tim grumbled.

"Sorry, I didn't compile a manual." Nate was having way too much fun with this.

"Maybe you should have." Tim drummed his fingers on the table distractedly then blurted, "I want to go."

Nate tilted his head at the random comment. "Where?"

"To that ball thing."

"The Plate Ball? Okay. Really?" he said, his gaze narrowing as if he wasn't convinced Tim knew what he was in for — and rightly so. Tim had been the five-year-old kid who cried when he went to birthday parties, and other than not crying anymore, similar feelings when faced with anything that involved over three people remained.

"Yes," he said, with what he hoped was a reasonable degree of conviction. "What do I have to wear?"

Nate was still looking at him like his body might have been invaded by an alien being, but the joking stopped.

"Well," Nate said. "They made it more casual this year. Last year it was full on formal. You'd probably be okay in what you were wearing on the plane. Or maybe what you'd wear before a game."

He nodded. They always dressed to look sharp walking into the arena. "And what about the race?"

"The Plate?" Nate asked.

"Yeah."

"That's a bit of a different story. I mean, you can wear

whatever you want, but," and he hesitated with a lift to one corner of his lips that would have been unmistakable to nearly anyone but the brother he'd once been close with. "If you want to impress Em, then yeah, you want to dress up."

There was no point in denying it. "You've got to help me," he pleaded.

Nate leaned back, meeting Tim's eyes. "You know who would do a better job than me?"

The unknown frightened him, but he had to ask. "Who?"

"Faye Taylor. She could hire out her services as a fashion consultant if she wasn't so busy with the café. The café is great, don't get me wrong, but she might have missed her calling. Even if she just wanted to make a bit more money on the side."

But Tim had tuned him out. That might not be so bad. Faye was all right. "When?"

Nate's mouth was open, like Tim must've cut him off. There was that restrained smile again. "Do you want me to ask her for you?" his brother said in the same tone he'd used so many times when they were growing up.

"You're such a jerk."

"That's my job as your older brother, right? Funny, it's what Emilie says now too. Nice to have things in common, isn't it?" He shielded his face with his arms when Tim reached for a salt shaker, threatening to throw it. "How about you come down to the city on Tuesday? A few guys and I get together with Will to play some music and Faye usually comes. It's pretty low-key. You could hang out for a bit if you want, then she could take you shopping. I doubt she'll say no."

"That's great." His tone didn't exactly make him sound enthusiastic, but inside he was exhilarated because of the end goal: the chance for a fresh start with Emilie.

"How'd the physio appointment go? Are you done with

those?" Nate nodded at the crutches, which Tim had left next to Holly's kennel before he'd taken her out. It seemed Tim was the only one who'd thought he should keep them around.

"I guess I don't need them anymore," he admitted. "And I have to up my exercises a bit."

"If you're going to the ball, it's not because you want to be a wallflower, am I right? It's only a week away."

Nate knew what Tim was thinking. They exchanged a look, skepticism etched all over Nate's features.

A week. A week to get his confidence back; to not worry with every step that something would give and he'd undo everything the surgery had fixed. Ligaments were tricky that way. Tim swallowed. Dancing wasn't exactly skating, but his knee was weak. He couldn't believe he was considering risking it for a girl.

"Maybe we can keep each other motivated," Nate said. "Be accountability partners."

Trust Nate to sense his worry, though the way his face was all scrunched up was likely a tip-off.

"You don't have a problem with that. You look pretty good for an old guy," he countered. Nate looked better than Tim had ever seen him, but he wasn't going to concede that. "Pushing thirty, aren't you?"

"That's a pretty cheeky thing to say to the guy who's trying to help you save your career and get the girl of your dreams."

Tim scowled. "Now you're pushing it."

"Am I?" Nate grinned. "Didn't I tell you about Emilie? I think thanks are in order."

"Nothing to thank you for, yet." *She'll barely even talk to me.*

Maybe he was delusional to think he'd make everything up to her by going to this ball; like he thought he was a Disney

Prince. His lack of charm was his downfall. Some days he'd trade a couple inches with Nate for half his brother's charisma.

"Will and I have a car lined up for you too," Nate said. "I didn't want to say anything until you weren't so reliant on the crutches because it's standard. You can drive a stick, right?"

Tim pressed his lips together into a tight line. "Sort of."

"I guess you're going to have to get better at it then, or just keep relying on someone else to cart you around."

"I just need practice," he said, convincing himself. "Then I can drive the Porsche too, right?" He grinned. That would be extra motivation to figure it out.

"Ha! No." Nate rose. "Make sure you put the dog back in her kennel. Emilie might let it slide once, but heaven help you if you screw up again."

He batted Tim's shoulder with the back of his hand as he left.

Screw up. Again. It's all he seemed to be able to do with Emilie, even when he was trying to be nice.

Somehow she'd forgiven him for his ineptitude at the wedding, where it had first gone wrong. The way he'd become a cardboard cutout when expected to dance with her, then made it worse by chasing her away.

It was easier to do that than get into all the reasons he shouldn't like her. He'd watched guys on the different teams he'd played with act like idiots because of girls. Heard about the reputation young hockey players had for doing bad things. That had always made it simpler to convince himself to maintain his focus on the game; keeping his nose clean, keeping his father happy. Keeping his distance from Emilie just seemed the right thing to do. *Strike one.*

Except he hadn't been able to get her out of his head. So when he'd seen her on the other end of that video call at Christmas, he'd sent the friend request, counting on her being too nice to ignore it, only to ghost her three months later. *Strike Two.*

This was it. He couldn't afford strike three.

CHAPTER TWELVE

"I HEARD you'd joined Ben's practice." Liv stood at the window of the vet's SUV, arms crossed, smiling. "Deserting your father?"

"Diversifying my experience," the man said as he climbed out and offered Liv his hand. "I'm sure I'll be taking over when my dad decides to retire."

Emilie didn't recognize this vet, and glanced at Liv who obviously knew him. His blond hair was cut short and in any other context he'd probably look like he was in good shape, but when the men she saw most were serious athletes, he seemed soft.

"They always send the new guy for the fun jobs, eh Chad?" Liv said.

"You could probably do this one yourself." The man grinned.

"This is Chad Winters, Em." Liv finally turned to her sister. "We were in vet school together. We weren't each other's biggest fans back then, but he turned out to be not so bad."

Liv's grin piqued Emilie's interest. She would know if Liv

had entertained an attraction to anyone before Nate, wouldn't she? Liv could be pretty secretive — and when she'd been in school, she hadn't had time to breathe let alone keep Emilie current on her state of mind — but surely Faye would have known. Faye and Liv had carpooled to Guelph nearly every day for classes. Either way, there was a story here.

She did recognize the assistant who jumped out of the passenger side, shorts reaching her knees and the navy polo shirt with the name of Ben's clinic embroidered on it untucked. Her blonde ponytail, a touch of pink running through it, bounced at the back of her head.

"Ava!" She skipped up and gave the young woman a quick hug. "I hadn't heard you were working for Ben."

"Summer job." Ava smiled, tucking a clipboard under her arm while she rummaged behind the seat for an extension cord. "I'm off to the University of Guelph in the fall!"

"Congrats!" Emilie said. "Let me guess: BioSci?"

Ava nodded, the ponytail bobbing with each dip of her chin. While not the only way there, Biology was the traditional undergraduate path to vet school.

"We'll do the ultrasound first, Ava," Chad called across.

Liv led the way into the cool darkness of the training barn, down to the stall of a bay filly, the name Wishonakiss written in bold block letters on the information card tucked in the metal keeper on the stall door.

"We're at eight weeks today," Liv said, attaching a long leather lead shank to the filly's track halter before pulling her out as Ava ran the extension from the closest outlet.

Chad prepared the ultrasound unit then crouched next to the filly's right foreleg. He squeezed gel onto the transducer.

"Want me to hold her, Liv?" Emilie asked.

"Sure. Thanks, Em."

The filly stood perfectly, so Emilie let her gaze drift to

where Liv leaned, hands resting on her jean-clad knees, watching the black-and-white screen as Chad ran the transducer along the length of Wish's tendon. No... they just looked like colleagues, Liv reaching over to snap a still shot when Chad nodded at her.

"Looks good," Chad said, then grinned at Liv. "Though you've probably seen more of these than me."

"Maybe," she replied, straightening and stepping aside with a wry twist to her lips as Ava rolled up the extension. "Either way, I agree. You can start her on some light work, Em."

"Are you sticking around for the rest of the fun?" Emilie asked Liv as she put Wish back in her stall, removing the halter and hanging it on the door.

"As much as I'd be happy to witness that particular event, I have to go."

"Good to see you, Liv," Chad said.

"You too, Chad. Let me know how it goes, Em."

As Liv reached the end of the barn, a silhouette appeared. Emilie knew that silhouette, even before she heard Liv's greeting trail back to her. Tim's stride was even, no hint of his injury. He'd been hanging onto the crutches to protect the knee. If she let herself, she could understand that. She'd watched Nate last summer oscillate back and forth between wanting to push, and being afraid he'd never be right again.

Determined to stick to her plan to be civilized despite yesterday's fiasco with Twizzle and Holly, she said, "You're walking great!" and hated how fake she sounded. Best to barrel on, she decided. She could say she had a professional interest after all. "How's it feel?"

"Pretty good," he answered, his tone cautious, but not unfriendly.

"You'll be ready to tackle Plate Day no problem. We'll probably have two horses running. It'll be fun."

He gave her one of those tentative smiles — not enough to produce that dimple again. A good thing, because that dimple had threatened to melt her.

She would do her part to make his visit pleasant, nothing more. Not sightseeing or grocery shopping or driving him around. And, probably, ensuring he wasn't in this barn for what happened next. His timing was awkward, and she needed to tread carefully to keep with her new resolve. She'd been so erratic around him, chasing him away too abruptly would only make everything worse.

"Tim, this is the vet, Dr. Winters," she said, remembering to make introductions. "And this is his assistant, Ava. Ava's worked for us here on the farm. And Dr. Winters went to vet school with Liv."

Chad thrust his hand toward Tim. "Call me Chad. Please."

"Have you met Nate, Chad?" Emilie asked, curious about how well he knew Liv and if they'd kept in touch.

Chad looked confused for a moment, glancing at Emilie as he released Tim's hand. "Liv's husband? The jockey?" His gaze shifted back to Tim as if sizing him up and wondering if he should be putting pieces together when those pieces didn't really fit. "No, I haven't."

"This is his brother, Tim. He's visiting from Calgary." She might have stressed the word *visiting* too much, but her clarification wiped the uncertainty from Chad's features.

"Nice to meet you, Tim." Chad turned back to Emilie. "We'll take this stuff out to the truck and be back for the colt."

She estimated the time she had to shoo Tim out of here as he sauntered over to the nearest stall and said hello to Wish. Every time he greeted a horse she felt a flutter in her stomach. He was so gentle; so intuitive with them. He definitely shouldn't stick around.

"What's the vet here for? Is someone sick?" There was a little wrinkle between his brows; concern in his eyes.

"No, nothing like that. This filly here had some tendonitis, so he was just checking it to see if it's healed enough for her to start training again."

"Is it?"

She nodded. His interest in the horses kept surprising her, though it shouldn't have. He was obviously an animal person even if he didn't work with them like she did. Maybe she'd been too hard on him.

She shook her head, earning herself a strange look from him. *Don't go there, Em.*

"What's her name?" he asked, eyes returning to the filly.

"Wishonakiss."

The heat was creeping up her neck even before his gaze shifted, meeting hers a beat.

"That's a pretty name," he murmured, once again settling safely on Wish.

Good. Then he approached Trop.

"Watch him," she said. "He'll try to bite you."

"Why?"

"Because he's a clown and refuses to believe humans are not his playthings."

As Chad and Ava returned carting the necessary instruments, supplies and medication, she realized she'd missed the window of opportunity to move Tim along before he discovered what was next.

"What's happening now?" he asked, turning his back on Trop.

She saw the light in Trop's eyes, the toss of his forelock as he wound up, and she dragged Tim so swiftly out of reach of the colt's teeth he staggered into her. *So close.* Close enough to hear his sharp intake of breath, to smell the clean scent of the laundry detergent weaving through the fibres of his shirt. She glanced up to catch him staring at her and stepped away.

"Sorry. Danger zone." Her words were garbled as she forced them from her throat. The action of removing him from one had landed her squarely into another.

Answer his question, Emilie. That would squash her surge of adrenaline.

She wasn't going to lie to him. This was a farm, and these things happened on farms. She had to warn him.

"He's being castrated," she said as matter-of-factly as she could.

Tim stood stock still a second. The cartilage in his neck bobbled. "Oh," he said in a quiet voice. "Can I watch?"

His response caught her off guard. "Be my guest," she answered, thinking the reason he was on this farm was not because he was her guest, so she'd put him to work. That would keep him out of trouble. She pushed the unsuspecting Trop back from the stall door and wound on the shank. "Could you grab his water bucket, Tim? Just set it in the aisle."

It was a relief to focus on Chad and the horse, holding Trop as Chad injected the anesthetic. Emilie took a certain amount of pleasure watching the bratty colt get sleepy, then start to sway, his knees buckling. Chad stepped in to ease his descent to the straw bed as best he could with a thousand pounds of dopey Thoroughbred.

From there, Chad worked efficiently — he might be new to Ben's practice, but he'd obviously cut his share of horses before, deftly slicing with the sharp blade. Emilie couldn't help stealing a glance at Tim when the distinctive crunch of the emasculators came, crushing the thick cord.

Tim flinched, sliding his eyes her way, muttering, "Remind me not to try to bite you."

Emilie ducked her head, covering her mouth to smother a

laugh. Had he just flirted in the middle of a castration? She sneaked another look at him, but he was focused on the operation again with a look of horrified fascination while Chad quizzed Ava.

"What do we do in case of eventration?" Chad drilled.

"What is that?" Tim interrupted.

Ava smiled and recited, "When part of the abdominal contents come through the incision site."

Emilie snagged her lower lip between her teeth to keep from smiling at the way Tim's eyes widened.

"Does that happen?" he asked.

"It's rare, but yes," Chad answered.

"Push everything back in, pack it and get him on a trailer to the clinic," Ava said.

"Have you ever seen it?" Tim asked Emilie.

"No, thank goodness. And I hope I never do."

"Wait — you're not going to stitch that up?" Tim asked a few minutes later when Ava and Chad began collecting the supplies and leaving the stall. The scene probably looked to him like someone should call 911.

Chad used his still-gloved pinky finger to carefully scratch the side of his nose but still left a smear of blood behind. "No. We leave the incisions open to drain. Infection is more likely if it's closed."

Emilie watched Trop carefully as the sedation wore off. The newly minted gelding rolled onto his belly then rested his nose in the straw, snuffling noisily.

"Good boy," Emilie cooed, relieved Trop was being sensible. The recovery was the part that scared her the most. "Take your time."

In a few more minutes he lurched to his feet, then stood, head hanging low. His innards thankfully stayed where they belonged. Chad waited until he was satisfied the gelding was out of immediate danger before preparing to leave.

Ava proffered the removed jewels, the same blue gloves as Chad had just peeled off covering her hands. "Where do you want these?"

"On the roof, I guess," Emilie said, then grinned at Tim. At least he wasn't green. "You want the honours? You probably have a better arm than I do."

"Honours?" Tim said, backing a step away from Ava and looking suspicious. "For what?"

"Throwing them up there," Emilie said.

"Them?" He stared at Ava's hands and didn't seem to be able to look anywhere else.

"Come on, Ava. Let's show these boys how it's done." She grabbed a pair of exam gloves for herself before relieving Ava of one of the egg-shaped sacs.

The sun beat down from a hazy sky and she tossed the dense organ from hand to hand before pulling her arm back and pitching it. It landed halfway up the slant of the metal roof, rolling a few inches before coming to a stop. Ava's landed a few feet away.

"They'll cook up nicely up there today," Emilie said.

"Lunch?" Ava suggested.

"You two are disgusting." Tim grimaced while Chad grinned, then, shading his eyes with a hand, peered upward. "Why do you do that?"

"Isn't that a racetrack tradition?" Chad said.

"Sure," Emilie replied. "But we're closely affiliated with the track and it's supposed to be good luck. With horses you can never turn your nose up at anything that might bring more of that."

"I wonder who started it?" Ava asked.

"Who knows," Emilie said. "Racetrackers can be crazy.

Really superstitious. The jockeys are the worst. Get Nate to tell you some of those stories sometime." She slid a glance to Tim. Now he'd really think she was nuts. That should fix everything.

"That was fun." Ava began walking to the passenger side of the truck. "See you next time, Emilie!"

Chad paused, his hand on the door handle, turning back to Emilie. "I don't suppose you'd want to have dinner sometime?"

She almost laughed. What a strange time to be asked out.

When she hesitated, Chad said with a wry grin, "Unless Liv's told you too many bad stories about me."

Before today I didn't know you existed. But that probably wasn't the best answer. "I work evenings," she responded. "But how about lunch sometime?"

"Today too soon? Barring any emergencies."

"Two o'clock?"

They exchanged numbers and Chad smiled, ducking into the SUV. He had a great smile.

So. A date with a vet. That was all right. She'd be happy if all she got out of lunch was the dirt on what had happened between him and Liv in university.

It wasn't till she waved as Chad backed away that she noticed Tim a few feet behind her with an expression she couldn't read, but the approach of another vehicle didn't give her time to dwell on it.

"It's Sylvie," she said, and had to fight back a fresh flare of irritation. Was she back for another go at Tim? *Says the girl who just agreed to go out with Chad.*

A vet made so much more sense for her life than a distant — both physically and emotionally — hockey player. *The hockey player you are not entertaining thoughts of anymore, remember?* It would make a great story if she ended up with a vet after Liv dropping out, and a former fellow student of Liv's no less.

Sylvie carried a white cardboard box that could only contain baked goods, and Emilie forgot her indignation.

"Red velvet cupcakes?" she said, her mouth falling open as she grabbed one, like she expected Sylvie to rescind the offer.

"We had a special order for them and there were extras. Tim?" Sylvie pivoted toward him.

Tim frowned. "I'm not really hungry right now, thanks."

Emilie almost choked on the mouthful she'd just taken of deep, red cake.

CHAPTER THIRTEEN

WHAT A SLAP IN THE FACE. Watching Emilie blithely accept Chad's invitation — right in front of him — had taken his justification for enduring a shopping trip out at the knees. If her lack of feelings hadn't been obvious before, they were now; a reminder he was only visiting while the vet was around all the time. The bump, the look; that moment after she'd pulled him from the reach of the horse and she hadn't moved right away — it hadn't meant a thing. He should probably be grateful she hadn't let the horse bite him.

He had half an hour before Faye was supposed to pick him up; not nearly enough time to invent an excuse that wouldn't trigger a line of questioning. Maybe he could feign food poisoning or a migraine. But Faye was sitting across from Liv in the kitchen when he reached the house, so there would be no backing out. They both clutched coffee cups from the café, the distinctive aroma filling the room.

Well — it was probably easier to stick with the original plan. He had a feeling Faye wouldn't let him off the hook, anyway. He could use some new clothes, and even if he skipped the ball, he still wanted to go to the big race.

"Hey Tim." Liv said, smiling.

"Want one?" Faye held up a white paper bag, also from the café.

Stewing about Emilie's exchange with the vet had pushed away his queasiness, at least. He should have grabbed one of those cupcakes, so he wasn't missing out on whatever was in that bag.

"Yes, please." He reached inside, extracting a butter tart. The sugar rush would pick his head up.

Faye set the bag back on the table between herself and Liv. "Are you ready to go?"

He shrugged. "Sure." Might as well get it over with.

"Just let me finish my coffee," Faye said.

When he went to the fridge for some water, Holly thumped her tail against the side of her plastic kennel. Tim could imagine her eyes, beseeching. The dog liked him, even if Emilie didn't. He wanted to let her out, but he didn't dare after yesterday. Even if he could dredge up the nerve to ask Emilie for permission — he'd willingly let her give him a lesson — he doubted she'd agree. Maybe he could find a way to talk her into it. It could be part of his rehab. He needed to walk before he could run, didn't he?

"All right," Faye said, draining her cup as she slid off the bench, swiping her car keys from the table. "Sure you don't want to come, Liv?"

"You know I adore shopping," Liv said, her tone saturated with sarcasm, "but playing with the guys is Nate's time to disconnect. He sees me all day. I don't want him to get sick of me."

Faye snorted. "It's much too early for that, sweetie."

"I'd rather give him reasons to miss me so it stays that way."

She gave Faye a coy grin.

Faye pressed her lips together, her eyebrows pinching. "I'm pretty sure taking Just Jay to England will accomplish that." Faye deposited her coffee cup in a small blue bin under the sink with a subtle shake of her head. "Let's go, Tim."

On the drive down he could tell Faye was dying to drill him about Emilie; she was just too smart to indulge herself. Faye and Emilie were close. He should be asking her questions. Just how much did Emilie hate him? Did Faye know the vet? Was there any hope at all, or should he give up?

"We'll stop and say hi to the guys first, then hit the stores. I know you're excited." She gave him a wicked grin then reached over and patted him on the arm when he rolled his eyes. "I'll try to make it as painless for you as possible, promise. Just leave everything up to me."

Nate had gone down to Will's apartment straight from the racetrack so he was already there when Faye showed the way in. Right away Tim felt at home. It was such a comfortable space, reminding him of hanging out with Nate and Will and their friends as a kid when they'd get together, the talk always coming around to how their garage band would make it one day. Nothing had changed, really. They were just older. They had jobs now and their friends were different, but they still joked about being discovered. He was sad when Faye whisked him off, promising to return in a few hours with takeout.

"Emilie's going to be busy, so you're going to have to stand out to be sure she notices you," Faye said as she herded him into the first shop. "We'll need to dress you up a bit."

It was the first time Emilie's name had come up. He'd take Faye's comments as encouragement — she wouldn't put him through this if she thought it was a waste of time. She had better things to do. If he was competing with the vet, he wasn't going down without a fight.

Faye glanced around briefly before her vision narrowed with laser focus. He followed her to a stack of shirts and after eyeballing him, tugged first one, then another loose, holding each in turn against him.

"Try both of those," she said, pushing them into his arms. "And this one." She added a third. "Now, some slacks."

When he emerged from the change room with the first combination, she looked him up and down, thumb and forefinger spread on her chin. She made a twirling motion, and he did as he was told even though he felt silly, rotating three-hundred-and-sixty degrees before stopping and tucking his fingers in the pockets.

"A vest maybe?" she pondered. "And I'm betting your brother didn't warn you that you might need dress shoes, did he?"

Of course not. He'd thought he was coming to lounge at the farm-resort. Nate hadn't mentioned anything about an outfit appropriate for a dance or a fancy horse race.

"Next!" Faye commanded, and he complied, ducking back into the change room to try the next ensemble.

"Nope. Try the blue shirt." Then, when he did, a smile spread across her face. "Yes. That one. A jacket, I think. Like I said, we need to dress you up. Wait there."

As Faye helped him into the black jacket she'd selected, he felt eight years old again, his mother buying him new church clothes. When she stood in front of him and adjusted the shoulders, then tugged on the lapels, he almost expected her to say, "Such a handsome boy," and give him a peck on the cheek — but he wasn't disappointed when she didn't.

"I'm having a good time, even if you're not." Her mock-sweet smile made him crack up. "You're my kind of horse. A clothes horse!"

Satisfied, she ushered him to the cash register. "You know

what they say, right? A guy looks at a woman in a bar and tries to picture her with no clothes on. A woman looks at a man in a bar and tries to picture him with better clothes on." She laughed at her own joke. "Not that I'm trying to pick you up or anything. We're just making you irresistible to Em."

Here's hoping.

It didn't seem like they bought that much for what it cost, but Faye didn't bat an eyelash when she pulled a platinum credit card from the wallet in her purse.

"You can't pay for my clothes," Tim said — not that it stopped her inserting the card in the bottom of the wireless machine and punching in the PIN.

"I'm not," she said in an exaggerated whisper, holding up the card for him to see, then added, pouting, "Nate never gave me his credit card when we were together."

Great. He was going to owe Nate this entire trip. That should light a fire under him to get fit again so he was at the top of his game come training camp. He needed a spot on the team. A contract. The poor younger brother thing was getting old.

The salesperson carefully folded and bagged the items and he took them when she handed them over the counter. She smiled at him, catching his eyes under long, thick lashes that had to be fake.

"Thanks," he muttered, gaze falling to his shoes before he turned away, looking for the way out.

Faye looped her arm through his, resting her other hand on his biceps. "I wonder if she thought we were together. I don't look too old, do I? Though, you could be my boy toy."

He laughed and grinned at her. He didn't know how old she was, but it wasn't as if she was forty. Now why couldn't he be this relaxed with Emilie?

He felt like a character in a movie after being bustled from store to store, collecting bags along the way. Nate was right —

Faye was good at this. All he'd had to do was try on the clothes she selected. He didn't even have to offer an opinion. Everything she picked looked great and was stuff he'd have no problem wearing. If Emilie didn't want him, it wouldn't be because of a lack of fashion sense.

"Thanks Faye," he said, relieved when she finally declared their mission complete, but grateful too. Instead of adding to his sense of futility, the trip had revived his determination to be the kind of guy someone like Emilie deserved.

"It was fun. We'll grab some food — also on Nate — then hang out while they play."

As he watched and listened, he wished he'd learned to play an instrument. The piano would've been too much work. He had to hand it to Nate — he was so good, pounding away on Will's keyboard. Maybe he could get Nate or Will to teach him guitar. How hard could it be? Then he could try to put music to the lyrics he wasn't writing.

"Guess we have to get you back for your physio appointment, eh kid?" Nate said, helping Faye pack up the leftover food as they wrapped up late afternoon.

Tim had rescheduled to allow for the foray into the city. Sam had said she didn't need to see him again so soon, but he was eager to speed up his progress in any way he could. And right now it wasn't about hockey: he needed to be sound if he was going to dance with Emilie at the ball. If he was going to do this thing, he wasn't going to be standing around eating food and talking to strangers, especially if the vet was going to be there.

"We picked up the car when you were gone," Nate said. "Think you can drive home?"

"I don't know if that's the best idea, to be on the highway yet," Tim said, though it was all the stops and turns on the minor Toronto streets Faye had used to get here that worried him more. "It would be easier to practice around the farm, wouldn't it?"

"You've got a point." Nate looked at Faye and Will. "One of you want to drive it back?"

"I've got a better idea," Will said, looking smug as he crossed his arms. "I'll drive the Porsche and you can introduce Tim to the car."

"Ahem," Faye cleared her throat loudly. "I think I should drive the Porsche. Women are safer drivers. That's why you guys have to pay so much for insurance."

"Why is everyone trying to separate me from that car?" Nate asked with a scowl.

"We're not, buddy," Will said. "We're just helping you remember the importance of sharing."

Nate dug into his pocket for the keys. "Fine. The two of you fight it out," he said, placing the keys between Faye and Will on the round kitchen table. "Let's go, Tim. Your chariot awaits."

Tim could feel the heat rising from the sidewalk through the soles of his running shoes, scanning the vehicles lining the street, wondering which one they were headed for. When he recognized an old-model blue car, his mouth fell open.

"Your old Mustang!" he exclaimed. "This is brilliant."

"It is. I love this car." Nate's smile was nostalgic. "I couldn't let it go. It was great to get it fixed up right this time, even if I had to pay someone else to do it. You sure you don't want to drive?"

"Nah. I know you want to."

Nate grinned, unlocking the passenger door for Tim. "You're right. I really do."

He wasn't going to tell Nate all he knew about how to drive standard was what Nate had taught him, in this very car. He'd see how much he remembered later, on his own, when he wasn't overcome with reminiscing. Nate snapped his seatbelt into place, turning up the stereo and pushing the stick into first.

He had a distinct vision of Nate, Phil and their father fixing up the Mustang after Nate had bought the car, the images as clear in his mind as if he had a photo. He'd tried to help, handing them tools, running into the house for cans of pop for him and Nate, beer for Phil and their Dad — a rare family bonding moment, like something from a fifties television show. Sometimes Nate drove him to hockey practice and games when Dad had to work. Dad hated missing their games, but hockey was an expensive sport so overtime helped pay for it — though sometimes Tim wished Dad had let him get a part-time job so he could contribute, just so Dad could have been there more.

"Is everything okay with you and Liv?" The words slipped out, thoughts of home stirring a vague sense of worry.

Nate glanced at him with a smile that brushed away some of his fears. "Yeah, everything's great. Why?"

"Faye said something about Liv going to England."

Nate's smile faltered slightly, but his tone was matter of fact. "For a couple of weeks maybe, with Jay, for a race. I'll go over and ride him, I just can't justify going for the whole time. Don't worry, she's coming back."

Tim nodded, bolstered by the confidence in Nate's words, the grin he tacked onto the end. He wouldn't tell him about Mom and Dad. Not yet. But a pang hit him, deep in his chest, until Nate's voice shook it out. Only Nate could get him singing at the top of his lungs, air rushing by the open windows as the old Mustang flew up the highway — song after song both of them knew by heart, flooding the car with layers of memories.

CHAPTER FOURTEEN

THE LAST TIME Emilie had been in this restaurant was the reason she hadn't been on a date since, and if she'd known Chad was going to bring her here, she might have thought twice. It was lunch, at least. A late lunch, but still lunch. Lunch seemed less serious than dinner. There was less risk of things ending badly.

She didn't have fond memories of that night last December and blamed Tim for her decision to accept Austin's invitation. After the whole wedding fail — when Tim had told her point-blank he wasn't interested in her while all she'd been doing was trying to make conversation as they fulfilled their first-dance duties as bridesmaid and groomsman — she might have agreed to have dinner with their, at the time, farm manager, for the wrong reasons.

Like letting herself get carried away with the possibility of her own fairytale future, made more fantastical by the wedding's romantic beach setting; Nate and Liv's barely contained passion after the ceremony, and the admission she wanted all that. If a hopeless case like Liv could find true love, why not her? Seriously, why not?

Then Tim had held her like they were in sixth grade gym class. At least he hadn't stepped on her toes. If he had, she would have known it was on purpose. She'd seen him on skates, watching him play on TV. He was incredible. Shuffling around in the sand was a far cry from that.

It had been all downhill for her love life — such as it was — from there. After the wedding she'd gotten drunk with Faye's brother Dean and thrown herself at him in his hotel room, only to have him gently turn her away. No surprise there. Dean would forever think of her as a little sister. When she'd returned home, suddenly Austin hadn't seemed as bad as she'd remembered. He'd kept the farm afloat in her absence, and at dinner had been a perfect gentleman. And they'd talked. Not just about horses; about all sorts of things. It had been a pleasant outing. But when he'd moved in to kiss her when he'd dropped her off, she'd bolted.

And the next day, he was gone, leaving her high and dry on the farm. Had it really been that offensive that she didn't let him kiss her on the first date? Or did she just scare guys away? At least the ones who might see her as more than just a friend or little sister.

Now she sat across from Chad, wondering if she was making a similar mistake. She was counting on him being more professional than Austin if things went poorly, but maybe it hadn't been smart just the same. It looked as if he'd be out to the farm on calls a lot, and it would set them up for awkwardness.

Oh well. She was here now. She felt better about the arrangement this time. Chad had picked her up at the farm, but she had to work at the clinic this afternoon so he'd drop her off there. That should preclude any kisses. And if she found she wanted to kiss him, she'd just have to hope he felt the same way and asked her out again.

"Liv didn't have much to say about you," she said as she took a sip of water before starting her salad. "I was disappointed. I need stories."

She'd quizzed her sister, but had got little out of her other than a laugh when Emilie had asked if there had been something between her and Chad. *That's hilarious, Em. No. We were rivals, I guess you'd say. We didn't like each other.*

"I'm hurt," Chad said, but a smile pulled at the corners of his lips. "I have many fond memories of her."

"Uh-huh," Emilie said. "Tell me more."

"We gave each other a hard time. Always battling for top position in our year. I think we had mutual respect, though. I hope it was mutual, anyway. She was a worthy opponent. I admit I was kind of knocked sideways when she quit. Took a lot of the fun out of it."

"Why didn't she like you?" Emilie prodded. "Being rivals isn't a good enough reason. Liv's competitive, but she won't say she doesn't like someone unless there's a good reason for it."

"She said she doesn't like me?"

He looked affronted, but Emilie laughed. "She said you didn't like each other. Past tense."

"I guess that's true. I didn't like her because she was entitled, which was really the pot calling the kettle black. I expect she didn't like me because I really didn't have a good reason for not liking her. And... I slept with a lot of girls. Because there were a lot of girls."

"Ah, there it is." That would rub Liv the wrong way.

Chad leaned back in his chair, turning his water glass. "Vet school was stressful. I was under pressure to get the marks and impress my father and the faculty, because they all knew him and I was expected to join his practice. There was no time for a relationship. At the end of the day I had nothing left for a girl-friend. But like I said, there were a lot of girls in our class, and hey, they were all in a similar spot. So it was mutual stress relief, right? It only went bad once or twice." He cracked a grin that had probably melted the heart of a lot of female vet students.

"That makes it very clear why the two of you didn't get along." Liv had different ideas about managing stress; at least she had in those days. "Even without the whole pressure cooker environment, she would have despised the guy with a harem. And you would've been mad she wouldn't sleep with you. Liv's never been the type to fall at a guy's feet." Unlike her. Liv's approach had worked better; maybe she needed to be more like her sister.

"I didn't ask her outright," Chad said, as if defending himself for not having added Liv to his list of conquests.

"Lucky for you," Emilie said. She was getting a taste of the Chad Liv had disliked. "No one can shoot a guy down like Liv. Except maybe Faye."

"But Liv's married and I'm not."

"Never stop believing in miracles, Chad." Emilie grinned. Long, drawn-out miracles.

"Faye — that's her friend, right? The one she was always with any time I'd see her out of class? What's she up to these days?"

"She and her brother own Northwest Stables, just down the road from us. They use Ben too, so I'm sure you'll go there at some point. Faye also owns the café here in town, and it's the only place around to get takeout cappuccino." If she started raving about the butter tarts, she'd sound like a lunatic, so she refrained. "We should go there after, if you have time, though Faye's off today so you won't get to meet her. You can leave me there. It's an easy walk to the clinic."

"Great idea. I could use a decent coffee to keep me going on my last few calls."

She was glad she hadn't ordered more than salad; it was a meal all on its own with slices of fresh strawberries and chunks of goat cheese. Cappuccino and a treat from Triple Shot would be a perfect end to their afternoon.

"So, you're reformed now? What made you decide to grow up? If that's the case." She gave him a wry smile, hoping he'd be as candid as he'd been so far. Her dating life had been full of guys who were big children. Tim Miller was no different. At least she hadn't had to date him to learn that.

"Let's just say my life is marginally more conducive to a relationship now."

"We'll have to find you a good match, then," she said.

"Which isn't you." He sat back, setting his fork on his plate, but didn't seem surprised or disappointed. Their connection was companionable, but that was all. It was a relief he could see that.

"A little pointer? It's probably best not to talk about how you slept your way through your graduating class."

He grinned that vet school bad boy grin. "Hey, you asked."

"Take heart in knowing Liv only has one sister, so if you avoid the sisters of all your other classmates you won't have the same problem." She twisted the linen napkin on her lap between her fingers. "You don't hate me, right?"

He laughed. "No. Thanks for taking pity on me and agreeing to have lunch. I don't know anyone around here. I know it's not that far from home but it's not as if I get back much with this job so it's nice to have some friends."

"Okay good. I've already chased away a farm manager. Liv wouldn't forgive me for causing problems with one of our vets."

His eyebrows crept up. "Sounds like it's your turn to share a story."

She grinned. "All right. I'll tell you on the way to the café."

She let him pay for lunch when he insisted and told him the Austin story as promised as she directed him to Triple Shot.

"Thanks for lunch, Chad. That was fun," she said before getting out. And it had been, even if it turned out not to be anything romantic. "You should come to the Plate Ball. You probably won't meet many single women, so think of it as a networking thing. Lots of farm owners and managers will be there, plus it benefits the New Chapter aftercare group. Ben's paid for a table, so claim a spot."

"Only if you save a dance for me."

She laughed. He did have a nice smile. "I'll try."

Sylvie was serving another customer when they entered. Emilie saw her look over and smile, then tilt her head as she noticed Emilie wasn't alone.

"This is my friend Sylvie," she introduced. "She's the daughter of Roger Cloutier, who was our trainer at the track for a long time." Roger hadn't officially retired yet but his decision to travel instead of coming back to train when it was looking like they'd have two starters in the Plate didn't bode well for his return. "Sylvie, meet Chad. He's a vet who's just started working with our old farm vet."

"Don't let Ben hear you calling him old." Chad chuckled.

"That's not how I meant it," Emilie said, elbowing him. Sylvie's head tilted the other way, but Emilie ignored it. "What do you want, Chad? A cappuccino?"

Chad nodded as his phone rang. He excused himself, wandering toward the door as he picked up the call. Sylvie placed the drinks on the counter, still wearing a question on her face as Emilie paid for them.

"Sorry, Em, I've gotta run. Emergency," Chad said, tucking his phone in his pocket.

"Go," Emilie said, waving him off. "Don't forget your cappuccino."

He swept it from the counter, raising it slightly. "Thanks, Sylvie. Nice meeting you."

Sylvie crossed her arms and drummed her fingers against her elbow. "I need to hear more about that. Most importantly, what was that?"

"We went out for lunch. He's nice, Sylvie. He and Liv went to school together, can you believe it?"

"For lunch — on a date?"

"Yes, a date. At least it started as a date. I'm pretty sure by the end it was not, though."

Sylvie frowned. "I'm sorry. Nice, and cute."

Emilie shrugged. "Easy come, easy go." Then her eyes lit up. This might be the summer fling Sylvie was looking for. He said he was reformed, but, old dog, new tricks? She wasn't convinced. "I can set you up."

CHAPTER FIFTEEN

THERE WERE no cars parked in front of the physiotherapy clinic, though further down the lot he spotted a white van with a rusted bumper that looked as if it had been left there to die. Tim engaged the clutch and let the Mustang roll between the faded yellow lines, hitting the brake carefully before the curb. He'd wanted to think driving standard was like riding a bike, but it wasn't. Maybe it would have been, if he'd driven one as much as he'd ridden a bike. Either way, he'd assured Nate he could make it from the farm to the clinic. It hadn't been pretty, but here he was.

The sign on the door was still flipped to "open" and there were lights on inside, but the little bell jingling as he slipped in didn't summon anyone. No one sat in the waiting room; no one was at reception. The usual music wasn't even playing. He stood in the doorway wondering if he'd got the time wrong or if he'd missed a cancellation message. A quick check of his phone told him no, but the place felt deserted.

He wandered to the rack of magazines and ran his eyes over the rows, hoping someone would appear. Maybe the office manager didn't work after six and Sam was busy with paperwork.

"Hey. Tim. Come on in."

He spun, starting, and stared, his pulse picking up extra beats. *Emilie.*

She smiled conservatively; a professional front. Her deep blue-green scrubs made her eyes more vivid, and she dropped her gaze before he did. "When Sam told me you wanted to change your appointment, I volunteered to do it this time. I'm almost always here in the evenings and she works days because she's got kids. I hope you're okay with that. If not, I understand and we can reschedule something with Sam."

Her words came in a rush, and she almost sounded hopeful, speaking the last part as she slipped behind the reception counter, her hand curling around the mouse. Was she nervous too? That made him feel better. She still had the advantage, knowing he was coming.

Recover. "No, that's okay," he said. " As long as you promise not to hurt me."

Her laugh was like soft music and he thought he saw a hint of pink rise in her tanned cheeks. "I won't do it intentionally, anyway."

He kept his gaze on the walls instead of her as he followed her because watching her from behind? Yeah. Bad idea. She was the therapist; he was the patient, that was all. She led him to a room, similar but different from the one Sam met him in.

"Have a seat," she said, motioning to a chair without looking at him, her eyes instead scanning the contents of a folder. "How did it go today, without the crutches?"

He eased slowly into the plain plastic seat, resting his hands on his thighs. "Pretty good. Still a bit stiff, and it's kind of sore. I was walking around more than I have been." He flushed, thinking of the jaunt into the city to buy clothes that were supposed to capture her attention, when it didn't matter what she wore, she always siphoned the breath from his lungs.

"Be careful not to overdo it. I'm going to check your range of motion, okay?"

His chin bobbed in consent but his heart leapt erratically as she approached, just when he'd thought he had it back under control.

Her hands were warm on the bare skin below the hem of his shorts, and he stared at them as she manipulated the leg. *Think of something else.* Like that poor horse's balls on the barn roof. This was why he should have agreed when she'd offered to reschedule his appointment with Sam.

"Does it hurt here?" She grasped his knee with her thumb on the patella and fingers on the soft flesh at the back, applying gentle pressure. His sharp intake of breath brought her eyes to his with a flash of concern. Good. Let her think it was pain.

"It's not that bad, but it's there." That wasn't the problem at the moment. He forced himself to exhale, counting to three.

"Is it okay with you if I tape it? Have you ever used Kinesiology tape before?"

He shook his head but stammered, "Yeah. It's great. That's great."

Emilie's brow furrowed for a split-second before she spoke. She dropped her hands, pressing them to her thighs as she rose. "Sam was actually excited when you said you needed a later appointment because she wanted me to tape it. She doesn't know how to yet, and, well, I — wasn't around when you had your first appointment. The downside of a small-town clinic."

The way her voice faltered gave her away. She'd been avoiding him.

"I'm sorry," he said, a muted release of syllables.

"About what?" She was trying to make her voice nonchalant, like she had no idea what he should be apologizing for, but the tightness around her mouth and eyes was suspect.

"About this. About Nate inviting me here."

With a shrug she walked to the table. "He's your brother. I'm glad you're getting some time together." But she didn't sound glad, her tone too controlled. She sounded like he should have been apologizing for so much more. Which was true.

Pulling a length of blue tape from a roll, she cut it and returned with various pieces draped between her fingers. "Could you pull your shorts up a bit on that leg, please?"

Her face was set, professional mien intact, and he did as she requested. When she crouched next to him she paused, her finger tracing the line of his scar.

Balls on roof. Regret. Remembering how to drive standard.

He followed the movement of her fingers — confidently stretching and laying the tape in place. When she'd used up all the pieces, she rubbed it. With both hands. He stared at the ceiling, leaving an indent from his teeth in his lower lip. *Yep, those balls had probably cooked up nice on that roof today.*

"You have to rub it to activate the adhesive," she explained, and he felt it warming, the pain easing, but he wasn't sure he could give some fabric and glue all the credit. "This application will last a long time. You can shower with it. Some people experience irritation. If it starts to itch, take it off. I'm going to warn you though. It'll tear your hair out and hurt like a —" She pressed her lips together, suppressing a smile as she got up. "Questions?"

He shook his head, the questions he had completely unrelated to the tape. *How was lunch with the vet? Do you like him? Am I out?* He tried to catch her eyes, but she ducked away again, returning to the table and scribbling some notes in the folder.

"You just saw Sam yesterday so I don't think we need to go through your exercises. Do you swim?"

She looked up just long enough to see him nod.

"You should use the pool at the house. It would be good therapy." She tucked the folder under her arm and headed toward the door. "Give the clinic a call tomorrow to set up your next appointment."

"All right. Thank you," he said to her back. She wanted to get rid of him. He wanted to fix this. *Think, man.*

When she ushered him to the waiting room, she peered around at its emptiness with a puzzled expression.

"I do have a question," he said.

She paused, turning, though not quite to face him, her expression neutral as she waited.

"Would you give me a lesson with Holly like you did Nate? So I could take her out? It would be good for both of us, right?"

A shadow passed over her face, an eyebrow twitching like she was thinking *you should have thought of that before.* He would have, if he'd had any idea.

"I'll think about it."

It felt like a tiny opening. "How late do you work?" he asked, jumping in.

"It depends on the night. Today, I have one more appointment, then I'm done. They must be running late." She ducked behind the counter to the computer, scanning the screen. "Nix that. They cancelled, so I guess I'm finished. I'd better call Faye so she can come get me."

"That's stupid."

She straightened, the furrow of her brow as she glanced at him just shy of a scowl. "What? Why?"

"I can drive you home, can't I?"

The way her lips pressed together was almost a frown. "You drove?"

"Yeah." It didn't matter what she thought of him; it just made sense. Logic was on his side.

She stood, hands on hips, looking perplexed, as if it was a major decision. "Nate came through with the car, did he? Well, that's cool. I have a few things to finish up. Can you wait ten minutes?"

He kept from grinning as he nodded, saving it for when he turned away. His arm seemed weightless as he grabbed a magazine while she took care of whatever she had to do. It wasn't long before she said, "Let's go," heading for the door to flip the sign to closed. Which was fine, because he hadn't been able to focus on the words in the article he'd supposedly been reading.

"Were you humming?" she asked, a twinge of humour lifting her lips as she held the door open for him.

"Me? No," he lied, muttering, "You're hearing things." But he smiled into the dusky parking lot as she locked up.

Her eyes widened, that perfect mouth falling open. "The Mustang! It's back! So awesome. Good job, Nate."

He tried not to feel frustrated that an old car could make her smile like that, so gorgeously unreserved, and led the way to the passenger side to open the door. She hesitated, her look as she met his eyes almost shy, and he had an overwhelming urge to step in, reach for her face, and kiss her. When she broke the gaze and ducked in, he blew out a long breath and swung the door closed. He should have kissed her the first time he'd thought about it — on that beach in Florida.

Once he was behind the wheel, he could feel Emilie watching but didn't dare so much as throw a glance her way. He needed to concentrate on the car or he'd flub the whole thing. It rumbled to life and Emilie grinned, but the next part was the tricky part. Reverse. Was that it? He eased out the clutch and exhaled when it rolled backward instead of lurching through the window of the clinic. When he pulled out from the parking lot with only a bit of a shudder as he shifted into second, he was grateful there was no one behind them. Time to contemplate third.

Lights. Where were the headlights? Things you were supposed to locate before you were moving.

"So," Emilie said, her voice distracting him. "The high school parking lot is right here. Why don't you just pop in there and drive around a bit? Get used to it?"

It had been ridiculous to think she wouldn't notice his inexperience. He wasn't trying to impress anyone here, which was a good thing because this wasn't the way to do it. He glanced at her, then ahead to the building that had to be a high school and gave a quick nod, zeroing in on the entrance like Luke Skywalker flying his X-wing fighter into the Death Star. The Mustang bumped over the low curb and he shoved his foot on the clutch, pressing it to the floor and letting the car coast, looking out for lamp posts. Brake. *Gently. Let's not give everyone whiplash.* He slid her a sheepish look, expecting a mocking one in return, but there were no sharp edges to her features.

"This is what I did when I got the Civic. Liv and I spent some pretty hilarious hours in this very parking lot. At the farm I was worried I'd drive through a fence or something, and the horses didn't need to be subjected to me trying to figure it out."

The thought of the horses judging her erratic driving made him chuckle, and the twist of Emilie's lips helped him relax.

She pulled out her phone. "Don't mind me. I'm just going to sit here and listen to music. Nate always had a great stereo in this car. Did he connect your phone?"

He nodded. Of course. That was the first thing they'd done before Nate sent him on his way.

"Let's hear what you've got," she said, focused on him with expectation.

Oh. He had no idea what to play. "What kind of music do you like?"

"I want to hear what kind of music you like." She crossed her arms, shifting slightly toward him. "All I know is that you don't know who Poe is."

"Poe?"

She scrunched her lips together, shifting her jaw like she was trying to decide whether she should explain something he was supposed to know.

"Never mind," she mumbled.

Mental note: *Google it or ask Nate.*

She tilted her head, waiting for him to take action. With the stereo, that was. He flipped through the music on his phone and tried to figure out what wouldn't scare her off. It was funny that they hadn't talked about music at all when they'd been messaging last winter.

He settled on something that was more about the sound than the lyrics. Something melodic instead of clever. Background noise. When he rolled the window down, resting an arm on the door, the warm night made her feel closer instead of helping him breathe.

"Who is this?" Emilie asked, her face mostly in shadow, backlit by the tall lamps in the lot.

"I can't remember. It's just a mix I put together."

"Can I see?" She spread the fingers of one hand wide, hovering in the direction of his phone.

He shrugged. It wasn't as if he was sharing a secret. The phone was locked; she'd only see the song information on the screen. "Sure." He placed it in her palm.

"Takénobu." The light from the device reflected on her face. She set it aside as she opened her own and typed something. "Writing that name down to check out later. I like them. Him?"

"Don't ask me."

He was supposed to be practicing his driving, but somehow this felt like a moment he shouldn't let pass — the two of them, alone; the gentle sound of the cello and soft vocals filling the sultry summer air. But where did he start? He curled and uncurled his fingers around the steering wheel, praying he didn't mess things up again.

"The other day. With Sylvie, in the café. Why did you do that?"

He didn't know why that was what he thought of, but the scene stood out. Until then, she'd been either aloof or bordering on mean to him, so the way she'd interceded before he found himself being Sylvie's date for the ball had caught him off guard.

"Do what?" But he saw her eyes waver and duck from his. She knew what.

"Come to my rescue."

She looked out the window, squeezing the phone in her hand before meeting his gaze. "I've lived with an introvert with anxiety my whole life. I recognize an SOS when I see one."

He hadn't thought his reaction had been obvious until she'd stepped in. He was so used to others not understanding; not seeing how cornered he felt sometimes. Her intervention had made him think that, despite everything, all was not lost — but then she'd gone out with the vet. So maybe it had only been because she couldn't help being a nice person and had recognized his distress. That's how her explanation made it sound. He couldn't tell her how he felt after that. It was too risky. He needed to win her over; be sure she felt at least a bit the same.

His playlist took that instant to betray him.

San Fermin's "Emily" warbled through the speakers and he only hoped it was dim enough in the car she didn't see his ears redden, his lips wedging together involuntarily as he glared at the stereo's display. A more obvious response — like reaching for the volume or poking a finger at the arrow that would advance the track, which is what he really, really wanted to do — would just give him away more. Why did that song have to show up when it so accurately pinpointed what was inside his head — something he was sure she wasn't ready to hear?

When he shifted his eyes just enough to see her face, she was grinning. He couldn't tell if it was genuine, or if she summoned it to relieve his embarrassment.

"I do like my rabbit holes," she said.

They had gone down some, when they'd been messaging. Silly exchanges about nothing; discussions that had made him feel at home. He'd been able to trust her to give him a break from the stress in his life, to get him out of his own head by letting her into it.

Until like the song said, it wasn't enough.

But when she'd attempted to push past the superficial, when he needed someone to do that, exactly that, what had he done?

He was the one who had stuck them here, leaving things hanging like George RR Martin never writing the last book of *Game of Thrones*. The TV series didn't count. The ending had sucked.

It was up to him to get them out of this place; move them forward.

He didn't realize his face must be showing all of it until her smile faded, falling into something wistful, then melancholy, and landing on disdain.

"Just drive," she said.

Because she wasn't doing this; sitting here with eyes locked to his, wondering why he didn't lean over and kiss her already. She wasn't hung up on the guy having to make the first move but with Tim, it would have to be that way. Their short, weird history dictated it.

He jerked his head away, his nod a heavy drop of his chin, and she left him to focus on practicing — watching but not watching. This had been a bad suggestion. It should be Nate here doing some brother-bonding time, not her. Because whatever had caused his horror when that song had come up — he wanted her out of his head. Either for the same reason he'd stopped messaging her back in March, or because he liked her and clearly couldn't deal with that.

If he liked her, how long had he liked her?

She gave a rapid little rattle of her head, like a horse trying to shake off a fly, grateful he was too engrossed in sending the Mustang stuttering about to see it. He'd probably think it was a reaction to his struggles with the car, anyway.

After a few minutes, he was getting a little better, the starts and stops not quite as jarring. It was going to take more than this, though, and it was getting late. She needed to wrap things up here without conveying her frustration, because it wasn't about him learning how to drive on her time.

"I remember I thought I knew how to drive standard after doing this," she said the next time he brought the car to a halt. "Then I got stuck in Toronto traffic and realized that wasn't true. Stop and go for half an hour. It was do or die. Thankfully, I didn't die, and I've been good since."

"So what you're saying is, I'm wasting your time?"

She sighed, turning to the window, because it was better than snapping at him for so quickly turning defensive. "I should probably get back to Holly." She almost added, *do you want me to drive?* But that probably would have just amplified the pall.

Maybe all of this was a waste of time. The driving part. The trying to come to a middle ground between them; trying to figure out the topography of this. They'd crossed the "your brother is married to my sister" line and hadn't managed to be friends, and there was nothing saying they needed to be. It was probably time to accept that and go about their own ways. Every time they tried to be civil they ran up against a brick wall.

He was better on the way home — his driving was better, anyway. His mood, maybe not. He'd shut off, and she had no desire to change that. Fewer cars on the road took the pressure off and it wasn't a hard trip. Lots of long stretches, not much stopping and starting. *Always end on a good note!* But she didn't believe that was always possible, because sometimes it meant you'd be there forever looking for it.

The maple-lined laneway of the farm didn't lead to refuge the way it always had before. He was messing with her tranquility. She was only barely aware of the music now, but still infuriatingly aware of him. She hoped he couldn't tell.

"Do you want me to drop you off at the barn?" he asked as he navigated the turn behind the house with reasonable success.

"Holly's at the house," she said. "So here's good." She craved her walk with the Black Lab tonight, desperately needing to clear her mind.

He parked the Mustang without incident and followed her in. It was just habit to go through the door of her apartment — even if it wasn't hers at the moment. If he was off crutches, did that mean she could take it back? She'd talk to Sam and see if it was okay for him to be doing those stairs. She wouldn't be responsible for sabotaging his recovery.

"Good night, Tim," she said, not hesitating as she reached the door to the main part of the house. He gave no response as she clicked it shut behind her.

Holly heard her coming, tail thumping against the wall of her plastic crate. Emilie sprung the bouncy Lab.

"Sorry, girl," she said. "I was busy wasting my time. But I know you spent the evening with Liv, so you had good company. Let's eat first, then we'll go for our you-know-what."

Her shoulders dropped when she opened the door of the fridge and there was no plate of food. Now she remembered Nate had been in Toronto with Will and their friends so he hadn't been cooking tonight. She wasn't that hungry, anyway. Tim had ruined her appetite. Some yogurt and berries would do while Holly ate her kibble.

The night was beautiful, in spite of her state of mind. Holly didn't care about her mood. She went about her business with her usual enthusiasm as they walked. Chique snorted at her in the darkness like she always did, convinced Emilie was a goblin. The horses still demanded their late-night treats. That was the great thing about them. They didn't care if you were feeling sorry for yourself. Neither did the trees and the stars. Humans were the problem, always. No one had to convince her of that.

She should have asked him. It wasn't as if she had anything to lose.

Why did you ghost me, Tim?

Quid pro quo. I answered your question.

That song. She'd let it go; let him off. She didn't want to make him uncomfortable. Why not? Why did he get a pass?

She climbed the steps to Nate's apartment, Holly bounding ahead of her with all the joy she lacked. That was what she hated most about this. She was used to being happy. She wasn't used to — this.

But it was like it was out of her control, the compassion that rose in her; that sense he was vulnerable, even though he would never admit it, preferring to encase himself in a hard shell. It was why she'd been so surprised he'd asked her about that time in the café.

She was capable of dealing with it. Just like she'd told him, she had experience. But did she want to? Did she need to? Was it worth it?

Because it wouldn't be for her. It would only be for him. He was going back to Calgary. He'd return to his regular life and just ghost her again.

She wasn't his friend. She didn't want to be his friend.

She wanted to be something more.

She was in so much trouble.

CHAPTER SIXTEEN

It was wrong that he was so unfit. He was a professional athlete. It was his job to be in shape. Shouldn't he have retained more lung capacity than this? And his good leg was overdeveloped, his bad leg weak — of course. Imbalance was unhealthy. Right now, imbalance summed up his whole life.

The tape was amazing, though. His knee felt great. It would help him get his balance back.

Except — Emilie. Her hands on the weave of the tape, on his skin, warming under her touch — it totally unbalanced him. *Cheap thrills, Tim.* They weren't, really. They cost him, those thrills.

He pushed the speed on the treadmill, a burn in his chest, legs pumping faster and faster — left, right, left, right — focusing on strength and equilibrium. Just like in the Emily song, running on empty, down the rabbit hole...

Don't overdo it. Words of wisdom. He couldn't afford a setback.

He gradually slowed to a walk, the hum of the treadmill less frenetic, and it didn't take long for his heart rate to drop.

Maybe he wasn't in as poor condition as he thought. Mopping his face with his towel as the belt slowed, he stepped off the deck and hit the weights. He'd been able to maintain his upper body, but the lower needed to be carefully rebuilt.

He stretched out his muscles at the end, then flopped down flat out on the mat, staring at the ceiling and trying to figure out what had gone wrong last night when it had felt for a while like progress.

He should have. He should have just told her. He should have just kissed her. Less thinking, more doing.

He had to make this Plate ball count; use a perfect setting to create a perfect evening. Show her and tell her. It was becoming an obsession. It wasn't as if he was planning a proposal; he was just trying to set everything up in his favour. Seeing her last night, he hadn't been prepared. He was going to be prepared for the ball.

Vibrations travelled through the floor — the dull thud of the door opening and closing, then the soft pad of footsteps. He pulled out an earbud and rolled his head to see Nate sauntering over. Tim crunched into a sitting position, crossing his legs. He had to stare at his knee a moment, still in awe of the tape. But the tape always brought him back to Emilie.

"Good workout?" Nate asked, straddling the weight bench.

Tim tried to rearrange his expression to something less preoccupied. "Pretty good, yeah."

"The knee must be feeling okay if you're sitting like that."

He rubbed his hand over it. Over the tape. "This stuff's pretty magical."

"I agree. Whenever I do something to myself, I just get Em to tape me back together." Nate grinned.

"That's handy for you," Tim said, feeling his face fall back into a frown. *Magical Emilie.*

"What's up? Working out is supposed to make you happy. Endorphins, and all that."

Tim balled up his sweaty towel and threw it at Nate.

"That wasn't smart." Nate twirled the towel then snapped it expertly, coming just short of Tim's kneecap. "Get off your butt. I've got something to show you. Follow me."

Nate still wielded the towel, so Tim pushed himself to his feet and did as he was told. If Nate connected with that weapon, it would leave a welt.

Six steps took them to a door that opened to the outdoors — and a pair of old hockey nets sitting on the driveway. Both were a little bent, the nets frayed, but that didn't matter; they'd serve the purpose. A hard plastic red street hockey ball waited on top with two sticks. Nate tossed him one, grabbed the other, and dropped the ball to the asphalt, where it landed with minimal bounce.

Tim just watched Nate at first, admiring the way he stick-handled then sent the ball into the net with a quick wrist shot. Nate scooped it out, popped it in again, then tipped it to Tim.

More memories. A scene, clear in his mind, of the street in front of the house in Calgary. A group of them gathered to play; mostly guys, a couple girls. Team jerseys of favourite NHL players. Stopping play and dragging the nets out of the way when someone yelled, "Car!" They were all future pro hockey stars then.

He began slowly, reminding himself: *don't overdo it*. Body angled casually over the stick, the ball travelling six inches, back and forth. Control over speed. Accuracy over power. There was nothing wrong with his wrists — he barely had to shift to flick the bright sphere into the net. Nate fired it right back at him and he deftly took control again. It felt good to have control over something.

He shot the ball again, bottom right corner. A little faster.

A little harder. Nate wasn't volunteering to stand in the net like a goaltender. He just retrieved the ball and returned it.

Bottom corner, left side. He could hear it whiz through the air, almost blowing through the netting from the force of the shot.

"Little bit of anger management happening here?" Nate asked, an eyebrow peaking. This time he just rolled the ball back.

Tim didn't stop it; he just fired. *Top left corner.* "Shut up."

"What are you angry about?"

The ball sizzled through the air like a fluorescent orange comet. *Top right corner.*

Nate sent the ball Tim's way. "It wouldn't be Em and the vet, would it?"

Tim stopped, mid-shot. "You know about that?"

"Did you forget about the sisters thing?"

He scowled. "Shouldn't that be like lawyer-client privilege?"

Nate snorted. "No."

"Do you have intel? Like how it went?" He straightened, leaning on the stick, needing to know.

Nate mirrored him. "Why would I?"

"For the same reason you knew about it! What good are you if you can't find stuff out for me?"

"Some stuff stays between them. I don't tell Liv everything we talk about." Nate swept in, batting the ball away, and back-handed it into the net, this time leaving it there. "Something happen last night? You want to tell me what's going on?"

"Nothing. Exactly nothing. I might as well go back to Calgary. I was stupid, thinking I could salvage anything coming here."

"I thought you were here to see me?" Nate gave him a crooked grin.

Tim smirked. "All of this is your fault."

"You're not giving up that easily, are you? You've been here less than two weeks. Trust me, from someone who's been there, with far worse prospects, whatever is going on, it's not beyond salvaging. I am the poster child for 'never say never.' And you've got the easier sister." Nate grinned.

"So why is it so hard?"

"Baby steps, kid. Admitting you like her is the biggest one."

"Do you think the vet is a problem?" The vet had taken her to lunch, but Tim had that moment in the car, a flash of connection over and above ordinary attraction. Who was the winner here? He'd probably been imagining that closeness, though, because she'd shut it down abruptly.

"Sounds like he was an ass back when Liv knew him at school, but who knows," Nate said. "People grow up."

"When is that ball?" Like he didn't know exactly when it was.

Nate crossed his arms. "Monday. Last year it was the night before the Plate, for some insane reason. I was a wreck."

"But you still won the race."

"Going for three for three." Nate grinned.

"How am I going to change how she thinks of me?" he moaned. "Every time I try, it goes sideways."

"Don't try. Be yourself."

"Thanks Yoda. Or Mom. Not sure which."

"I'll take either as a compliment," Nate said.

"Still... you know how that goes. I'm not sure there's much about me to like." He was always going to be the guy who preferred his own company to that of others; who'd rather spend his spare time working out or with his nose in a book than being sociable. Going to this event was going to take all his determination to overcome the discomfort of it. But he would do it, for her. Except — would he have to be someone else to pull it off?

"I think there's plenty about you to like," Nate insisted.

Tim scowled. "You have to say that."

"No. I don't."

Nate's stare was so intense it hit Tim between the eyes, and he remembered then. Phil and Nate. There was no love lost between those two brothers. But Phil had earned that estrangement. Nate had every right not to like him. He wondered if Nate's feelings had changed since Phil's death. Time healing all wounds, and so on.

"Listen," Nate said, his face softening. "You don't know Em like I do. All the things you think are negatives about yourself are plusses. She might seem like a social butterfly, but when it comes down to it, that's not what's most important to her."

"What is?"

"You're going to have to figure that out for yourself. But I think you're already doing that."

Was he?

"Still, she does like to dance," Nate said, tipping the blade of Tim's stick out from under him so he lost his balance.

Tim found his feet and grabbed Nate's stick but Nate dipped away and broke his hold. He might not be big, but he was strong.

"When was the last time you danced?" he asked.

Tim tried to remember. He wouldn't count the wedding. "Last summer? At one of Mom's things."

"Guess we should practice then, eh?" Nate grinned, and held out his hand. "Give me your stick."

CHAPTER SEVENTEEN

The Queen's Plate Ball.

It sounded fancier than it really was, though it was definitely grander than last year. She'd talked the board into holding it in a hotel instead of the trackside tent at Woodbine because it better suited the Big Band theme they'd concocted — complete with a real big band. The hall looked amazing. The food was fabulous. It was going to be a fantastic evening.

She'd been so busy getting ready for it that it had been easy to avoid Tim without being intentional about it. Tonight would be more of the same. She was here to work, not to enjoy herself. Dean, always a good sport, was officially her date. He didn't mind filling the role so she could turn down anyone else who'd asked because an actual date wasn't practical.

She'd come early, so Dean arrived when he wanted and left when he wanted, which was completely his speed. No one, not even Faye, knew if he'd dated in recent years. If not for the fact that at last year's ball he'd revealed feelings for Liv, Emilie might have believed he had no interest in a relationship. And maybe he didn't. Maybe Liv had been his one and only but it hadn't been important enough for him to speak up until her relationship with Nate was tossed into the spotlight. Either way, he remained single, which Emilie was starting to think wasn't such a bad idea.

Tim came with Liv and Nate, and they shared a table with Faye and Will and Dean. Emilie joined them for brief moments when she could. She could deal with Tim — mostly — when they surrounded him. She had trouble keeping her eyes off him, drawn to the brilliant cobalt of his shirt. In some bizarre coincidence, it was remarkably like the colour of the dress she wore.

It wasn't as if he purposely commanded attention. If it were up to him she guessed he'd want to just blend into the background. That he couldn't was beyond his control; the blessing or curse of the genes that had combined to make him the most drop-dead gorgeous guy in the room. *Sorry, Nate. You've been upstaged. I still adore you — just not like that.*

Dinner was a buffet, so she grazed while fulfilling her duties. The silent auction was just warming up; it would build steam as the evening progressed, mounting to a fevered pitch in the last minutes. She always loved seeing that happen because New Chapter silent auctions were never the kind where participants hoped for a deal. It was a competition, a show of who had the most money to throw around — all of it for a good cause. Honour and pride were at stake, and some of these folks had deep pockets.

The band played backgroundsy music while people were eating, but when it was time for the dancing to begin, a vocalist joined them. Couples tentatively drifted to the floor — a little more alcohol, and people would get braver. She popped a carrot stick in her mouth and took a rare break to sneak away to the bathroom to freshen up, hurrying back and stopping in the doorway to take in the scene, allowing herself a sense of gratification.

That blue shirt grabbed her right away. In the middle of the dance floor?

Stupefied, she watched as Tim held a middle-aged woman in a formal ballroom dancing stance until another elbowed her out. He danced with that one until another cut in. In most cases it appeared he was instructing them, their husbands and partners gawking on the sidelines with the same mixture of awe and discomposure she did herself. The women looked up at Tim with delight and adoration. Who could blame them, really? That face, wearing a patient smile — yes, a smile — was impossible not to adore.

It was so, so, cute. And infuriating.

As she made her way across the room, she nearly bumped into several couples attempting to glean what they could from his direction, because she couldn't stop staring. When she reached Faye, arms outstretched, palms face up, her lips parted for words she would never find to account for this development.

Faye shrugged. "His mother did competitive ballroom. And we know Nate can dance. Properly." Then she leaned into Emilie and whispered, "Do you think I should join the line?"

Emilie smacked her on the arm. It was true: there was a line forming, waiting to dance with the smoking-hot guy in the nifty blue shirt.

"Tell me why I'm not supposed to take it personally that at the wedding, I might as well have been dancing with a stuffed bear?" She wasn't going to lie. It stung. If he could fake it with a bunch of women he'd never met before, why not her on the most significant day of his brother's life? Because that wedding had been bigger than all the Queen's Plates and Dubai World Cups. Anyone who knew the history between Liv and Nate understood that.

"The night is young, Em." Faye patted her on the shoulder. "He might redeem himself yet."

She wouldn't hold her breath. Besides, she planned to be too busy to dance, unless there were a few minutes near the end of the night when Will, who would take over as DJ later with some music that was more relatable to the majority of this crowd, played something modern so she could blow off some steam.

She hadn't expected there would be many people who knew how to dance to this stuff so she'd predicted a lot of shuffling about and laughing. She certainly had not anticipated Tim Miller giving impromptu lessons to strangers on how to dance to old school jazz. Who was this guy? Why hadn't she met him?

"Gotta go," she snapped, whirling away. "I need to check on the silent auction."

As if that was the most pressing task in the world. On the edge of the floor, Nate was cajoling Liv into joining him. She'd do it. Emilie knew she would. Nate was good at coaxing her sister out of her comfort zone. She stopped and watched for a few minutes, the silent auction obviously not in desperate need of her attention. When Liv forgot herself a little, she was fine. Dancing was really just another sport, wasn't it? That strength and grace Liv displayed on a horse would translate, with a little help from Nate.

Faye and Will had joined in but they weren't even trying to look impressive. They were just participating, and Emilie laughed when Will tried some moves. All of it made her feel left out.

"Would you like to dance?"

She twisted toward the voice, then grinned. "Hey, Chad. Having fun?"

"Sure," he said. "Do you know how to do this stuff?"

"Nope."

"Good," he said with his winningest smile. "Let's go make fools of ourselves."

She ran her eyes over him, handsomely turned out in a jacket and tie. "I'd love to."

They tried to copy Tim and what he was teaching his most recent partner, but Emilie kept getting distracted. Chad was attractive, but he was no match for Tim. She got caught up in how relaxed Tim's body was, in a way she'd never seen it; the movement of his feet as he led his partner so effortlessly, making the woman look way better than she had any right to look.

The broadness of his shoulders.

The subtle shift of his hips.

The way the fit of his slacks showed off his butt to perfection.

The exquisite line of his jaw, that slight dimple as he looked down with what she now thought of as his trademark careful smile. A smile that, coupled with the deep and delicious coffee-brown of his eyes, had the potential to make any woman swoon.

At least if they were in his arms, which she was not.

She tripped, stumbling into Chad, treading clumsily on his toes and clutching his arms as she tried to recover. When he caught her by the waist, she righted herself and released her grasp, stepping back, a hand flying to her mouth.

"I'm so sorry!" she gasped, then broke into a giggling fit.

He laughed, but there was something in his expression that made it clear she'd given herself away. "Maybe we should go watch some YouTube videos."

"We achieved our objective. Or at least I did. I've success-fully made a fool of myself!" she said.

"Want a drink?" Chad asked.

"Yes, please." Desperately. "I really do need to check on the silent auction though."

"I'll meet you over there," he said.

Chad hadn't looked hurt or like his ego was bruised, so her

initial assessment about the two of them was reinforced. She'd officially added another guy friend to her collection.

With just half an hour left, the silent auction tables were busy, individuals making the rounds. She scanned the most recent bids, the numbers pleasing her. Another successful event. Chad reappeared and handed her a seltzer.

"Ah, perfect," she said. "Thank you. I worked up a thirst out there." Chad slid into a nearby chair and she joined him. "How are your feet?" Her own were aching from running around on them all night, but at least no one had stomped on hers like a baby elephant.

"I work with horses all day, and I come to a charity event and get trampled by the organizer." He shook his head, but a good-natured smile tugged at the corners of his lips.

"Just another thing I'm never going to live down."

"I'm sure not going to let you forget it." He grinned.

"You will be okay to work tomorrow, won't you?" She rested a hand lightly on his knee with a wry twist to her mouth.

"If not, I'm telling Ben it's your fault," he joked. "Good thing Triple Stripe is one of our best clients."

"We should probably stand you in some ice, just in case," she quipped.

"Are you introducing traditional racehorse therapies into your physio practice?"

"And vice versa," she said with a nod and a prim smile.

The seltzer was refreshing with just enough alcohol to even out her tension; tension she couldn't entirely blame on her responsibilities. The lineup for Tim's Dance Class was petering out — he'd worked his way through most of the women — but the one stepping forward made Emilie sit up with a start. She checked herself, taking another sip — okay, so maybe it was a gulp — and demurely crossing her legs at the ankles.

Sylvie didn't look as if she knew exactly what she was

doing, but she had enough natural ability and eagerness to be coached to look better than most of Tim's previous students. Emilie simmered. It was only a waltz. Even she could fake her way through a waltz.

At the end of the song he released her, and Sylvie came over, laughing and breathless. Tim didn't follow. He didn't even cast a glance their way as he sauntered over to Liv and Nate, hands in pockets, the band tapering off the last song and pausing, talking among themselves.

"Why aren't you over there, Em? So much fun." Sylvie said. "Ooh, can I have a sip? I'm parched."

I'm parched, Emilie mimicked in her head. *Stop being catty.* She handed the glass to Sylvie. "If Tim Miller wants me to dance with him, he's going to have to ask."

"That's not how things seem to be working tonight," Sylvie said. *Now who's being catty?*

Liv joined them, leaving Tim and Nate behind, their heads together. She sat next to Emilie, crossing her knees so the slit of her sleek ice-blue dress fell open enough to show the defined muscles of her calves.

"One day Nate will make a dancer out of you," Emilie said.

"I'm hardly a worthy partner," Liv demurred.

"Who is, though? Besides their mom, of course."

Liv slid her a glance. "Well..." Then she jutted her chin toward the dance floor, just as the band started up again.

Emilie's jaw dropped, and she snorted a laugh. This was going to be the best. Tim stood, straight-faced, posture-perfect, one foot posed in front of the other, and offered his hand — to Nate.

He might have been trying his hardest but Nate couldn't keep a straight face. He grasped Tim's hand and did something between a bow and a curtsey, then let Tim pull him into a formal ballroom stance. Then they took off with the music.

They flew with the flourish of the professionals you saw on TV.

Nate was probably having a hard time letting Tim lead, and Emilie wondered if their mother had made them practice together, or if this was spontaneous entertainment. When Tim dipped him, Nate's feet slipped and there was a tense moment, a gasp escaping from the rapt audience as Tim held him suspended there, Nate's hands blanching as he gripped a little tighter. Their lips were moving — words were exchanged. Emilie guessed Nate was saying something like, *Please don't drop me on my head,* Tim responding with *But it would be payback for all the times you tortured me as a kid*; brotherly love stuff like that. Then Tim pulled Nate back up, and they carried on to a flutter of clapping. They finished to thunderous applause that nearly rattled the chandeliers, both of them bowing before Nate dragged Tim into a laughing, back-thumping hug.

Will started up the recorded music and Nate and Tim wandered over to their group. The other guests dispersed, some dancing like mere mortals, others hitting the dessert table and refreshing their drinks, or heading outside for a smoke.

Emilie stood, leading a small standing ovation, Liv, Faye, Sylvie and Chad joining in. She clapped because it gave her something to do with her conflicted energy, and kept her eyes pinned on Nate. She didn't know what looking at Tim would do to her.

"That was brilliant!" she said, throwing herself at Nate because it was safe. His shirt was damp. It was pretty gross, which helped distract her from all the thoughts ricocheting around her head about Tim.

"I hope someone videoed that," Nate said, grinning.

Faye waved her phone around. You could always count on Faye to catch the important stuff.

"We need to send that to Mom," Nate said.

Emilie tried to stop herself from following the turn of his head as he looked at Tim but it was an ingrained response. Those eyes were staring at her, not at Nate. She gulped, and dropped hers to her feet.

"I totally messed up the dip," Tim said.

"We forgot to practice it," Nate admitted. "Want to dance, Em?"

She smiled at him gratefully and dragged him to an open spot.

She didn't want to talk about the performance he and Tim had put on. There was no way to iron out her emotions, and she struggled for something, anything else. Or she could just stay silent. Nate would let her do that, not try to get into her head. And so she did. She would just enjoy being with one of her favourite people in the world; someone she didn't have to worry would misinterpret her words or actions. Someone who didn't send her brain into unexplained turmoil.

The crowd was already thinning; this was a late night for most of these people. She let her arms wrap around Nate's neck and pressed her face into his shoulder as they swayed until the song ended and they walked back to the seats.

Liv looked ready to leave, and Nate reached for her hand, pulling her from her chair. He kissed her and eyed Tim. "Time to go?"

Tim stood, his eyes flitting from Nate to Emilie, but she was already planning her escape. She had a lot to finish up before she could go home.

"Drive safe, guys. Thanks for coming," she said with a smile and a wave, and marched off to help settle the silent auction.

"Emilie. Wait."

She took a couple of steps before coming to a halt, spinning to face Tim.

"I get it Tim, it's fine. You dance beautifully. You just don't want to dance with me. Which is great, because I don't want to dance with you either." She flipped her hair over her shoulder. "You'd better go. You wouldn't want them to leave without you, because I'm sure not going to drive you home."

And she stormed off, not letting herself look back. She had things to do.

CHAPTER EIGHTEEN

His NYLON SHORTS skimmed the tops of his knees, the tattered edges of the tape, lifting and peeling, exposed below the hem. It was sore after last night. He'd iced it when he got home, and this walk around the farm should help, but he wished he could ask Emilie to tape it again. The effect of the first application was probably wearing off, right? But given how the evening had ended, he wasn't optimistic she'd agree — if he ran into her today.

The ball hadn't exactly gone as planned. Emilie had been so busy he'd hardly seen her — though sometimes he thought being busy was her way of avoiding him. She'd floated about like the social butterfly Nate said she wasn't all night long, though she'd found time to dance with the vet. The two of them had laughed and fallen over each other looking as if they were having a great time while he'd been stuck teaching a bunch of older women how to waltz, foxtrot and rumba.

It had started when Nate asked him to dance with a widow he rode horses for after Nate had done so himself. How could he say no to something that would help his brother, after everything he'd done? Things had steamrolled from there, more ladies jumping on the bandwagon. At first it had given him a purpose; something he was confident doing in a situation in which he'd otherwise feel out of place, but it had gotten out of control and he'd ended up just as occupied as Emilie. And when he'd tried to explain at the end of the night, she wouldn't hear him out. He couldn't win.

The evening had given him flashbacks to his mother taking him along to help when she'd taught classes at church for fun. Fun for her and the ladies, maybe, but not for teenaged Tim who was sure the whole thing would keep him from ever meeting girls his own age.

Nate had been her first pupil. He and Mom had a special bond — somehow even at a young age Nate had realized Dad wouldn't dance with her and had asked Mom to teach him, because he knew how much she loved it. It had been a normal scene in their house, the two of them practicing steps in the kitchen, those early lessons among Tim's first memories. He tried to entice Tim to learn too by claiming it was an amazing way to improve his footwork on skates. Tim hadn't believed him until he stepped in to replace Nate — Mom had been so mopey after her middle son had moved to Ontario, he'd felt sorry for her. When he'd really started devoting himself to it, much to his mother's glee, even his father had shrugged off his disgruntlement because Tim's skating had improved exponentially. Anything that helped his game was worth keeping up.

The demonstration last night, as he was choosing to call it, had been Nate's idea. A "let's show them how it's done," to which Tim had only agreed because Nate let him lead. Once he'd gotten over his self-consciousness, it had been fun, and a great workout, though it had probably crossed into the overdoing it category, as his knee was pointing out this morning. Mom had loved the video — Faye was the best for getting that

— so that alone made the whole night worth it. Of course Faye had posted it on TikTok and last time he'd checked, it was threatening to go viral. Maybe he and Nate could make some money as social media influencers on the side. *The Miller Brothers...*

As he sauntered along the lane, it wasn't about elevating his heart rate; he only wanted to be moving. Emilie's red Civic was parked outside the smaller barn that had the apartment over it, but the building seemed empty — no horses, no sounds coming from upstairs, the office door locked. He peered up the narrow staircase. It would have been aggravating with his crutches. It had been kind of Emilie to trade. She did nice things in spite of herself; she couldn't help it.

He walked through and stopped a moment to visit with the horses in the closest field. The little black one was Nate's super-horse, though she looked more like a round pony instead of a famous racehorse right now because she was carrying a baby. He couldn't expect her to maintain a more athletic shape.

There was activity at the other barn. The Balls on the Roof Barn, he'd forever think of it as. He glanced up cautiously, but didn't see anything. Birds had probably taken them away. All that mattered was that they were gone now.

He stopped to admire the motorcycle parked just to the side of the entrance on the jaunty tilt of its kickstand, keeping himself from running his hands over the shiny chrome and black paint. A helmet and heavy leather jacket hung from one handlebar. Maybe once he'd mastered the stick shift, he'd get a bike. After his walk he was going to practice in the high school parking lot with the car. He would conquer this thing. For himself, though. Not for Emilie.

Someone was riding in the outdoor ring while another person shouted at them, her tone sounding a lot like one of his coaches; encouraging in one breath while demanding his best in the next. When he drifted from the bike, following the voice — and the plumes of dust — he recognized Emilie on the horse. The person standing in the middle had to be the bike owner, her legs clad in black leather, a black tank on top, and a black cap pulled over her hair, the long thick braid poking from the hole at the back trailing to her waist.

"And, walk," the coach called.

As if the horse had understood, it slowed, Emilie unmoving. After a few steps, she let the reins droop and the horse stretched its long neck out with a wet snort.

"That was good!" the coach praised. "Much better this time."

Emilie reached forward, stroking the horse's brown neck. "I can't get my leg back!" she said with exasperation, then added in a drawn-out whine that almost made Tim laugh, "Whyyyyyy?"

"That jump saddle is not making it easy for you to have an ideal leg position," the coach said.

"So I need a dressage saddle," Emilie said, then cracked, "How about an exercise saddle?"

"Sure," the coach said. "Let's try it. You wouldn't be the first. Your saddle isn't doing your horse any favours, so either way it would be best to try something different."

Emilie brought the horse to a halt in the middle of the ring, the dust settling on and around them. Her black helmet looked more like it was a warm grey with the resulting film.

"Hi Tim!"

The girl on the horse sounded nothing like the one in the blue dress at the ball who had scorched him last night. Forgiven, just like that? He needed to buy that horse some carrots.

She kicked her feet out of the stirrups and threw her leg over, landing gracefully, the slight bend of her knees cushioning the impact and showing the perfect curve of her butt, the tight line of her hamstrings, those grey riding pants leaving just enough to his imagination. She did something quickly with the saddle, then something else with the bridle before pulling the reins over the horse's head and starting toward him, the coach alongside.

"This is my brother-in-law's brother, Tim. Tim, this is Jodi. She's paid to kick my behind."

He offered his hand. "Nice to meet you. Nice bike." Tim wondered if she would take him for a ride, then wondered if asking would come off as suggestive.

"Thanks," Jodi said, checking him out before turning to Emilie. "Same time next week?"

"Sounds good! You'll get back to me about judging the show?"

"I'll check my schedule," Jodi said, and they left her sliding her arms into the heavy jacket as they entered the dark barn.

"Want me to turn on some lights?" he asked.

"Thanks. They're just behind the door on the left." She continued down the dark aisle, the horse walking placidly next to her.

When he rejoined her, the bridle was off and looped over her arm as she put something else on the horse's head and snapped a line to it on either side of its face.

"That's the halter, right?" he asked.

She raised her eyebrows with a crooked smile as she unbuckled the part that went around the horse then ducked under the horse's neck to do something on the other side. "Right. You taking notes?"

Soon the long belly band thing was resting over the saddle. Girth, he was pretty sure it was called. They had lots of them at the racetrack.

"Can I take that?" He held out his arms as she slid the saddle off.

"Uh — sure. It goes on one of those racks in the tack room." She took the pad out from under it before he carried it away. "Careful now," she called after him as he went into the room. "If I ever horseshow again, I may hire you as my groom."

His forehead creased as he returned. "Horseshow is a verb?"

"Sure. Why not"

"What is wrong with people? It sounds stupid." He scowled, coming around to her side and leaning back against a stall, arms crossed.

Emilie laughed. "What are you, a linguistics freak? Or just old?"

"I'm younger than you," he said.

She began picking up each of the horse's feet and scraping the bottoms with a hooked tool. "How do you know?"

"I know things."

She rolled her eyes as she straightened after doing the two back feet. "Stupid Facebook."

When he grinned her eyes stayed on him for a second before she tucked the tool into a plastic tote. He kept from reciting that her birthday was March fifteenth because he'd sound like a stalker.

"When's your birthday?" she asked, glancing his way again.

He'd hidden that information from the public, but didn't mind her knowing. "January."

"January what?" she asked.

"Third."

"Hmm. That's almost enough to make me believe in that astrology stuff."

"Why?"

She reached down for the rope that lay next to the tote.

"Because Liv's birthday is December thirty-first, so you're in the same time zone or whatever. You're a lot alike."

"I think sign is the word you're looking for."

"I think perhaps you're right." She smiled at him as she snapped the rope to the halter and unclipped the side lines.

"What are those called?" he asked, pretty sure they weren't "side lines."

"Crossties." She walked the horse forward a few steps before turning him around and heading in the other direction.

This is how things had been between them last winter when they'd been messaging. Only this was in person; the same easy back and forth. The real them. Last night hadn't been either of their normal states. It made him giddy — all was not lost, if he could figure out how to keep them here, just the two of them — and the horse, who he was convinced might be the conduit.

She tied the horse up again with crossties in a white-walled wash area, rubber mats on the floor and a drain at the back, then sprayed the animal all over, pausing to let it drink from the little fountain she created by kinking the hose which she presented to its grabby lips.

Tim laughed, and when she unkinked it and started spraying again, he stepped forward and offered his palm, letting those wet lips nuzzle, then lick. "What's its name?"

"His name is Excursion," she said with emphasis on the "his."

"He looks like a Curtis," Tim decided.

"Is that a family thing, giving everything a nickname?" She tried — and failed — to suppress a smile. "Nate does that all the time. Doesn't matter if we call a horse one thing, we all end up calling it whatever he decides it should be instead."

"How come he didn't find a nickname for this one?" The horse bobbed his head when Tim withdrew his hand.

"Good question."

She unsnapped Curtis — because Tim was going to make sure he was called Curtis now — and took him outside to a patch of grass. They watched in an uncomplicated silence as the horse mowed the turf, occasionally stomping at a fly and shaking his head.

"I should have sprayed him," Emilie said, brushing an insect from Curtis's side. "How do you feel about holding him?"

Curtis looked pretty chill, so he inched forward, reaching for the rope.

"Don't worry," she said, heading back to the barn. "He'll just keep eating. All you have to do is keep the slack out of the lead without restricting him. I'll be back in a sec."

It was fascinating, the way Curtis tore off the blades, bite by bite, turning his head slightly or moving forward a step to find a fresh patch. He was selective, chomping at the dandelions but leaving behind other weeds, and the sound of the tearing and chewing was soothing. Tim followed him, just like he seemed to be following everyone right now. It had been nice to lead for a while last night; to be the one who knew where to go.

"You look good on the end of a shank."

Emilie stood in the doorway, a spray bottle dangling from her fingers as she watched him. She blinked, and came forward, training her eyes on Curtis.

"Lift his head?" she asked.

He had to pull hard to get Curtis away from the lawn, then slid his hand up to the snap like he'd seen them do at the track to keep the horse from moving while Emilie sprayed fly repellant over all four legs. Curtis rubbed his nose against Tim's arm, leaving a trail of green slime, seeming not to care as she continued to cover his body.

"Thanks," she said, and traded him the spray bottle for the horse.

He was rubbing the green slime on his t-shirt when an SUV drove up and his spirits plunged. The vet.

"Come on, Curtis," Emilie said, tugging the horse's head away. The grin she gave Tim almost made up for the vet's arrival. He followed her again. He was going to follow her until she told him to stop.

"There aren't going to be any more balls on the roof, are there?" he asked, tossing the fly spray bottle from hand to hand.

Her laugh trailed back to him as she led Curtis to his stall. "No, you're safe."

"Hi Em," Chad said, walking up as Emilie came out of Curt's stall. "Hey, Tim. You were amazing last night! Too bad you didn't have time to give Emilie a lesson."

He cringed as Emilie scowled. *Thanks, Chad.* Mentioning the dancing seemed to bring whatever had set her off last night seeping to the surface, now that the horse ride vibes had worn off. Just when he'd made up ground.

Emilie swung the lead, her lips pressed tight together. "I don't know why you're even here. Liv could remove those sutures. I could do it, for that matter."

Chad laughed at her and Tim unsuccessfully tried to analyze their interaction. She turned on her heel, tall riding boots hugging her long calves, and brought out a horse that seemed to be mostly legs.

"Where'd you and your brother learn to dance like that, Tim? You could be on *Canada's Got Talent.*" Chad crouched beside the racehorse and snipped bright blue stitches from the animal's knee. Tim was pretty sure he could have done that, too.

"My mom used to be a competitive ballroom dancer when

she was younger. She taught us both. Me and Nate, I mean." Not that they'd ever danced together like that.

"Well, it's pretty cool. I should get you to give me lessons, come to think of it. It's probably good for impressing girls."

"That's what Nate always said." And that had been the whole idea of the Plate Ball. He'd needed to impress a girl. *Fail.*

Emilie was busy tickling the horse between the nostrils, looking completely disinterested in the conversation.

"It looks good, Em." Chad straightened, pulling off his blue gloves. He waited for Emilie to put the horse away. "Listen. I'm determined to get to my parents' cottage for a couple of days and I could use some company."

Was this guy serious? Emilie's eyes shifted.

Chad tapped the handle of the little scissors he'd used to remove the stitches against his palm. "The two of you should come. Invite Sylvie, too. It'll be fun."

Chad's offer threw Tim for a loop. Did he like Sylvie now, or was he just trying to double his chances by playing both women, inviting Tim because he knew neither of them would agree otherwise?

"I'll ask her," Emilie said, her eyes travelling to Tim. "Do you do cottages in Alberta?"

"Not my family," he admitted. "The closest I came was going to Will's grandfather's farm sometimes. That's where Nate learned to ride." And where Tim had been on a horse a few times. After what he'd seen here, he wasn't going to call that riding anymore.

"I can't imagine Nate ever needing to learn how to ride," Emilie said, like his brother was some kind of hero — which he kind of was.

"Do you want to go?" Emilie asked.

Tim couldn't read her look. It was as if she was trying hard not to have any expression at all when there was a hidden question behind it.

He shrugged. "Sure."

He wasn't sure. But he was sure he didn't want Emilie to go without him.

CHAPTER NINETEEN

THERE WERE A LOT OF PEOPLE.

But it gave him an excuse to stay close to her; sometimes letting himself bump into her — and sometimes having no choice because of the press of bodies around them.

"The best part is, we get to go in the walking ring," she said, tipping her head back to him, her face bright. "Then all the people on the outside will look at us and sigh, wishing they were us and thinking we're important."

The way she said it made it sound as if her family wasn't important, when they were. The horse they were here to watch in this next race had won one worth twelve million dollars in March. He only got seven million of that, though, Nate said.

Only. Emilie should be some rich guy's wife. She was already organizing charity fundraisers. Bottom line? On paper, out of his league.

Except she was so real. There was nothing fake about Emilie. She wafted effortlessly from one world to the next, looking comfortable getting splashed with water while spraying a horse, or sitting on top of one wearing those tight pants that showed off her long thighs and nipped-in waist; and now, in her fancy race day outfit, the feathers bouncing on her head staying put by some force of magic while she chatted and weaved her way through the throng. Her dress was classy, skimming her form in a way that highlighted her shape without being glued to her like cling wrap. There were enough outfits like that around, and he didn't need any help to picture Emilie more evocatively dressed.

He'd seen her. In December, back at the hotel, after the wedding. By the pool.

She'd pulled off her oversized t-shirt like she was taunting him as payback for his earlier behaviour, revealing the bikini under it — something meant for maximizing sun exposure, not swimming laps. The light around the pool had been dim, shadows accentuating shapes. He'd had to retreat to his room. He hadn't seen her again, in real life, until she'd picked him up at the airport.

She waved at someone now, arm stretched high in the air, her heels adding a few inches to her usual reach. Tim spotted Will, one of the taller people in the sea, and breathed out a sigh. With his long-suffering expression, he looked just as dragged along as Tim felt. Faye's arm was wrapped around his elbow, her face flushed with the same excitement radiating from Emilie.

"You look fabulous!" Faye exclaimed, breaking away from Will to shuffle up on dangerously high spikes.

"So do you!" Emilie returned as she gave Faye a careful one-armed hug, angling her head so that the brim of Faye's hat didn't take out her eye.

"Naturally," Faye said as she stepped back, her eyes roving over Tim with a slight tilt to her head. "And who is this?"

"I know, right?" Emilie said, and Tim almost jumped out of

his skin when one of her hands curled around his biceps, the other stroking it. "Sharp, eh?"

He didn't miss Faye's wink and found himself smiling. It wasn't lost on him that his crisp white shirt and grey vest complimented Emilie's outfit. The striped tie was a nice touch, and rolling up his sleeves made it just a bit less formal. Not that he minded wearing nice clothes, especially when he got a reaction like that. They looked good together.

"Did Liv get you two paddock passes?" Emilie asked. "She said she would."

Faye nodded. "It takes some of the sting out of Dean not having a horse running today. We still get to be in the middle of it. Ride on the Triple Stripe coat tails."

"Faye and Dean's horse won the Plate last year," Emilie said to Tim, her vivid blue irises travelling in an arc like she wasn't feeling all that sorry for them. "But that's okay, we'll still take pity on you, Faye. It does take some fun out of our little rivalry though, so I really am sorry."

Faye smiled. "Your horses better run one-two to make up for it."

"I will die if Reba wins," Emilie said, looking as if she was already visualizing it. "Come on. Let's get in there before the horses do."

Faye and Emilie led the way to the area closed off from the crowd with a metal fence and hedge. It was dotted with weeping willows and small groups of people, a path made up of rubberized bricks around the perimeter. Emilie and Liv's parents were already there, and they greeted him warmly without being effusive. He'd met them too at the wedding, but that hadn't required anything quite like this: standing in a cozy group making small talk. They managed to make him feel part of everything without demanding too much from him. Nice people. Just like Em.

Then the horses began arriving, breaking from their single file one by one as they found the spots corresponding to the number they each wore. More people were added to the already busy space, including Liv and Nate, picking their way across the grass. Nate was wearing the required uniform: light, white nylon pants tucked neatly into flat black boots, his top white, blue and red. Liv looked as elegant as the other women, though she wore slacks and a sleeveless red blouse of something shimmery instead of a dress, her hat navy. Nate said something in her ear that made her smile. Tim slipped his phone from his pocket to take a photo for Mom.

He'd met Jay, the horse who now strode easily around them next to his groom, Michel. Jay was big and gleamed a rich reddish-gold — brighter than copper, redder than brass. Tim didn't know horses, but this one had the unmistakable aura of an athlete. Michel reached up and rested a hand on the side of Jay's powerful neck for a few circuits, obvious pride and dedication on his face.

Emilie sighed. "He's so hunky."

She was talking about the horse, of course. But he didn't mind. If it was a competition, he'd rather the horse than the vet.

"Hard to believe a year ago I was riding him around the farm for fun, isn't it?" she said, not taking her eyes off Jay.

"You did a good job with him, Em," Liv said. "If not for you we wouldn't be standing here."

"If Nate hadn't stepped in, it might have been him I started Jodi's boot camp with!" Emilie said.

"Missed opportunities for sure," Nate quipped. "Glad you found someone else to torture yourself with and let this guy do the fun stuff."

"You rode him?" Tim asked, staring at her. Jay was huge, and she was tiny. The horse was so powerful he made Tim feel paltry, yet she could handle that brawn. And a manual transmission. He should probably be afraid of her.

She tore her gaze away for a glance at Tim. "He's a big puppy. Anyone could ride him."

By anyone, she didn't mean him. This horse was nothing like the Quarter Horses he'd gone trail riding on back home when he was a kid. He'd just sat there. He hated to think where he'd end up if he just sat on this horse. The horse would probably deem him unworthy and dump him.

Even though he didn't know exactly what was involved in riding properly, it seemed so much more impressive than learning how to skate while holding a stick and moving a chunk of rubber about. Hockey was just him, the ice, and trying not to get hurt by players whose job it was to stop him. His teammates were human and wanted to cooperate. A horse was a partner who may or may not want to play.

When Emilie skipped over to say something to Liv, it felt like she left a hole, so much so his eyes dropped, sure the ground had opened up in the space she'd vacated. He stared at it for a moment, the cool pocket of air redistributing to ambient, the sensation passing with it. Lifting his gaze slowly, he stopped when it found her again, wishing she'd look at him, then forced his eyes away, running them around the whole circle — only hesitating at Nate's subtle, wry smile, directed right at him. He gave a small headshake, lips pressed together tightly, and carried on with fresh determination to Not Look At Emilie.

Will stood behind Faye as she chatted with Emilie's mom, his hands shoved in his pockets, and for once Tim felt sorry for someone else. He looked as if he was enduring it all while Tim could watch the horses — and Emilie — all day. He stepped back, needing to feel occupied.

"You look thrilled," he said.

"I'm just here for the eats," Will grinned. "Want to check out the food trucks after this race is out of the way?"

It didn't sound as if Will was looking forward to the race as much as he was. "Sounds like fun," he responded, even though he didn't really want to commit to anything without knowing Emilie's agenda — because she seemed to be operating on a very specific one.

From somewhere a voice commanded, "Riders up!" then everything went from quiet conversation to excited motion — colourful jockeys heading for their mounts, trainers assisting their ascent onto glowing horses as the grooms at their heads kept them walking, all of it like an elaborate stage production.

Nate's knees, perched on top of Jay, were tucked up so tight it made Tim's hurt, and he absently rubbed the injured one. The tape was still there, tattered edges and all. He forgot about it most of the time, but whenever he had a shower, it warmed again as it dried.

Emilie. Shower. He tried to shake off the tangent his brain ran with, shooting a quick glance in her direction. Her eyes followed Jay and her body moved in small steps with the press of the crowd as they gathered near the point where the horses exited, starting down the path he assumed would take them to the racetrack. Her face sparkled with anticipation, hopelessly beautiful. When they were finally able to head for their seats, he was shuffled to the back with Will when he really wanted to be up there with her; to absorb some of her light and glean some of her knowledge — about this sport, this race, this horse.

"It would be too much to expect them to wait for us, wouldn't it?" Will feigned exasperation at being left behind by his girlfriend. "We have to keep them in sight so we don't get lost. I'm not sure I could find my way to where we're supposed to go."

"Wish you'd told me that sooner," Tim quipped. "I thought

you were a veteran of this game. If I'd known you were almost as clueless as me I would have been sure to stick closer to them."

"Don't worry, I've got Faye's hat in my sights. As long as she leaves it on, we're good. If she doesn't, all bets are off."

"Should we bet? I want to bet," Tim said.

Will shrugged. "Okay. Let's make sure we know where they're going first."

The lines were long for the mutuel windows, which weren't windows at all. Emilie had loaned him her program, and he tried to study it as he waited, wishing she'd come with him instead of Will. So did Will, by the looks of him, but Tim couldn't ask Emilie to miss even a second of the pre-race stuff. He was sad he was missing it himself. Maybe Will would have stood here for him, because he looked bored either way — here or there.

He knew what horse he was betting on, just not what he should bet. So when he reached the front of the line, glancing nervously at the television screen that had just updated to two minutes to post, he slapped a twenty-dollar bill on the counter and said, "Just Jay to win."

The clerk raised a tired eyebrow. "Number three in race three?"

Tim glanced at the program numbers. "Yes. Sorry. Thanks."

She nodded, punching it in, and traded him a printed ticket for his money.

His heart did a little blip when he saw the seat beside Emilie was empty. Faye and Emilie half-stood to let Will in, and Will settled next to Faye and pulled out his phone. Tim sat on the edge of the vacant seat, the thermal ticket paper slippery between his fingers, his toes bouncing as he located the starting gate, just in time to see the last horse go in. Then they were off.

He could feel Emilie vibrating beside him, perched expectantly as she locked onto the colourful stream of horses and jockeys far on the other side of the track. They were racing on the grass course, and Tim's eyes flitted from the big screen that showed a close-up, to the live race and back again. It was like watching a hockey game in person versus on TV. You got a much tighter view on television, but you missed so much of the bigger picture.

Liv and her father had binoculars trained on the race and he wished he did too. He wanted to see them up close, not have to rely on the camera person's crop of the action. Where was Jay? Now and then he caught the announcer's rapid stream like a play-by-play. It sounded like Jay was last.

"Where is he?" he asked Em, having to raise his voice to be heard over the buzz of the crowd.

"At the back. Don't worry. Just wait for it."

She gave him a quick smile and flash of her blue eyes and like always, he had to pull away from them because he could get lost there and there was a race to watch.

The stretch was way, way long, and he shaded his vision with a hand, hoping to see more clearly — trying to zero in on the red, white, and blue Nate wore, and the big copper horse beneath him.

Soon it wasn't a problem. Just Jay zoomed down the middle of the wide green strip like an orange torpedo, flying past the other horses with Nate low and barely moving on his back. Even Tim could tell he wasn't asking for any of the effort Jay was giving him. They cruised past the finishing point first and rollicked away, Nate scrubbing him heartily on the neck.

"Wow!" Tim gasped.

"I love him so much." Emilie beamed, then Tim overheard her as Faye congratulated her with a big hug. "He's the most reliable man in my life."

Faye laughed. Tim frowned.

"See Tim, all that effort to dress nice paid off because you're getting your picture taken," Faye said as they began the procession to the stairs.

This time they had to walk all the way across the track to get to a semi-circle in the inner part of the oval. Halfway there, Emilie rested a hand on his arm and turned him, pointing toward the grandstand. The tiers were draped with blue and white, packed to the gills with people; the whole place humming like it was a living thing. He supposed, in a way, it was.

"And this is just part of the opening act. Now, ever been in a photo with an international celebrity?"

When she smiled up at him with her infectious joy, he thought this might be the best day of his life.

CHAPTER TWENTY

Emilie escaped to the barn with Liv after Jay's race. She
needed to see the big horse come back; make sure he was okay.
She needed to see Reba before the Plate. And she needed to
step away.

Tim looked good — and smelled good. Yes, she'd inhaled
deeply as she'd stroked his arm. Stoked his arm! She'd had to
keep separating herself from him because it was too much. It
would be too easy to let herself be taken by the sheer physi-
cality of him. Her muddled feelings were already being tossed
about like a white water raft going through the rapids after
those moments they'd spent hanging out after her lesson with
Excursion. Never mind how natty he looked today, and that she
wanted to hang off his arm. She loved watching him experience
the festival atmosphere, learning to love what she loved about
this day.

Leaving him with Will and Faye assuaged her guilt for
running off — the three of them planned to scout out the tents
and trucks. It wasn't Saratoga with its row of vendors, but they

might find some interesting food (in case they still had room after they'd stuffed themselves at the buffet upstairs) or some new signature cocktail the track was trying to sell in a souvenir glass.

Jay's effort in the King Edward Gold Cup hadn't come close to pushing him to the full extent of his talent. Liv had big plans for the five-year-old horse, and today's victory propelled them forward. But Liv had already tucked away her satisfaction with Jay's win to focus on what was next: running two horses in the Queen's Plate.

Nate would ride Cam — Can't Catch Me — the second-favourite on the morning line, the odds set by the track handi-capper. Reba, in the program as She Sings, would have Emilie's friend Cory MacDonald, whose hard work last year had earned her the title of top apprentice jockey in the country. Cory was more excited than any of them; this was her first Queen's Plate mount, and she had a good chance to win. Emilie didn't want to play favourites, but her heart was with Reba and Cory.

Last October, Reba had been sent home after a brief stint on Woodbine's backstretch; too small and too lazy to justify keeping at the track. Emilie had fallen in love with her over the winter, slowly and steadily putting a foundation on her with hacks in the snow and easy gallops on the track. The filly hadn't grown, but her increased fitness had flipped a switch and Liv had taken it from there, awakening the dormant talent. When Reba won the Oaks, Emilie was ready to burst with pride. She'd lose her mind if the filly came home first in the Plate.

Not that it wasn't just a tiny bit bittersweet. Back when Reba had looked as if she was going to be a turtle instead of a racehorse, she'd entertained the idea of keeping the filly for herself, but winning the Oaks meant when she retired she'd be a broodmare, not a riding horse. Playing with Jay last summer, she'd just been fooling herself. With his pedigree, he was going to be a stallion, somewhere. Now all the big farms in Kentucky wanted him.

I just have a knack of wanting things I can't keep. Like Tim, because no matter how much she was enjoying his company today, she had to remind herself: he wasn't here to stay.

Liv drove first to the test barn where Jay was being cooled out; the attendants there would take samples for the required drug screening. Once Liv was content all was well with their big horse, they headed back to Barn Five. With a couple of hours yet to go before they'd be called to bring their runners over for the Plate, there wasn't much going on. The crew waited with expectant tension, and Liv and Emilie joined in.

Reba snoozed in her stall, standing with her nose pointed toward her feed tub, hind leg cocked, but when Emilie approached, leaning on the frame of the door, the filly pivoted, pushing her head over the screen. Emilie didn't flatter herself; it was probably only because Reba wanted treats and was convinced Emilie would provide them. Being deprived of food in the hours leading up to a race was horrifyingly unfair to a peppermint monster like Reba.

Liv came up next to her, probably thinking the same thing as Emilie: that six months ago neither of them would have imagined this quiet filly would be waiting to run in the country's most famous race.

"So... Tim," Liv said instead, catching Emilie entirely off guard.

"What about Tim?" she snapped. *Why so defensive, Emilie? Because you've been caught.*

Liv laughed. "He cleans up nice."

"Like we've ever seen him get his hands dirty."

"Is that important? Because it wouldn't be too difficult to arrange."

"What's the point, Liv? Even if I was letting myself think

that way again — and I'm not." She returned a pointed look to Liv's wry smile. "He'll be leaving soon, right? This is just a visit for him. Visits end."

"Do you remember, two Christmases ago, when we were over at Faye's on Boxing Day? Nate was in California, and Will was in Calgary, and you were telling us both off for being idiots. This may not be an exact quote, but you said, 'if I'm lucky enough for that kind of guy to fall into my life, I pray I have the common sense to grab him.' So you're up, sister."

Emilie scowled. It had seemed so easy then to proffer advice, watching Faye and Liv screw up their lives. How ironic to find herself in the same spot. "Just... don't remind me. And reality is a way different story than theory. Besides, he's hardly the perfect man."

"How do you know? You haven't even given him a chance."

There was truth to that. And every time she felt she'd been shown another piece of him, she thought she could like him enough. Then something else wiped it away and convinced her to stick to her resolve. Sure, he looked pretty darn dreamy today, but contrary to the old saying, the clothes did not make the man. As if clothes had anything to do with it at all.

Reba, Jay, Tim. Maybe her knack for wanting things she couldn't have was really an unconscious tactic for protecting her heart.

"Have we finally taken our rightful places?" Emilie asked, crossing her arms and eying Liv with a droll slant of her lips as she leaned back against the cinderblock wall.

Liv grinned. "Do you mean, am I finally sounding like the big sister? Maybe so."

After all the waiting, everything happened in a rush. The grooms prepared both horses, then assistant trainer Jo sprayed each of them with water to cool them before the walk over. Liv and Emilie hopped back into the Porsche to beat them to the paddock while Jo walked over with the runners.

Jo saddled Reba while Liv put the tack on Can't Catch Me. Cam was a handful, taking all of Michel's finesse to keep him safe enough for Liv to get the job done. When Nate and Cory appeared, it all got real — fast. Emilie stopped Cory, who, despite having ridden enough races in her career at this point to have plenty of experience, looked pale.

Emilie grabbed her by the shoulders. "I am so proud of you! Have fun!"

Cory hugged her, a flush of colour returning to her cheeks. "I've got you to thank, right?"

"I don't know about that. All I did was chat you up to Liv and introduce you. The rest was up to you. Good luck! See you outside."

She wished Nate good luck too, even though they both knew she was cheering for Reba.

She was too nervous to be distracted by Tim, but that didn't mean she didn't see him, standing on the other side of the rail in front of the saddling stall, observing. She couldn't ignore him; when the paddock judge called for the riders to go out to the walking ring, she waved him in. He'd get lost in the crush out there and not make it through in time.

"Come on," she said. "This way. It's faster, and you can't miss any of this." She almost grabbed his hand, but that would have been too familiar. In the last few days though, sometimes it felt as if he had always been here; a part of this life; a part of hers.

She barely remembered the mayhem of the walking ring and the walk up to their seats. Once again Tim was next to her; if he'd been there all along she couldn't recall. So that's what it took to wash him from her mind — two horses running in the Plate.

It wasn't until he squeezed back that she realized she was gripping his hand. She flashed him an apologetic smile and released it, lacing her fingers together in her lap so they wouldn't stray again, then focused on the starting gate, the drone of the packed grandstand surrounding her. When the horses exploded from the barrier, the drone crescendoed to a collective cheer.

The field sped past the grandstand in a wave of colour, flowing into the clubhouse turn, kicking dirt up in their wake. Cam and Reba ran side by side toward the back of the pack while a speedster named Done At Noon blazed on the lead. Were Nate and Cory talking? Commenting on the weather while they bided their time? Stablemates would become rivals once the real running began. Emilie dug her fingernails into her palms.

The roar of the grandstand became thunderous when the horses reached the top of the stretch. Done At Noon wasn't done at all, his lead opening to three, then four lengths. Reba was hanging, Emilie's heart pounding. Was she okay? Was this too much? Nate asked Cam for another gear, and he wore away at the pacesetter's lead. Maybe it was his day to shine.

But Reba and Cory hadn't given up. Emilie jumped to her feet, screaming as Reba made up the ground, catching up with Cam. They battled hard, eclipsing, then passing Done At Noon.

"Come on Reba!" she yelled. "You can do it! Come on, filly!"

Liv, next to her, dropped her binoculars muttering one word. "Nope."

What? Why? Then she saw the horse sneaking up the rail, slipping past Done At Noon. She wanted to yell like a movie-goer at a horror flick. *Look! Over there!* She prayed both Cory and Reba sensed the impending danger and weren't so wrapped up in the duel with Cam to miss the real threat.

"Big Sensation," Liv said, reciting the name of the race favourite who whittled away at Reba and Cam's advantage.

Emilie's voice was gone, sounding like a mew of a pitiful kitten. *Hang on, Reba. Hang on. Just a few more jumps. Maybe he won't get there in time.* At the wire, the three horses swept past the big white finish post together — Big Sensation, She Sings, and Can't Catch Me.

Her pulse kept racing as they galloped around the turn. She looked down at her hands, the knuckles of one of them white, the fingers wrapped around Tim's. *Oh, no. Not again.* "I'm so sorry!"

Tim's lips pressed together in a grimace, but a grin tugged at one end when she let go.

"Good thing your nails aren't very long," he said, rubbing his palm slowly against his thigh. "Who won?"

"We'll have to wait for the photo," Liv said, edging her way out of the box. Either way, she was headed trackside to talk to Cory and Nate. She seemed too calm to Emilie. Liv didn't think either Triple Stripe horse had won, and a heaviness settled in Emilie's stomach.

"I'm going down too," she said. She had to think positive.

Maybe she was secretly pleased when Tim followed, close enough behind her that every now and then she felt the brush of his arm against her back. Liv hovered on the asphalt apron, watching for her horses — and looking to see where the red-coated outrider was, because he would go to the winner once he knew who it was. Instead of keeping her eyes on the infield board, Emilie's gaze remained on Liv. The instant Liv tipped her head back, eyes closed with an oh-so-subtle shake of her head, Emilie knew.

"Augh!" she yelled at the sky. Not today.

Moments later, the result went up. Big Sensation had won. Reba and Cam —

"Does that mean a dead heat?" Tim asked, a look of enlightenment on his handsome features. Emilie was disappointed, but seeing his face as he took in those details did happy little things to her.

She laughed. "Now we don't have to listen to Nate or Cory crow that one of them beat the other! Just please tell me there's an inquiry sign and they're going to disqualify Big Sensation so they've dead-heated for the win?"

It would have been a great story, but it wasn't to be. She wanted to run out onto the track and join Liv in welcoming them back; throw her arms around Reba's neck because even though they weren't gathering in the winner's circle today, she'd run a tremendous, gutsy race. So had Cam, but Emilie wasn't going anywhere close to him or she might lose a piece of her face. The colt was pumped, squirming as Nate removed his saddle. It was as if he knew he'd lost, only just, and was mad about it. Nate sure was.

Cory waved, almost dancing as she rushed past on her way to the scales. She came over once she'd weighed in, flushed with the conflict of a great ride that had come just short of winning Canada's most prestigious race.

Emilie crushed Cory with a hug. "Ugh, so close, I'm sorry! At least you won't have to listen to Nate complain he gave you his Plate winner!"

"It would have been worth it!" Cory laughed. "I'll see you back at the barn! Hi Tim!" She winked at Emilie before she dashed off.

Emilie flushed and glanced up to see if Tim had noticed. If he had, he wasn't showing it.

"Now, see?" she quipped to hide her embarrassment. "If you'd tossed one of those testicles up on that roof, maybe we would have won!"

CHAPTER TWENTY-ONE

Emilie and Sylvie climbed into the back seat of Chad's Nissan X-Trail, balancing cappuccinos from the highway rest stop as Tim folded into the passenger seat. He'd done that thing at Starbucks again, this time ordering a London Fog — for Bobby. Chad and Sylvie hadn't been close enough to hear, and when Emilie raised an inquiring eyebrow, Tim ignored her. Amusing as it was, the fact he didn't drink coffee was probably a red flag.

She'd spent far too much time trying to figure out Chad's motivation for the invite. He wasn't into her; she knew that. Had he decided to take a run at Sylvie, or was it just a friends thing? He had talked about not having any in the area, but his hometown wasn't so far away for it to be difficult to arrange a getaway with his old friends. She'd spent even more time wondering why Tim had wanted to come. He didn't seem to like Chad, particularly, though he wasn't outright hostile. Was he interested in Sylvie after all? They had danced at the ball. She'd forgiven Sylvie for that — because it wasn't as if Sylvie had actually done anything wrong.

Either way, she'd found herself in the position of squashing the whole thing if she declined, so she'd agreed. Naturally the prospect of spending a couple of days with a shirtless Tim didn't have anything to do with it. There was nothing wrong with helping him discover what their province had to offer. Plus, a friend with a cottage, like Chad, was a relationship worth fostering.

"How are things coming with the charity show?" Sylvie asked, taking a sip from her cup.

Now that both the ball and the Queen's Plate were over with, Emilie was ready to dive into preparing for the show. "Jodi agreed to judge it for us, so that's taken care of. Will said he'll arrange a food truck. We're going to need jumps, but we can borrow the show jumping ones. I just have to figure out what to do for cross-country fences. We have to build them. Maybe I can hire someone."

"Faye said we're making lots of stuff for it," Sylvie said. "Like a bake sale, almost. That'll be fun."

"Bleachers." Emilie punched the word into the notes app on her phone after it popped into her head adding it to her list. "Do you think we can rent those? And Chad — you'll be our on-site veterinarian, right?" She grinned.

"Give me the date and I'll see what I can do," he said over his shoulder. "If I'm on call, I'll try to swap."

"If you're on call, we'd be calling you anyway, right? It's going to be great, though, so if you can make it, you should."

It was dark by the time they reached the cottage, Chad backing the X-Trail into a spot at the base of a hill. He was prepared with a powerful flashlight, holding it while the rest of them walked up the gentle incline, carrying their gear, which included enough food for more than the two days they'd be there. When they reached the top, the lake met them, lights from other cottages reflecting on its dark, glassy surface, the sunset a faint glow on the jagged, treed horizon. Emilie peered up at the indigo sky, stars popping everywhere, and breathed.

Chad trudged past, letting the beam fall on a modest cottage. It wasn't exactly rustic, but she'd expected something more elaborate, considering Chad's father was a very successful veterinarian. Each of them had their own small room and once they deposited their bags and put away the groceries, they gathered in the kitchen, a long counter dividing it from the dining area.

"Anyone need anything?" Chad asked after pointing out the bathroom.

When they all responded with shaking heads, they agreed to call it a night.

The double bed in Emilie's room was surprisingly comfortable; after the mattress in Nate's apartment on the farm, it seemed luxurious. She read a page and a half before she had to put her book down and turn off the lights, her lids heavy.

She woke the next morning to the patter of rain on leaves, steady drops pock-marking the lake. It almost lulled her back to sleep, but she rolled out of her cozy cocoon, zipping a hoodie over her pyjamas, gathering her book, and peeking out to see if anyone else was up.

Someone had found the pastries Sylvie had brought from Triple Shot, and she spotted Tim on the screened-in porch with the same thick fantasy novel she'd seen him with before, the cover worn, like he'd made several trips through that world. Sylvie had also brought a French press so they'd have decent coffee. Emilie ate a croissant as she prepared the brew, then silently joined Tim, wondering why he hadn't claimed the couch. Wrapping a fleece blanket around her legs, she settled in with the book she'd so rudely abandoned last night.

Her TBR list was a mile high because when did she ever take the time to read anymore? Life at home was so crazy; it was nice to have nothing to do but relax. Soon Sylvie appeared with her own cup and croissant. If Chad had been looking for friends to party with, he'd brought the wrong ones.

"Well," he said when he finally surfaced, staring out at the rain before his eyes travelled to each of them. "I'm going to have an early nap, then."

"I think that's called going back to bed, Chad." Emilie laughed.

He'd told them there was only one place to get a decent signal, so their cell phones were nowhere to be seen. There were ancient ways of receiving messages here. Chad had provided them all with a number which she'd given to Liv and Nate for emergencies. If they needed her, the marina owners would dispatch a note via boat. Yes, really. She loved it.

It was liberating to be unplugged. She spent so much time on her phone, updating the various social media accounts she managed — for the farm, the physio clinic, the New Chapter Thoroughbred Retirement group. It was such a big part of her daily routine; it wasn't until she stopped she acknowledged what a big time suck it was. She needed more days like this. It was easy to forget to step back when she loved her life so much but it ate away at something foundational in her to always be on the go.

It wasn't until she felt a gentle nudge and a quiet, "Emilie. Wake up," that she realized she'd fallen asleep.

She cracked her eyes open, pushing herself up slowly from the cushion her head had landed on. She didn't even remember repositioning herself. Tim loomed above her, the long-sleeved t-shirt and sweatpants he wore hiding his dream-worthy body. But she hadn't been dreaming about him. She'd been dreaming of Excursion-now-Curtis, braided up with big fat dressage braids, light in her hands as she trotted confidently down the centre line. Jodi was wearing off on her.

Tim held her book out. "This fell."

She gave him a sleepy smile, accepting it. "Thanks."

"It's clearing up," he said, depriving her of his macchiato-coloured eyes as he turned his head to look out at the trees. The oval leaves of the poplars rustled in a gentle breeze, whispering to the pine needles.

"What time is it?" She stretched, yawning, unzipping her hoodie partway. It was warming up, too. Or maybe that was just her.

"Almost ten."

The creak of the floor and approaching footsteps preceded Chad's reappearance. "It's swim time!" He burst onto the porch looking a thousand times more refreshed than she'd ever seen him, already dressed in trunks, a concert t-shirt for U.S.S. covering his top half. He disappeared as quickly as he'd shown up.

"Well?" Tim said, the way he quirked his right eyebrow just like Nate. He didn't have the same grin, but there was a softness to his lips; that same almost-smile he allowed from time to time.

"I'm in," she said, getting to her feet with an injection of energy. "Where's Sylvie?"

Sylvie emerged from her room as Tim and Emilie came in from the porch. "I'm ready to go. See you at the beach!"

Sylvie's bikini and wrap-around skirt were far more stylish than the sporty two-piece she tugged on, the upper portion coming to her collarbone and hugging her midriff, her bottoms boy-short style, because if there were going to be water sports of any sort, she wasn't wearing ones that would end up wedged in her butt or a top with the potential to part company with her. *No wardrobe malfunctions, thank you.* Either Sylvie hadn't considered the practicality of her beachwear, or she wasn't planning on taking part in anything except wading and sunbathing.

That was a good place to start, though. Carrying her camera with a short lens, she left her towel on one of the lawn chairs and joined Sylvie on the small strip of sand, dipping her toes in the cool water.

This was not a South Florida-style beach like the one on which Nate and Liv had been married. Chad had raked it, removing most of the seaweed and sodden leaves, but the strip was all of twenty feet across and four feet wide, the lapping water washing up the odd pink stone or small shell. The other side of the lake was visible, with a few small islands between here and there.

"It's cold," Sylvie said, clutching her elbows, her feet barely covered, toes curled into the sand.

"Bet it was colder in May," Emilie said, holding the camera up and focusing on Sylvie, who tilted her head and smiled. *Click.* Cottage memories.

"I bet it was too," Chad agreed. He was messing about with the speedboat, stripping off the top and the cover that snapped over the open front. "I was up here one time in May. Before I started vet school. Vet school put a whole crimp in my cottage visit schedule."

Emilie snapped a couple of photos of him, too.

Tim wandered along the dock to the end, staring down into the water. "How deep is it here? Deep enough to dive?"

Emilie paused, viewfinder to her eye, framing a shot, then slowly dropped it without taking a picture, holding it to the side in one hand.

"Sure," Chad said. "A shallow dive."

Tim nodded and peeled off his shirt. Emilie heard Sylvie's sigh as her own shoulders rose and fell in an involuntary response to the perfection of his back and shoulders. If she could get him to turn around, she might be able to snap some shots that would make her a little cash on the side, selling them as cover images for romance novels.

"Well," Sylvie said, sounding a little breathless.

"Well, well," Emilie agreed.

She'd seen him shirtless before, in the dim poolside light at the hotel in Florida, after Liv and Nate's wedding. It had been easier to hate him then, and that hate had helped temper the heat that had crept through her, like it did now.

Such a lie, Emilie. It had been after that episode in the bad comedy that was their history that she'd tromped upstairs, talked Dean into sharing his cheap American alcohol with her, and subsequently propositioned him. Not any misdirected lust there. Not at all.

If Tim knew they were ogling him, he didn't show it, staring straight ahead over the smooth water, arms hanging loosely at his side. Then with a slight bend of his knees and swing of those arms, he dove cleanly into the clear water. When he surfaced, he began an easy crawl; languid, thoughtful strokes pulling him toward the small raft that floated twenty metres out.

She'd asked if he could swim. He could. Good therapy, she'd said. She was going to need therapy if she kept watching the way he twisted from the hips as he skimmed through the lake. The motion was mostly upper body, his legs only kicking enough to stay afloat, so it didn't hide his torso with splash. She imagined steam rising from his back. *Hot, hot, hot.*

"All right. I'm going in," she said. The water would cool her off.

Sylvie gave her a knowing look, but Emilie wasn't following Tim to the raft. He could have his space.

Leaving her camera behind, she waded up to her waist, holding her breath with elbows raised shoulder-height, her skin breaking out in goosebumps. There was merit in the way Tim had done it, diving head-first. Getting it over with. *One, two, three...* she sucked in a breath and dropped, crouching, submerging her whole body, then popped up, gasping.

"It's not so bad!" she squeaked.

"You're crazy." Sylvie laughed.

Instead of the raft, she swam toward the big rock that was part of the bay. It wasn't far, and soon the silty bottom of the lake turned slippery-solid as she made her way out of the water.

The rock was huge, beautifully decorated with moss and lichen, sloping upward; part of the natural waterfront of the property. A circle of stones marked a fire pit, chunks of charcoal and white ash supporting evidence. It was the perfect spot, away from the brush and trees, right next to the lake where it would be easy to scoop up a bucket to douse the flames.

She perched carefully on the hard, angled surface, wrapping her arms around her knees as water dripped from her body and hair. The sun bathed her shoulders, the big rock warm underneath the soles of her feet. She'd been avoiding looking at Tim, but she was helplessly drawn to him. He lay flat on his back, an arm across his eyes, legs angled, the now-ratty kinesio tape standing out against his skin. She should offer to do a fresh job. It would be a good excuse to touch him. But he looked perfectly content to be on his own.

CHAPTER TWENTY-TWO

"HAVE YOU EVER WATER SKIED?" Chad asked over a lunch of sandwiches and iced tea.

Tim flashed a grateful look at Emilie as he peeled off slices of veggie ham and arranged them on the thick rye bread. Had she volunteered to do the grocery shopping because of him? She'd probably overcompensated on the cheese, though. Not mere cheddar or Monterey Jack; there was Swiss and Gouda and a big hunk of Brie, too. He opted for Swiss, slathered on some Dijon mustard, and topped it all off with red onions and field greens.

"Just downhill," he replied, "but I'm game to try."

"What about you, Em?" Chad asked.

"Sure, I'll give it a go."

"Don't look at me," Sylvie said, trying to bite delicately into her sandwich creation. She was going to fail at that. "I'll watch."

"Designated lookout," Chad said, pointing at her with a grin.

Neither response surprised Tim. Sylvie didn't look the type

to try potentially embarrassing things, whereas Emilie was the perennial good sport.

Emilie made a face at Sylvie. "What have I gotten myself into?"

Sylvie shook her head. "You're on your own, honey!"

"Be careful with your knee though, Tim," Emilie said, her expression more serious. "You'll get me in trouble if you wreck it."

It was a logical warning. She was a physiotherapist. Her concern was professional. But she'd opened the door. "Maybe it needs to be re-taped. Do you have any with you?"

She'd been just about to take a bite of her own sandwich, and her eyebrows arched toward her hairline. He'd overstepped.

"Sure," she answered slowly. "I don't go anywhere without tape. After lunch?"

He nodded, controlling his mouth so he didn't look too pleased. It would seem suspicious.

Chad watched as she did the application, and Tim didn't feel the gratitude toward her he should have. Resenting Chad's proximity distracted him, though it also kept his mind from going places it shouldn't.

"Can you use that on horses?" Chad asked, intent on every movement of Emilie's hands.

"Yes, for sure," Emilie said. "I do it all the time. It's great for lots of things."

"And you find it really helps?" He turned to Tim now with the same studious expression.

"It's pretty remarkable, yeah," he said, disappointed when Emilie stood. It might have been his imagination, but he was sure she didn't rub it as thoroughly as she had the first time. He ran his hands over it absently, like he could prolong the sensation, the heat lingering, the analgesic effect immediate.

"Let's go," Chad said, changing gears and jogging to the beach. They followed, and he tossed a lightweight life vest to each of them. "Try these on."

"Where are the helmets?" Emilie quipped. "I feel there should be helmets."

Tim laughed, and she looked at him like that was inappropriate.

Chad went through the steps of a water start, then familiarized them all, including Sylvie, with the hand signals they'd need to communicate with the boat — *speed up, slow down, go home I'm dying; I'm okay even though I fell flat on my face.* Tim volunteered to go first. Sylvie climbed in the boat with Chad while Emilie elected to stay behind.

He made it up no problem, the power of the boat pulling him from the water as it accelerated. For the first while, he tested out the feel of the skis, the way they handled, buoyant with the surface tension. Then he experimented with going over the wake, to one side and back again, repeating it for the other side. It was fun, but he wanted to go faster, learn how to do tricks or something. It got boring pretty fast. They didn't keep him out for long, looping back and zooming around the raft, and he tried to use the centripetal force to propel himself, gliding before he sank into the water.

Emilie watched from the end of the dock, legs dangling. "Not bad, hotshot."

He pushed the skis in front of him, frog-kicking his way toward her, and beckoned. "Your turn."

She slipped off the end of the dock into the water with a pretty grin, floating over.

"It's not that hard," he said. "You'll probably do better than me because your legs are in such good shape."

"We'll see about that." She struggled under the water to slip her feet into the rubber bindings. "I think they're too big."

"Take them off, then. They're adjustable." The skis popped up to the surface, and she didn't need his help to slide the rear part of the bindings forward to make them smaller. "I'll grab the rope for you." He swam back with the handle in his hand, the boat idling behind him, and floated it close enough for her to reach.

"Keep your back straight," he said, treading water close enough to touch her, the thick vest keeping it from being intimate. "Shoulders back."

Her lips rose to a jaunty tip on one side. "You sound like Jodi."

"The riding coach?" He quirked an eyebrow. "You just like being bossed around."

He hadn't meant for it to come out like that, all raspy. Her jaw clenched and her fingers gripped the handle harder, making him step back in case she let go and walloped him.

"Good thing I'm not sensitive," she muttered through clenched teeth.

A chuckle escaped from his throat as he dared inch closer. "Arms outside your knees. The boat will pull you out of the water. Then use your core. Keep your arms straight, and stand up."

"You make it sound so easy."

"It'll be a breeze for you. When the boat takes the slack out of the line, lean back and kind of sit on the skis. Like when you're keeping one of those racehorses from going too fast."

"It's almost as if you've been paying attention."

She locked onto his eyes with her lively blue ones, and he almost yelled, "Hit it," for Chad to take off, just to get her away from him before he made a scene and kissed her. But she'd end up drinking a lot of lake water if the boat zoomed away when she was unprepared — then she'd probably come back and dunk him.

"Ready?" He held her gaze.

She nodded, and he signalled the boat so she didn't have to take her hands from the rope. She made it up first try, despite a little wobble.

He watched her gain confidence as she first just skimmed along behind the boat, then crossed the wake. Chad took her on the same brief tour he had Tim before bringing her back.

She laughed as she let go of the rope, landing with a splash. "I didn't die!"

"What did I tell you?"

"It really does use a lot of the same leg muscles as riding."

"See?"

She bobbed, treading water, her grin owning her face, and it took all his restraint not to reach for her, see if those lips were as sweet as the rest of her. But Chad was idling the boat into the dock... and it was a stupid idea, anyway. He'd just get himself slapped.

Chad hopped out and tied the boat up. "Who's driving so I can have a turn?"

"Not me!" Sylvie smiled, and half-raised a hand. "Designated lookout, right?"

"Tim?" Chad asked.

His eyes shifted. "Uh, sure."

"As long as it's not a stick right?" Emilie quipped.

He turned to her slowly, then lunged for her, taking her with him under the water's surface, leaving her splashing and sputtering, staring daggers at him when she regained her feet.

"Just tell me what I have to do, Chad," he said, smirking at her as he hoisted himself onto the dock.

She trudged her way out of the water, unzipping the ski vest and spreading it on a rock to dry. Her wet bathing suit clung everywhere, and he dropped his eyes to study his toes.

Ugly toes. They'd spent too many hours stuffed into hockey skates.

"Okay, quick lesson," Chad said, waving him into the driver's seat to give him a rundown.

"I'm coming in the boat too!" Emilie grabbed her towel from the chair she'd left it on and wrapped it around her shoulders, tip-toeing along the wooden slats. She settled into the other rear-facing seat, across from Sylvie, hugging the life preserver that had been resting there. "You sure you're okay, Tim? Because I can drive if you need me to."

He glanced at her over his shoulder and briefly imagined picking her up and tossing her over the side; partly for being so cheeky, and partly so he could jump in himself to rescue her, because she was always rescuing him. But that was the problem. She didn't need to be rescued.

He forced himself to concentrate on driving, listening for Sylvie's voice when she translated Chad's signals. Now and then he caught a glimpse. The guy seemed to know what he was doing, wearing shorter, fatter skis and performing tricks: popping in the air and doing one-eighties over the wake, skiing backward, twisting side to side.

"Showoff!" Emilie called as they returned to the dock, Tim biting his lower lip as he focused on not beaching the boat.

"Yeah, but I'm going to hurt tomorrow," Chad said, swimming in with the skis. "I haven't done that in years. My arms and legs are jelly."

"You were spectacular," Sylvie said, beaming. "Bask in the glory while you can."

He was famished by the time Chad started up the barbecue, and once again Emilie came through. While Chad flipped burgers, she produced a couple of vegetarian patties, sliding them onto a separate part of the grill. Then she added a big tin foil package of veggies drizzled with olive oil and balsamic vinegar.

When he bit into the patty, dressed up on a bun, he moaned. "Black bean? And garlic? Where did you find these?"

She nodded enthusiastically. "Garlic aioli. Will made them. So good, right?"

After dinner Chad pulled out the board games and Sylvie produced dessert — a pan of decadent frosted brownies she'd baked at the café. Emilie started doing the dishes, so Tim picked up a dish towel and dried. Wouldn't Mom be proud of him? Even if it was only so he could stay close to Emilie.

She wore rubber gloves that reached three-quarters of the way to her elbows, hands submerged in sudsy water, intent on squishing the saturated cloth inside of a glass and twisting it around. His lips curved, amused at how intent she was on the task. Whatever she did, she did the best job she possibly could.

Her neck was tanned brown under her ponytail, all those hours on the horses responsible, and he wanted to trace his fingers down the smooth curve of it, feel the softness of her skin. Chad and Sylvie's chatter in the background was just a babble of words to his ears. When she rinsed the glass and placed it on the drying rack, she glanced up and he pressed his lips back into a straight line. Here's where being able to make normal conversation would come in handy. Usually she could be relied upon for that, but she was silent. Probably tired, like he was tired. But it was a good tired, from swimming, and water skiing; getting too much sun and eating too much food. He didn't know how he was going to stay awake for the board games, then the bonfire Chad had planned. For once he wished he drank coffee, like the others would have with dessert. He'd have to eat an extra brownie instead.

"You two almost done?" Chad asked. "Hurry up, Monopoly awaits!"

Emilie sloshed around the last two plates but still gave them a careful once-over to be sure she hadn't missed any grime as she rinsed them.

"Are you ready for Monopoly?" She grinned, running a hand along the bottom of the sink to pick up the last of the utensils.

"I am the king of Monopoly," he said, leaning in so he said it right in her ear.

She gave a little shake of her head as she rinsed off the cutlery and dumped it on the tray. "Is that so?"

"It is. You've been warned."

CHAPTER TWENTY-THREE

FLAMES ROSE, crackling and popping, and Tim used his stick like a poker, jabbing at the blaze, ineffectively trying to rearrange the branches. The end broke off, then the tip caught fire. He tossed it onto the pile and stared at it as it flared.

Emilie watched him, his face bathed in the golden light. It was like he'd run out of gas, his energy sucked dry from a day of peopling; either that, or he was mad at her for beating him at Monopoly. She didn't know if it was right to try to draw him out again, or just leave him to it; still afraid to cross that line in case it backfired. She missed Holly. Holly would have effortlessly bridged the gap. If she'd felt she knew Chad better, she would have asked if the Lab could come along — a cottage needed a dog — but she hadn't wanted to push his generosity.

Chad whittled away at the end of a stick, sharpening it to a coarse point. He handed his finished creation to Sylvie, then started on another for Emilie before doing the one he kept for himself. Emilie pulled the marshmallows from her cloth grocery sack full of junk food — everything from crunchy cheese puffs to red licorice twists — and passed them to Sylvie, who tore the bag open and skewered one of the puffy white blobs with her stick.

"Here, Tim."

Chad held out his stick, marshmallow in place, and it jolted Emilie's memory. Where was her brain?

"No, thanks." Tim lost some of his reticence as he said it, seeming to appreciate the gesture.

"Don't you like marshmallows?" Sylvie's expression suggested it was impossible. Who didn't like marshmallows? A travesty! She held her own stick so it caught the heat from the fire without burning, the white confection turning golden brown.

"I just can't — don't — eat them," he responded quietly.

"Why not?" Sylvie persisted.

Tim straightened, glancing at Emilie almost as if he was hoping she'd help him. She was trying too hard not to laugh to do that, though. Besides, it was more entertaining to see how this played out.

"You sure you want me to tell you?" Tim said, then added reluctantly, "They're made with gelatin."

Sylvie tilted her head slightly. "Like Jello?"

Chad snorted. A vet would know where gelatin came from.

Tim pressed his lips together. "It comes from the connective tissue of animals. Marshmallows are usually pork gelatin."

Sylvie set her stick down slowly, her mouth forming a small *oh*. "You've ruined s'mores for me forever, Tim."

"Some pig will thank you," Chad quipped. Sylvie glared at him.

"Sorry," Tim said, looking genuinely apologetic for being the bearer of bad news.

"Hey Tim! Catch!" Emilie said.

He snatched the squishy bag she tossed at him and

squinted to read the label in the flickering illumination. "Are these —?"

She nodded, feeling too much pleasure from his look of wonder. "Vegan marshmallows! Too bad you wrecked your stick." A wry grin took over her lips.

"Let me try one of those?" Sylvie pleaded. She'd given hers, toasted to perfection, to Chad. "I may have just decided to become a vegetarian. Or at least a marshmallow vegetarian."

Emilie handed her stick to Tim. "Seeing as you turned yours into kindling."

He met her eyes as he accepted it, light dancing off his, then dropped his gaze, holding one of the gelatin-free marshmallows between the thumb and forefinger of his other hand. "That's the nicest thing anyone's ever done for me."

"Oh, Tim, I hope not!" She laughed, and he gave her a most charming version of his almost-smile before sliding the vegan marshmallow onto the point.

She admired his technique as he toasted it over the embers, turning the stick with a practiced hand. When he finally slid the marshmallow from the tip after letting it cool for a moment, she waited patiently for the verdict. Did it melt?

He shook his head but smiled, reaching for another one. "Tastes good, though."

Chips were necessary next — they were all ready for some salt to balance out the sugar-sweet. The cheese puff package she handed to Tim differed from the one Chad and Sylvie shared.

"I read the ingredients," she said. She had, in fact, contacted the company to ensure the cheesy dressing on the snacks was made with microbial enzymes instead of rennet. Not vegan, but vegetarian-friendly.

Tim tasted one after scanning the label, appreciation

pulling at his lips and flickering in his eyes. "You did your research."

She shrugged, turning her focus to a bag of sweet-and-salty popcorn for a more gradual transition from sugar to sodium. Did a warm, satisfying feeling fill her from the inside out? It did. There were at least three things that made Tim Miller smile: Holly, the horses, and food. Maybe he wasn't so hard to figure out.

When Tim offered the bag to Sylvie, she held up her hand, shaking her head. "I don't want to know."

The rest of them laughed, and Chad left her with the popular brand and pulled out a guitar.

Sylvie crunched a cheese puff and joked, "Is this on the cottage list?"

Chad nodded. "And you all have to sing along. Those are the rules."

"You should've given us a playlist beforehand so we could practice," Emilie teased. "Sylvie and I grew up in Quebec. We don't know any English folk songs, except maybe Kumbaya."

"Well, you'll just have to do a French duet for me and Tim, then," Chad said, then pointed a finger at Tim. "I'm dedicating this one to you."

He started strumming simple chords with a twang, then sang an upbeat song Emilie had never heard about a marsh-mallow man that had her and Sylvie in stitches. When he morphed into "Down By The Bay" Tim actually joined in, Emilie trying not to let her surprise show in case she embar-rassed him; instead isolating his voice, listening for a few rounds. He even added his own variation when prompted by Chad. By then she and Sylvie had caught on to the tune and the part that repeated, Chad's smile wide.

"Now you can check that one off," Emilie said when Chad finally rested his fingers. She reached for her water bottle, the salty snacks making her thirsty, the fire getting too hot, then climbed to her feet, reaching for her hoodie. "I'm going to go look at the stars." If that didn't rate on the list of cottage pastimes, it should.

She climbed to the top of the slope where the rock flattened, using her hoodie to cushion her head as she lay back and stared up into the clear, dark sky, wriggling until nothing jabbed her spine; the rock still warm from the day's sun. The view was enough the same as at the farm for her to feel connected. But it was different, too; more expansive. Chad and Sylvie's voices drifted to her ears, a gentle ebb and flow, and she wondered if that revelation was symbolic. New friends. New experiences. New admissions about herself, as she tried to take something from this escape. Escape wasn't really the right word, because she didn't want to run away from her life, but she appreciated the time and space to reflect.

The quiet scuff of someone approaching muffled the voices, and though she caught movement in her peripheral vision, she didn't shift her gaze from the stars. He sat quietly next to her, her pulse leaping erratically, and she didn't want to tell it not to bother. A deep inhalation through her nose helped even the rhythm out, the initial rush replaced with something... comfortable. She focused on her breathing like she'd do with a flighty horse, trying to keep still; not saying anything, letting him dictate how they should be.

"Is this okay? I was feeling like a third wheel down there." The timbre of his words strummed a chord somewhere inside she struggled to dampen.

"Sure," she said, keeping her tone noncommittal. "I guess they bonded on the boat this afternoon." And, had she and Tim? The two of them bobbing in the water as Tim quietly instructed, supporting her back, her mind easily filling in the sensation the thick vest had blocked of his hand on her skin. The food wins. The mundane but amiable washing of dishes.

"It's nice here. Quiet." He wore the same smell of wood smoke she'd brought up from the fire with her, overpowering the pine and peaty scent of the mossy soil. It made her feel irrationally close to him, like they shared something organic.

"It's like being on top of the world, isn't it? Like the stars are right there." She stretched an arm upward imagining they were within reach.

He gazed down at her, that same small smile tugging at his lips. "Kind of," he said, like he meant to say something else but stopped himself, just to agree with her, to buy in. He carefully slid down next to her, his head level with hers, doing the same wriggle she had to find the best spot. "Do you know what you're looking at?"

A breathy laugh escaped her, his nearness affecting her oxygen supply. "Some of it. I wish I knew more."

"I wanted to study astronomy."

She tipped her head toward him, questions flooding her mind. "Why didn't you?"

His shoulder moved slightly; a shrug or position adjustment. "I'm not good at science. Not much better at math."

"What did you take at school?" She rolled onto her side so she could see him, propping herself up on her elbow, resting her head in her hand.

"English and history. A bit of psychology. Nothing you have to be too smart for."

She frowned. "You think only people who study science are smart?"

"Sometimes that's how it seems. No one talks about poetry, right? It's all about science and technology."

"And sports?" she quipped.

"Yeah. But that has a finite impact, doesn't it? The thought of being some used-up NHL player doing bad commercials or second-rate charity events kills me."

"What would you want to do if you didn't play hockey?"

"I don't know. Teacher, maybe? Summers off." He grinned, rearranging himself so his hands were behind his head.

"Like hockey?" She grinned back. "You'd be an excellent teacher."

"You think?"

"Sure. You were good with the water skiing stuff. Not too bossy." She nudged his side, trying to forget the way the resonance of that comment had affected her when he'd said it, the water rippling around them as they floated. "The boys would respect you because you played pro hockey, and the girls would fall all over you. You're set."

He chuckled, a rare sound from him, and she studied his face, a faint suggestion in the dark. He seemed to be aware, and accept he was attractive, while Nate had always been caught off guard when anyone mentioned his looks. Maybe it was Nate's height, his lack of it affecting his confidence.

Tim shifted to face her, the catch of her breath and thud of her pulse sending her heart and her head on a collision course; the rush of blood to her capillaries making her skin tingle. He was so close, looking at her like he was searching for something he'd lost.

"I know now I could do any of that. Now that I have this."

His words triggered a mild panic in her, even though she wasn't sure what he meant — but her brain wasn't exactly functioning at its best right now. His head rested directly on the rock. "Isn't that uncomfortable?" she croaked. But her attempt to derail his gaze failed.

"You're beautiful."

She almost said, *no, you are,* but words of any sort were beyond her at the moment. No one had ever called her that before, not to her face. Nate had told her she was cute, but beautiful was for models, not someone like her.

"Can I kiss you?" he asked, still with those scorching eyes.

Her lower lip became unstuck from its mate. She should say no, for all the reasons.

For the ghosting.

For the moodiness.

For being temporary.

Sure, she might see him again. They were almost like family now, thanks to a marriage that had happened against the odds. Unlike the two of them, who had been odds-on to end up together. If anyone had bet money on them in a backstretch pool, by now they had likely lost.

But she nodded, before he mistook her stunned expression and delayed response as no. She wasn't capable of speech. Her throat was parched, drier than it had been by the fire.

"Say it," he murmured.

Her lips twitched with a smile. "Bossy," she whispered, then grabbing what little air between them was left, said, "Yes."

He reached for her, grazing her chin as he thumbed her unruly lower lip before curling his fingers behind her neck. She didn't need further motivation to crumple her elbow and close the distance between them, steadying herself with a hand on his chest — except that only made her tremble more, feeling it rise and fall beneath her palm, his heart pounding with the same insistence as hers.

"Say it again," he said, his mouth near enough to hers the breath she sucked in was the expiration of his.

"Yes," she said, releasing it with conviction.

She had waited so long for this; banished it, buried it. For now, she was going to take it, make it hers, ignore the underlying sadness of the truth that nothing had changed; that there was a price to pay for her failure to resist. That she was willingly giving up a piece of her heart, knowing she would never get it back.

She felt him gulp for air when he pulled back from it, leaving her to breathe on her own again, but she kept her eyes closed, holding onto the sensation, though it was already slipping into the realm of memory.

I remember that time he kissed me. It was everything I always thought it would be. Mine, for a moment, like a stunned bird I cupped in my hands before it flew away.

And there were fireworks. No, really. Actual fireworks. She laughed, opening her eyes.

"Why are you laughing?" His expression flitted between concern and humour.

"Because there are fireworks."

He looked at her like she was crazy, and maybe she was. Then she dragged him up as a series of bursts erupted on the other side of the lake against the inky sky. He slipped his arm around her and she leaned in, resting her head on his shoulder and they watched until he kissed her again.

CHAPTER TWENTY-FOUR

THE MUTED LIGHT gave everything an ethereal quality, mist curling just above the surface of the waveless lake. Tim propped his pole against the edge of the boat, taking in the filtered landscape and the peace it offered. Today, everything seemed new and clear, like the soft blue sky overhead.

He had no interest in fishing — never had, and had never been — but it was on Chad's list, and Tim was too grateful for the last twenty-four hours to say no. Chad was a good sport. He'd agreed to weight the end of Tim's line — no hook — so he'd just sit here, provide silent company for the ritual, enjoy the tranquility, then hope Chad didn't catch anything. It wasn't as if there would be any male bonding over gutting fish, after last night's marshmallow revelation.

Last night.

He still wasn't sure it had been real. It was the stuff of movies, side by side with her, staring up at the Milky Way, insulated from the rest of the world under the starry dome with a feeling of harmony radiating between them.

The talking.

It had pushed away the fog; helped him see what he hadn't been able to, before. The balance he'd always lacked to handle the pressure of the high-profile career he pursued. He'd always felt it was necessary to keep his mind, his focus, on a single career track, believing it took everything to make it. There had never been a fallback plan, even though he'd started university. That had only been a way of pacifying his mother; attending with a goal in mind would have felt like planning to fail at hockey. When he'd finally been drafted — much later than he'd hoped — he'd walked away from his education without much thought. He was going to make it. No one had to boost his ego and tell him he had what it took, talent-wise, to play in the NHL. He knew he did. It was stupid to play humble. But then he'd been hurt, swamping him with uncertainty, until last night.

The kiss.

He'd asked first; he'd had to be sure it was okay, that he wasn't off track. After everything he'd done wrong, he wasn't taking anything for granted. The moment had been too precious to mess up; he didn't want to kiss someone who didn't want to be kissed. Maybe they were only supposed to be friends.

So he'd asked twice. Because he needed to hear it; to know she wanted it too. Assumptions got you in trouble. But the kiss itself said more than words ever could; filled in all the blanks, completed the puzzle.

He still wanted it, the hockey career, but now he wanted to fit Emilie into that picture, too. How, though? Love always found a way, didn't it? A bit of kissing under the stars and he was quoting sappy old love songs.

Chad dragged his line through the water, trying to entice would-be victims, creating a little ripple on the surface.

"What made you move?" he asked, if only to get Chad to

stop. "Do you not get along with your dad?" Tim did, maybe because he'd always toed the line. Nate did not, because he never really had. Things were better between Nate and Dad now; one good thing that had come out of Phil's death, if he was allowed to think that.

"I get along with him fine. I worked for him for four years, starting right after I graduated, like I was supposed to. Then I convinced him working for someone else for a while was a good idea. First, because he doesn't have much of an equine practice and wants to grow that, and I'd shown some aptitude in school. But also — not that I told him this — because you end up with a pretty narrow view when you stay close to home, right? Like how can you form your own opinions about stuff? If you dare have a thought of your own it can't possibly be right. And even if you're pretty sure it is, you don't dare share it."

Wow. That was some truth there. Wasn't that basically the same thing Nate had said, just in different words? From the time he'd met Chad, Tim had thought of him as a pompous jerk, and Nate's background info from Liv supported his view. As it turned out, the guy had some useful insight to share.

"Did you always want to be a vet?"

Chad shrugged. "It's just always what I was going to do. Almost as if I didn't have a choice."

"Same. Exactly. It was supposed to be Nate though. He was good. Like, really good. But my mom is five foot nothing, and my dad's only five-ten, and, well, he hit five-six and that was it." Either way, Nate was going to be good at whatever he did. He hadn't ended up in hockey, but still cast a shadow of success Tim always felt he walked in. "When Nate left to come out here, wanting to ride, it was all on me, thanks to inheriting Dad's genes in the height department."

"But come on, Tim. It's nearly every Canadian kid's dream

to play in the NHL. You were good enough. I'm having a hard time feeling bad for you," Chad said.

"Yeah, okay. I don't hate it." But he lacked security, having yet to establish himself. The last few months had filled him with so much doubt. "Did you ever want to be anything other than a vet?"

"I guess not enough to rock the boat. What about you?"

"Same," he replied. But his injury was a wake-up call. He'd never told anyone he'd thought of being a teacher — and he wasn't sure he even had until Emilie had asked last night. He wondered if she was up yet, and what was next; how to make the best of every moment to build this thing between them so they survived the obstacles he knew they faced.

"You sure there are fish in this lake?" he asked, hoping Chad didn't intend to stay out here much longer. He wanted to get back.

Chad frowned. "I think you scared them all away."

Tim leaned over the edge. "Swim away, fishies! It's not safe!"

"Sounds like we're done here." Chad pressed his lips together with a hint of scorn, but he couldn't maintain it, their edges softening and lifting as he drew his line from the water. "You'd probably just make me throw them back, anyway."

Tim grinned as the small outboard engine disrupted the quiet. "First, do no harm, right?"

He tried not to rush as he helped Chad unload the tackle from the aluminum fishing boat. It wasn't as if he knew where anything went, so all he could do was carry stuff, then wait while Chad put it away. When he stepped out of the boathouse, he stopped so short Chad almost ran into him. Emilie was there, in shorts and bare feet and a pullover hoodie, her hair in a messy ponytail — and the smile on her face wiped away the low-key anxiety he'd had that things might be weird after last night.

"I hope you're not expecting some hearty he-man breakfast, boys," she said, jamming her hands in the hoodie's pouch.

"I was supposed to catch it, wasn't I?" Chad said, pulling the door shut.

"No luck?" she said.

"None."

"I bet you're disappointed." She caught Tim's eye with a twitch of her brows.

"Heartbroken," he said, straight-faced.

"There might still be a stale croissant if you hurry, Chad."

"Guess I'd better hurry then," Chad's eyes shifted from Emilie to Tim with a wry grin before he left them alone.

She glanced over her shoulder as Chad strode away, then brushed past Tim, sauntering to the edge of the lake and dipping her toes in. He followed. Of course he followed. She didn't ask his permission before she reached up, hands slipping to his shoulders, stretching to kiss him.

"Good morning," she said.

"Even better now," he murmured. *Much, much better.*

"Hungry?"

That was a loaded question. "What's on the menu?"

She laughed, withdrawing her hands and starting toward the cottage. "I brought strawberries, and Faye sent some amazing-looking granola she made. And there's oat milk. Because oat milk tastes better than dairy on granola."

They took their bowls back down to the little patio area by the beach, bringing along novels, Emilie's camera around her neck. He wasn't a hundred percent sure the old nylon lawn chair would support his weight but decided to chance it. Would asking Emilie to tape his tailbone if he broke it be a good thing, or a bad one?

He'd made little progress on the book since yesterday morning — Chad had kept them hopping — but he picked it up once his bowl was empty. Emilie lifted her camera from the flat-topped rock that served as a table, and he heard the click. When he slid her a look to find the lens pointing at him, she didn't stop firing the shutter release until he jokingly put the book in front of his face.

"My turn," he said, holding his hand out.

She twisted away, clutching the camera with both hands. "No! You'll break it."

"You don't trust me with your camera?"

She rolled her eyes and handed it over.

It was a nice one, a DSLR. He'd seen her around the farm with it, using a longer lens, shooting photos of the horses. As he popped the back open and previewed the pictures she'd taken, he felt her watching him. He was sure she'd stop him if she thought this was an invasion of her privacy. She didn't say anything, so he kept going.

He looked at the ones of himself without much thought, running backward through the images on the small screen, past photos from yesterday to the previous ones on the farm — grinning at the seemingly endless pictures of Holly. Then he popped the cover closed and turned toward Emilie, her own paperback open in her lap, bringing the viewfinder to his eye. He felt the lens slip into focus as he touched the shutter release and framed the shot. Then he pressed it.

Her head popped up. He snapped again, letting the motor drive take a few frames, then set the camera back on the rock without checking them.

Her mouth curved on one side and she reached for it, too curious not to scroll through. "These aren't bad. You have a camera?"

He shook his head. "My dad has an older Canon I've played with a bit."

"Would you come to my next lesson? I don't have any photos of Excursion. I should probably get some to use for a sales ad."

He frowned, his brow tensing. "You're selling Curtis?"

"That's what I do. He's a project horse."

"You're never tempted to keep one?"

"It's just never worked out that way. Maybe one day, when I have more time." She looked off over the lake.

How could she not have her own horse? It wasn't about money. She could have any one of a number of them for her own if she wanted. It made him sad she trained them, knowing from the start they were going to someone else, yet she treated each one as lovingly as if it were her own.

"How can you do that?" he asked.

Her face snapped to his, like she thought he was judging her, though he'd tried to keep his tone from sounding accusing — and her expression changed when she recognized his. "The people these horses go to — they're fulfilling dreams. Finding their one-and-only, and the horses deserve that. I'm always spreading my attention over so much; it wouldn't be fair. Plus a horse like Curtis is wasted on me. He's so good. So uncomplicated. If I keep something, it should probably be one that needs me more."

"What does that mean?"

She sighed. "Curtis is the horse everyone is looking for. He's the right height, the right temperament and he's sound. Not every horse is as easy as he is. I can live with something smaller, or more challenging, or one that might need a little help physically. Something no one else wants."

"So you don't deserve a nice horse too?"

Her eyes, that gentle sapphire blue, dropped from his. He

understood wanting something he couldn't have. Holding a little piece of it, but having to let it go because he couldn't have it all, not right now. Last night's kiss; a taste of a future he hadn't been sure he'd wanted until that moment. A view of an alternate life from the one he'd been conditioned for since his father laced up his first pair of skates. Or at least a life beyond hockey.

"It's better for them," she continued, like she was trying to convince herself. "Not that I don't keep tabs on them all to be sure they're still doing well. And I'm lucky. I'm in the position to take them back if something goes wrong."

"Does that happen a lot?"

"A lot? I don't know. But I wish it didn't happen at all."

He almost picked up the camera, wanting to capture her faraway look as she stared at the horizon. "When do you think you'll have time?" he asked softly. "For a horse of your own, I mean."

"That's a good question." Then she met his eyes again. "You make time for the things that are important, right?"

A challenge, to both of them.

His knee was good, and he needed to give part of the credit to her. Not just for her magic fingers, the wizardry of that tape, but for her quiet encouragement; the kind that kept him bolstered, instead of the noisier push of his father, his coaches, his agent — and the voices in his head. But that brought the reality of this thing growing between them to the forefront. What would happen when he left?

Chad walked past, picking up a rake, and started cleaning up the seaweed and debris that had washed up on the tiny beach overnight.

"When do we have to leave, Chad?" Emilie called.

Chad stopped, turning with a rueful grin. None of them wanted this brief getaway to end. "As late as possible."

CHAPTER TWENTY-FIVE

Four AM hurt after two lazy mornings. It was amazing how quickly her body adapted to relaxation — much faster than it did to a high level of activity. She could go from frenetic to cottage time in the blink of an eye, but this morning she was dragging. Hard.

She skipped her usual coffee at the house because she'd slept an extra ten minutes instead. The lumpy bottle of instant in the apartment's cupboard would have to do it — it was all about caffeine right now, anyway. As she poured boiling water from the kettle and stirred, she wondered how long it had been up here; it possibly pre-dated Nate. She shuddered. Between it and the calcium-encrusted heating element at the bottom of the kettle, she could only hope for some kind of fantabulous alchemy that would give her the energy she needed to get through a morning at the track.

Their exercise rider/swing groom Marie had asked to swap her day off for a weekday, when Emilie usually only went in on weekends. Normally it wouldn't be that big a deal — she'd just rearrange her farm rides or give those horses a day off — but she wasn't usually up quite as late as she had been the night before. It was after eleven when they'd made it back from the cottage trip because they'd wanted to squeeze in as much time as possible at the lake. It was worth a bit of pain the next morning to prolong that feeling. The coffee kicked in once she was on the road, some upbeat tunes trying their best to pick her head up.

She always looked forward to galloping, so why not today? Why? Because of Tim. If she'd had her usual day, she'd be at home, and there was always a chance she'd run into him around the farm. But after spending time with him at the cottage, she didn't want to leave it to chance. Maybe they could take Holly for a walk together later; she needed to make up for her absence — not that Holly hadn't been perfectly fine with Liv and Nate. She could give Tim that lesson so he could play with her and walk her himself while she was at work. For now, though, Tim would have to wait.

By the time she pulled into the backstretch parking lot the sky was lightening, even though the sun had yet to make it above the horizon. Power walking to Barn Five helped put a spring back into her step, and she called "Hey, Jo," as she passed the assistant trainer's stalls on her way to the tack room. She paused to check the whiteboard for the schedule, happy Liv had put her on Reba first, then turned toward the voices in the room — and the first face she saw was Tim's.

He leaned against the cupboards, arms crossed and one leg hooked over the other at the ankles. She stopped in her tracks and grinned.

"Hey!" she said, too brightly.

Tim grinned back.

Liv and Nate looked at her, then at Tim, and grinned at each other.

The heat that assaulted her face was immediate, and she

ducked between them, muttering, "Nothing to see here, move along!" as she located her boots in the corner.

Liv and Nate filed out as ordered, so she and Tim were alone.

Suddenly it was awkward. How did they do this, here? How did she play it? Just because they'd kissed at the cottage didn't mean they would carry on like they were a couple.

The kissing had been nice. Sweet.

Who was she kidding? That first kiss, there'd been fireworks.

But it was an isolated event; special circumstances. She might as well forget about it.

Except how could she, with him standing right there, that cute little twist making his lips so irresistible?

Not now, Emilie. There are horses to get on. Not to mention too many people around. Gossip on the backstretch spread like wildfire.

"So, are you starting your hotwalking career this morning?" She straightened after pulling her jeans down over her boot tops and smoothed her red kerchief over her hair.

"Do you think they'll let me cool out something?"

"Why not? People with zero experience walk hots all the time. It's a learn on the job kind of thing. Jo won't give you anything that will kill you." She was grinning again. Had she stopped? She must look insane. *Helmet, Emilie.* "Reba, actually. She'd be good. She's a sweetie. Are you coming out to watch her go?"

"Yeah, absolutely."

"Great!" *Could you sound any more like a dweeb? Gah.* Then she saw her camera bag on the counter behind him. "You're stealing my camera again, are you?"

His eyes dropped to the bag, and she could see the pink tint in his cheeks. "Just tell me if you don't want me to use it. I thought you might like some pics of you and Reba. Just to have."

She wanted to hug him, kiss every inch of his face. Of course she wanted pictures of her and Reba. She was always the one behind the camera, so there were hardly ever any decent photos of her riding. Blurry iPhone images where you could barely tell it was her, sure, but not ones taken with a proper camera.

"That's the nicest thing anyone's ever done for me," she said, mimicking his comment at the bonfire after the marsh-mallow discussion.

Tim rolled his eyes. She zipped on her safety vest and dashed out of the room to Reba's stall, slipping in as Sue put on the bridle.

"Hey Em. Have a nice break?"

"I did, thanks," she answered, leaning against the stall wall, breathless and heart racing, trying not to sound as if she'd just run a hundred-metre dash. "How's everything with you? How's Leo?"

All Sue needed was an excuse to talk about her baby boy, three months old, and Emilie was off the hook. It helped distract her from thoughts of Tim. Reba needed her attention more than the mirage of that kiss on the rock.

Four of them headed for the main track. Nate joined them for the first set because Liv made him get on Cam. Nicole was on Wishonakiss, who must've shipped in from the farm when Emilie was cottaging. Liv was on Trop, the new gelding.

"We'll jog these two," Liv said, nodding at Nicole. "She can gallop an easy mile and a half, Em. And you do you with that beast, Miller. At least try to back up as far as the wire with us."

"Should've trained him yesterday," Nate grumbled. "If he kills me today, it's on you."

"You're not allowed to die, Miller," Liv said. "Who would get on him then?"

"Newlyweds in love," Emilie sighed, and Nicole laughed.

"There's Dean," Nate said, pointing ahead to the trainer's tall figure at the mouth of the tunnel leading to the racing oval. "You can stand by the rail with him, Tim."

Just the sound of his name made Emilie gooey inside. She needed to get a handle on this. She decided not to look back at him, reaching up to run a hand down Reba's neck instead, smiling as the filly snorted happily.

When they hit the track, the two fillies jogged politely side-by-side. Trop was a hundred times more settled without his mischief-inducing gonads, though Liv kept him to the inside of the fillies because it had only been two weeks since his little operation. Nate, on the other hand, had his hands full with Cam. The big colt was going to cause traffic problems, so Nate sent him forward into a floaty trot to get ahead of the other three-year-olds.

"Did you all have a nice time at Chad's cottage?" Liv asked.

Emilie caught the sly smile toying with her sister's lips but was determined to play it straight. "It was lovely. Chad made us do all the cottagy things. We swam, played board games, water skied, read books, ate too much. I feel like we packed a week's worth of stuff into two days. It was great. Maybe if you're nice to Chad, he'll invite you and Nate next time."

Liv laughed, but not before Emilie was sure she caught the flash of a wistful expression. Liv and Nate hadn't even taken a honeymoon, not really. They did live on the beach in Florida all winter, and they'd taken Just Jay to Dubai. But Emilie would now advocate that sometimes you needed to get away from the horses, if only for a day or two, no matter how much you loved them. Maybe she'd talk to Chad secretly and see if she could arrange something for the two of them.

Nate finessed Cam to a walk but the boisterous colt's patience was lacking — he merely hesitated when facing the infield before wheeling up the track in the direction he got to gallop. Emilie worried briefly the two of them were going to part company. Nate stuck though. She gave him plenty of time before she set off with Reba, who was far more civilized about the standing ritual. She didn't want to be anywhere close to Cam with her sweetheart of a filly.

Reba always galloped like a pony — all Emilie had to do was plant her knuckles at the filly's withers, her reins crossed. Sometimes Emilie couldn't believe this was the same filly who'd won the Oaks and dead-heated for second in the Plate. Unlike Cam, Reba saved her energy for race day. She glanced ahead as they turned into the backstretch, unable to keep herself from finding Tim on the rail. She saw Dean first, then Tim, who had a blonde woman Emilie didn't recognize leaning into him, trying to chat him up. Emilie scowled — both at the woman and the twinge of jealousy that twisted in her chest. Then Tim pointed the lens their way, and she scolded herself.

"Come on, Reba-girl. Let's smile for the camera!" And while she didn't look directly at him, she happily focused on the filly, because she'd be mad at herself if all he got were shots of her looking annoyed.

Nate was back at the barn before the rest of them were — in one piece, safe and sound. It was as if the entire crew breathed a collective sigh of relief after the brawny colt trained, because the opposite fate for their star jockey was a real possibility with Cam. Tim had walked back with Nate, and kept his distance as Cam's groom, Michel, took the big bay colt over to the sandy rolling pit. Cam was always good for a show, standing on his hind legs; hooves flailing like a wild stallion above Michel's head after he got up from grinding the sand into his sweaty coat.

"This is your chance, Tim!" Emilie called as she hopped off Reba.

He approached cautiously, taking the lead when Sue handed it to him.

"I'll bath her if you want to get your next horse ready Sue," Emilie offered.

"Thanks, Em," Sue said, disappearing.

It was easier to act natural with a horse between them. She wasn't worried about Reba, and Tim relaxed once she started sloshing soapy water over the filly. He appeared to take to horse handling effortlessly, like he had an innate ability. Where did it come from? Nate had it. He'd told her his oldest brother, Phil, the one who had died last year, did not. Neither did his parents — while in her own family it was generations deep. She imagined scientists one day identifying the horse lover's gene.

She made herself wait till all the horses had trained before looking at the photos he'd taken. Reba looked brilliant with the sun lighting up her bright chestnut coat, and after scrutinizing her own form, she decided she didn't look half-bad. He'd caught Cam at full height after his roll, Michel laughing under those terrifying front hooves. Then there was an assortment of shots that told the story of the backstretch, capturing the magical light and atmosphere. Maybe he should be a photographer.

"These are amazing, Tim," she said, her voice soft. She didn't dare look at him, or she was going to end up a syrupy puddle at his feet. "You have to see these, Liv."

Liv peeked over her shoulder as she flipped through them again. "They really are, Tim. Let Em put some of those up on social media." Liv hung her helmet on a hook and shook out her damp kerchief. "Can you take Tim home with you, Em?"

Can I, please? She controlled her features. "Sure. I'm just going to put Reba's bandages on for Sue."

"Okay if I watch?" Tim asked.

"Of course. If you learn how to do that, you'll really be useful around here." She grinned. Again.

It really seemed as if he was taking notes in his head as he watched her gather the bandages and a bottle of rubbing alcohol. Reba stood tied up in the doorway munching her hay while Emilie worked, and Tim crouched just outside the stall, leaning against the green metal of the doorframe. He wasn't in the way, and he was safe, but it was hard to focus with him so near. Good thing she could wrap a leg in her sleep.

She took Reba's halter off when she was finished and cleaned it before hanging it on the filly's door. "Done. But I have to stop for a coffee, okay?"

One of his eyebrows crept up. "Do you think you might have a problem?"

"Don't make me regret agreeing to give you a ride. What are you on, ginseng or something?" But she laughed.

She had a million things to do. People to call about the horse show, horses at home to ride — and she had to work later today. But it was so incredible to finally have this with him. This Tim was intoxicating. Maybe he should drive.

At Starbucks, when asked for his name after he ordered, he said, "Maurice."

Emilie laughed, finally figuring it out. "I see the pattern. Famous hockey players."

Her reward was a grin wide enough to bring out that dimple. "Just a bit of fun," he said.

"I like it," she said. "Then again, I'm easily amused."

"That one was probably too obvious for a Montreal girl."

"Pretty much a gimme, yeah." But she felt like he'd wanted her to know; wanted to share his goofy game and let her be closer to him. "You bring up an important point, though. I don't think I could date you, because when you play the Canadiens I won't be able to cheer for you."

"That's okay. I couldn't afford to date you. You like expensive coffee."

"Just wait till you sign your multi-million dollar deal. Then we'll talk."

When he smiled, truly smiled, her heart had no chance.

"Wait!" She flagged down the barista. "Don't hate me, but can I change my order? I'd like a macchiato."

Had she really just asked for a drink because it matched the colour of his eyes?

CHAPTER TWENTY-SIX

HOLLY EXPLODED FROM HER KENNEL, nails ticking on the slate floor as she bounced around Emilie. "I missed you too! Next time I'll tell Chad I'm not coming unless you're invited."

Tim grinned and followed them outside, feeling just as much like an adoring puppy. Holly sniffed around, both of them watching.

"Let's go for a drive," he suggested, feeling bold. "I want to show you how well I manage the Mustang now."

The corners of her mouth curved up, and she checked the time. It was cute the way she worried her lower lip before deciding. "Sounds like fun. We'll go for ice cream."

"Can Holly come?"

"That's a great idea. She loves the car. Meet you back here." She gave him another smile as she walked off. "Come on, Holly!"

He hopped into the shower, even though he liked the lingering horse smell that clung to his skin and hair — and Emilie wouldn't have minded. When she returned her hair was damp, pulled back again in a tight ponytail. He wanted to bury his face in it and smell her shampoo; learn the scents that made her Emilie. At least the ones he wasn't already familiar with, like what he'd washed away.

With Holly balanced on the back seat as they drove out under the canopy of maple trees, Emilie scanned radio stations, stopping at one playing Whitney Houston's "How Will I Know?"

"If you dare tell Nate I'm playing this station in his old car, I'll have to kill you." She slid him a threatening look, then her tone turned all sweet and light to ask Holly to lie down before they reached the road.

He gave a single nod, trying to look serious. "Your secret's safe with me." They both laughed when that was the next song to come on.

"How do we know these songs? Neither of us were alive back then," she said after motioning for him to turn right. She was his GPS, the clearest direction in his life.

"I know how I know them," he said. "I heard them all the time as a kid because my parents listened to this music. At least my mother did. Those were the best days of my life."

"Oh, Bryan Adams! Bonus points for Canadian content." She reached over with her fist and he obliged with a bump, resisting the temptation to capture her hand. He needed both his for driving.

He'd let himself forget about his parents, too captivated by these last few days with Emilie. He wondered if those had been the best days of his mother's life, knowing full well she hadn't met his father until the nineties. Had she been with someone else before? Did she have regrets? Was middle age making her nostalgic?

"What's your excuse?" he asked, needing to reset his thoughts. "Did your parents listen to English music?"

"I just like the oldies. We love to make fun of eighties

music, don't we? Like we're all sophisticated with our modern alternative." The expression overtaking her face worried him — eyebrows raised, mischief in her eyes. "This makes me want to do karaoke."

"Oh. No way." He shook his head quickly.

"Girls just want to have fun, Tim."

That made him laugh. "You can have that fun without me."

She scowled, then said, "It's just up here."

She pointed ahead to a dirt parking lot in front of what looked to be a country store, and he parked in the shade of a massive oak tree. Emilie was out of the car, promising Holly they wouldn't be long, before he'd even thought about jumping out to grab the door for her.

I don't think I could date you.

They'd been joking around, but that still implied they weren't dating. So what was this? Had the kiss at the cottage been just a bit of fun for her? *Because girls just want to have fun.*

Like Excursion, was he just a project to her? A thing she allowed herself to feel a fondness for, but accepted she would one day say goodbye to? Maybe all he could hope for was that she'd keep tabs on him, like one of her retired racehorses. Come watch his games when the team played in Toronto, like she might go to a horse show to see one of her graduates — taking photos to add to her testimonials.

He followed her to join a short line outside a large serving window with a big wooden cutout of an ice cream cone nailed to the side.

"What are you getting?" She was bouncing on her toes like a little kid.

He scanned the list on the other side of the window, feeling the pressure of making a snap decision, and picked the first two flavours he saw. "Tiger tail and bubble gum."

She scrunched up her nose, squinting. "Those don't even go. You really are twelve."

She'd called him that at the wedding, when he'd behaved like an adolescent and refused to give her even a little bit of an opening. But she was grinning now, not scowling like she had then. It was worth how horrible that ice cream combination was going to taste just for that.

"What are you having?" he asked, shuffling forward as the line advanced. Someone joined behind them and he moved up, near enough to catch a hint of the light floral scent of her hair.

"Don't stand so close to me," she said, tossing a smile over her shoulder at him. "That one's perfect, because it's totally going to be you if you ever become a school teacher."

"Hey," he protested. "I would never cross that line."

"I believe you." She turned slowly into him, her expression leaving no doubt she did. "But that's not going to stop the school girl fantasies."

Her mouth had a playful slant and the light in her eyes made it impossible not to dip his head with a light hand on her hip, dredging up remarkable restraint with the kiss he placed on her lips. Even that careful touch messed with his pulse and respiration. He hated to nudge her away, but the line was moving again. When she turned back to face the serving window, he closed the distance just enough to rest his fingers on her waist. What might look casual to onlookers threatened to make his head explode, but now that he had some momentum, he wasn't letting up. It was probably a good thing there were people around, because though the way she tipped her head and leaned slightly into him was a signal on the plus side, it just made him want to do more.

He couldn't remember what he'd said he was going to order, so he just nodded at Emilie's cone. "I'll have the same, thanks."

She grinned and elbowed him. "A much more mature choice." She checked the time again and nodded toward a vacant picnic table. "Let's sit for a bit. I'll grab Holly."

"We should've got her a cone," he said.

"I suppose she can have the end of one of them," Emilie conceded.

He saved Holly a generous portion and slipped it to her before Emilie could protest, then laughed as Emilie caved and gave her the last inch of her own. When they went back to the car, this time she let him get the door for her — and Holly, of course.

"You really are getting the hang of this driving a standard thing," she said as he smoothly pulled out. "Impressive."

"Do you think Nate will let me drive the Porsche now?"

"If he lets you drive it before me, I'm never speaking to either of you again."

"How is that my fault?"

"It just is." She gave him a cheeky grin.

At the farm he pulled up to the apartment barn as she'd asked. She freed Holly from the back seat, keeping an eye on her as Tim jammed his hands in his pockets.

"What are you doing now?" he asked.

"I really have to catch up on some of the prep for the charity horse show, after doing absolutely nothing for two days."

"Is there anything I can do?" He felt like a needy child. *Where are you going? Can I come? I'll help!*

"Are you any good at graphics?"

"I'm afraid not," he admitted.

"Then unfortunately, no. Don't you have an appointment with Sam this afternoon, anyway?"

"You're right, I do. I almost forgot." He grinned. "Thanks."

She laughed. "Glad I'm not the only one whose brain is scattered from a couple of days off."

"I think it was more than the days off, but…"

She dropped her eyes; her smile almost shy as she shuffled closer; her gaze when she languidly drew her face to his considerably less so. She kissed him, and he ran his fingers down her arms slowly, a silent request to prolong the moment.

"Well. Guess I'll see you, then," he said, exhaling, when he really wanted to ask *where* and *when*.

"I'm going to work early today," she said, backing away. "I might see you at the clinic. Let's go, Holly!" And the Labrador chased her into the barn.

He stared up at the overhead apartment's big window, wanting badly to follow. He wanted more of her, and it wasn't just physical. It was all of this; this borrowed life. A life with an expiry date.

As he pulled up to the house, his phone rang, the sound of it an irritation, but he couldn't ignore it. It was Erik, his agent. Leaving the Mustang behind, he stepped into the apartment, pausing by the door.

"Hey," he said, his tone dull.

"Hey yourself. What's the matter? How's the knee, all right?"

"Yeah, it's great. The physiotherapists here are top-notch. Not what I expected in a small town." He pushed inside.

"Good, good." He could picture Erik nodding. "So when are you coming back? We need to meet with the GM. Coach will probably want to see you skate."

It was too soon. But it was time. He'd put reality on the shelf these last few days to pacify his heart when his head knew he needed to get back on the ice. His knee was ready. Just when he'd finally shifted Emilie's perspective — shown her he wasn't the blockhead she'd met at the wedding — it was time to go.

His eyes drifted around the cozy apartment. The things that made Emilie, Emilie. Things he would leave behind. Photos of horses, a couple of original drawings, a few knickknacks. Comfy furniture with fat cushions and a dog bed she hadn't taken to the barn apartment with her — which was a dead giveaway Holly didn't actually use it. He'd put money on her being right next to Emilie on the couch. Right next to Emilie on the bed.

He sighed. "Okay. I'll check flights."

He didn't want to be in the apartment right now, surrounded. The main house was less personal. It didn't scream of anyone he knew, not even Liv or Nate; like they hadn't been here long enough to make it their own.

He almost jumped over the edge of the landing into the sunken living room, he started so hard when the front door opened, but it was just Liv and Nate, back from the racetrack.

"You all right?" Nate said, opening the door from the foyer, his expression half concern, half amusement.

"You just surprised me, that's all," he answered, his heart rate finally starting to recover. "Didn't know you'd be home so soon."

"Easy day," Nate said, dropping a small gym bag on the floor.

"Hi, Tim," Liv said, slipping past him, starting down the hall. "I'm going for a shower. See you in a bit."

"Sure," Nate said, and he watched her stroll away for a few moments before turning back to Tim.

"Good day at the office?" Tim asked, controlling the way his lips wanted to twist. Not that he was going to judge Nate for what was probably going through his head as he watched his wife leave.

"All right. A couple of winners." Nate was more focused on him now, studying him in that way that made it obvious he wasn't hiding his feelings well. "What's the matter? You had a good time at the cottage, right? Come and sit down."

"It was great. Better than I could have expected." His voice was quiet with the memory of it as he followed Nate to the living room.

"I saw the way you two were grinning at each other this morning," Nate said, his smile droll. "What's the problem?"

"My agent called."

"Oh." Nate's tone flattened, his smile with it, and he waited for Tim to continue.

Tim grabbed a cushion and kneaded it. "I've got to go back."

"Just to check in though, right?" Nate said. "Let them see you're good, then you can fly back here."

"What for?" he snapped, all his exasperation coming to a head. "I'm just going to have to leave again, and next time, for good. She's going to hate me either way."

"She knew you'd be leaving," Nate said cautiously. "She won't be mad at you for that."

He thrust the cushion aside and lurched to his feet, shoving his hands in his pockets and staring out to the patio. "This is my strike three, Nate. She's never going to give me another chance."

"Strike three? Hold up there, kid." Nate said it like he was talking to that big unruly horse, Cam. "It's different this time. This time you're going to tell her what's going on. You're going to talk. You're not going to leave her hanging."

He shot Nate an ungrateful glare. *Thanks for the reminder of my past transgressions, bro.* "Which doesn't really matter, because I'll be too far away." How could he go back to that, after this? "What's the point?"

"The point is, if you love her..."

Did he? Was it even possible after just a few weeks? But he knew the answer.

He hadn't noticed Nate come up behind him. "Take the risk, or lose the chance, kid," Nate prodded in his ear, then smacked him hard enough on the deltoid it stung.

What did that even mean, though? There were no risks to be taken. His path was clear.

So much for GPS. GPS could be wrong.

CHAPTER TWENTY-SEVEN

This was the price of her mini vacation.

She'd been run off her feet since she arrived at the clinic, trying to make up for the days off. Some of her patients had done their appointments with Sam in her absence, but others wanted to wait for her. It was nice she'd built those kinds of relationships, but now she was stuck trying to accommodate far more people than she should have. Trudy, the office manager, had gone a little over the top fitting everyone in. Clearly she thought Emilie was more efficient than she was, and didn't allow for the chatty patients Emilie had to shuffle gently out the door so she didn't run overtime. Trudy had also failed to compensate for the fatigue factor, which was definitely in play.

All she'd been able to manage was a brief wave as she'd glimpsed Tim when he'd come for his appointment. She didn't even remember when that had been. Trudy and Sam had finished at their usual time, leaving her to juggle everything for the rest of the evening. She glanced at her watch. Just another ninety minutes and she'd be out of here.

"Come to the front and we'll find a time for your next

appointment, Annie," she said, keeping a steadying hand on the elbow of an elderly woman recovering from a broken wrist.

She smelled him first — or the coffee, more accurately — and had to keep herself from leaping over Annie to hug Tim after he placed the takeout cup from Triple Shot on the counter.

"You are an angel." She beamed. "How'd you know?"

"Wild guess?" he said dryly.

"I'm that transparent, aren't I?"

"I like that about you," he murmured.

His low tone resonated in her like a tuning fork, warmth spreading from her fingers to her cheeks. She shifted her gaze to the computer, clicking the schedule to find a slot for Annie. "Back to your regular day? Tuesday at seven-thirty?"

"That would be lovely," Annie said, tucking the card Emilie handed her with the information into her purse. "Is this your young man?"

Another flash of heat assaulted her like she was sitting in front of the bonfire again. The only consolation was, when she glanced at Tim, he looked ten times worse.

"Ah," she began, grappling for words. "This is Tim, my brother-in-law Nate's brother." That was a mouthful, and benign enough to dampen the flames.

"Well, he's very handsome," Annie said. "I think you should keep him."

She almost snorted, and Tim stared at the magazines, scratching his neck and looking adorably uncomfortable.

"Tim plays for the Calgary Flames," she said, regaining her senses and catching Tim's eye. "I can't afford to keep him."

The look on his face wasn't what she'd expected. She'd thought she'd get one of those grins that was becoming more common; that funny little twist he tossed out when she said the ridiculous things she said. But he looked distraught, and turned away, fingering a dog-eared copy of *Sports Illustrated*. She frowned, staring at his back.

"That's too bad," Annie said. "See you next week, Emilie."

"Tiffany?" Emilie called to the red-headed sixteen-year-old girl in the waiting room. "Can you give me a minute? Go ahead in."

The teen had heard the entire exchange, of course, and hadn't taken her eyes off Tim the whole time. Who could blame her? He was extremely pleasant to look at. But right now, Emilie was having a hard time getting a read on him. At first he'd seemed fine; happy to see her, pleased she appreciated his thoughtfulness. Then something had shifted.

"Thanks for the coffee," she said to the breadth of his shoulders, the cut of his traps — or how she remembered the sight of them, because of course he was wearing a shirt. She wanted to gush, let out all the feelings she was holding onto, because they represented everything she'd given up on. They reminded her that sometimes first impressions were wrong. Sometimes, people should get a third chance.

He turned slowly, fingers tucked into his pockets, his expression frustratingly neutral. "I thought you could use it."

"You were right. What are you running on now, still ginseng?"

His mouth twitched in an attempt at a smile, but it didn't stick. "I had a nap. Almost done? You must be exhausted."

He looked too tired for someone who'd fit in a nap. "Two more. This will get me through." She lifted the cup gratefully. "Thanks again."

"I'll wait around, okay? Maybe I can drive you home. I'm kind of worried you might fall asleep at the wheel," he said, genuine concern in his tone. "Tomorrow's a more normal day. I can drop you off."

"That would be great." Her own smile was weak. It was a sweet gesture, but something wasn't right.

She tried to focus on her last two patients, though Tiffany didn't help matters by asking a million questions about "the hockey player." She knew far more about the players than Emilie did. Emilie liked the game, but had never been hung up on the athletes. At least, not until now.

"You like him, don't you?" Tiffany said with a sly grin.

"I might," Emilie hedged, "but Calgary is a long ways away."

"Maybe you could get a job with the team."

"There's a thought." She grinned. "It's a little early to be making plans like that, though."

"So you are seeing him."

"Did you miss the part where he's my brother-in-law's brother? I see him around." She laughed, but when she said it that way, it further deflated the high she'd been riding. All the stuff she'd been brushing aside to worry about some other time was tapping her on the shoulder now, thanks to Tiffany's inquisition. It might all be straightforward in the head of a sixteen-year-old, but the real-life logistics were more complicated.

So they'd kissed. So what? Maybe he was a fling after all. Was kissing enough to call it that? Because it wasn't enough to call this thing between them a relationship. It wasn't enough to think about uprooting her life.

At five to nine he reappeared, and she recognized the little bag from Triple Shot. It hit her just how badly she'd underestimated this man, the rush of affection battling with her sense of defeat. She hurried to finish up. She was certain of one thing: she wanted to know what was in that bag. With the caffeine kick dying, she could use the sugar rush to get her through what was left of her day. It should time out just about right, tapering in an hour and a half when she was ready for bed.

"There," she said, shutting down the computer. "Done."

He dangled the bag in front of her like a carrot and she pushed him through the door, locking it behind her. When he walked her to the passenger side of the Mustang she paused, but didn't know why; it wasn't as if it was the first time he'd opened a door for her. Maybe it felt symbolic, making her think of how he was opening up to her: this guy she still didn't really know, revealing little pieces of himself bit by bit. It was like she'd been given a colouring book for the summer holidays and each day she filled in another page. He handed her the bag after she ducked into the car.

"What is this?" she asked once he was in the driver's seat. "Faye doesn't sell these at Triple Shot." She pulled out a flakey brioche that looked and smelled divine.

"Will's been stress baking, I guess." He started the car, speaking over the rumble of the engine. "Nate says he does that sometimes."

"Go Will," she said, taking a bite of the pastry, moaning as the rich flavours of butter and caramelized sugar filled her mouth. "When Will bakes, we all win." Then she felt bad for not feeling bad about whatever was causing Will's stress. She'd been known to stress bake herself. She should be more sympathetic.

Tim palmed the gearshift, his other hand wrapped around the steering wheel. It was like the wind had shifted inside their atmosphere, and now was very, very still. He drove out of the parking lot, letting the silence linger.

She tried to ignore the mood; focus on the music coming from the stereo as she savoured the pastry. Conversation would go better tomorrow, when they were both rested — because that's probably all this was, and she'd wake up in the morning and realize her imagination had been feeding her doubts when things were fine; of course they were. It was nothing new that he wasn't inclined to talk, and she was okay with that.

Holly greeted them at the house with her usual joy, and the way she made them both laugh further dispelled Emilie's fears until she said, "Let's go, Holly!" and Tim asked, "Can I come with you?"

"That would be nice," Emilie said, when part of her wanted to say no. Because now she wanted the silence, afraid of what he wasn't saying. She could feel it. Tim, the guy who hardly talked, had things to say.

She preempted anything serious by explaining her routine, because her nightly walks had a dual purpose. He helped check waters and dole out peppermints in the training barn, and she didn't miss that Excursion — Curtis — got seconds.

The stars weren't as clear and defined here as they had been at the cottage, but that was probably appropriate, because neither were they. He chose the moment she stopped and peered upward — something that usually grounded her — to speak.

"I know it's late, and you're tired. But putting things off just got me in a whole lot of trouble with you in the past."

She held her breath, waiting for him to go on. Holly wandered back to them, checking in, then drifted to sniff along the treeline.

"I know I have so much to explain," he said, his voice almost monotone. "So much to apologize for."

So maybe that's all this was: him wanting to clear things up. It was long overdue, wasn't it? Once the *why* behind his past actions was brought to the surface, they could move forward.

"I know how horrible I was at the wedding," he continued. "I just — freaked out."

She almost reacted because the memory of it still got to her — despite the Tim she'd since discovered. But she understood better now, since that time in the café when Sylvie had almost asked him out. She'd had this idea of him in her head before the wedding, that he would be her Nate, when he was more like her sister than his own brother.

"It starts further back than that." He ran a hand through his hair and walked forward a few steps before he stopped, though he wasn't looking at her, his features filtered by the darkness. "When Nate came home for Phil's funeral, he told me about you. He didn't mention your name, he just said, 'I've got the girl for you.'"

She had to smile, just a little, at that, his words revealing he'd been teased about her like she'd been teased about him.

"I told him not to go setting me up; he had enough going on with his own love life." There was that twitch of a smile that made her heart flutter. "Then when it's obvious it worked out just fine for him, I meet you, and it's real. You're real. Beautiful and confident and funny, and so totally out of my league. That's a lot of pressure. So I panicked. You know how that went."

Wait, what? "You out of my league?" She stifled a laugh.

He shook his head; held up a hand. *Shut up, Emilie.*

"I felt bad about the wedding. Messaging seemed a non-threatening way to try to make up for it. And it was. It was comfortable. I liked it. I liked you. I tried to convince myself it was nothing — because our messages were about nothing — but it was something. At least, it was something to me."

"It was to me, too," she said, her voice barely more than a whisper. She remembered that night in the Mustang, when the song "Emily" had come on, and she couldn't keep quiet; couldn't trust him to answer the question she'd pushed back in her mind, letting this newer, nicer Tim cover it up with strokes of clean colour. When you put fresh paint over a layer that hadn't properly cured, it cracked. This fissure remained between them. The old Tim was still there; the unresolved layer just hidden temporarily. It didn't matter anymore how tired they both were. They were into this. "So why did you ghost me?"

"It wasn't like I meant to. It was just, when I got the news about being sent back down to the minors, it was such a huge disappointment. Even though they brought me up because one of the regulars was out with an injury, I thought I was playing well enough when he came back they'd keep me. But I guess I wasn't. It was pretty tough to swallow." His shoulders slumped, and he wouldn't meet her eyes. "You must've heard, because you asked if I was okay — but I couldn't answer. Because I wasn't okay, but when less than a year ago I'd lost a brother and sister-in-law, something that was legitimately devastating, it seemed so wrong to be upset over something so trivial in comparison. I didn't want to pretend with you — but if I told you the truth, I'd just sound like a whiny jock. We weren't about that. So I told you nothing at all."

He paused, like he needed to breathe, and her heart hurt, thinking *if only*. If only he'd taken that chance; shared with her. If only before that moment she'd given him a reason to feel it was worth the risk.

He exhaled. "And then I got hurt, and at that point I didn't really care about anything. Until Nate invited me here, and I thought, just maybe, I could make it all up to you; fix just one thing in my life. And I know now, Nate was right. You are the girl for me." He turned toward her, his eyes searching, and she wanted to see hope, the future. "But—"

Of course there was a but.

"When he first mentioned you, that day in Calgary, he told me to call him when I had my hockey career settled, like he knew I wouldn't be ready until I had that. And it's not settled yet. I have to go back and figure that out."

Her anger dwindled to nothing, melancholy replacing it. "You mean soon, don't you?"

"My agent called today. I'm leaving next week."

There it was. She'd known it had to come. She couldn't tell if what they had was real, or pretend; whether it was forever, or just for now. She'd run with it, wanting to believe until life told her otherwise, because reality would ruin it. And here was reality, doing just that.

"I think I might love you, Emilie."

The words made her light-headed and weakened her knees, but not the way they should have. "I think I might love you too, Tim."

"So how do we do this?" His tone was imploring now.

"We don't." Because no matter how much saying it drove a spear through her chest, she couldn't help thinking this thing between them wouldn't survive long distance. "You have to go back and see that through. And I have my life here. There's really no way it can work, is there?" She gulped and blinked, determined not to get emotional. "Go back and train hard so you make the team. Then Faye and Will have to get their act together and get married so we'll have an excuse to see each other again. And you'll get us tickets when you play in Toronto." She had to stop again, to breathe. "Now is just not the right time."

Maybe she should have said she'd wait. She thought of Liv and Nate, and how long it had taken them to get where they were now. Nate had done a whole lot of waiting, even if that had probably been for the best because he'd been able to get his own head sorted. But Emilie didn't know that she could hold on to a maybe. She didn't know if she had that kind of patience.

She put her arms around him, and pulled herself into the firmness of his chest, feeling his uneven breathing as his ribcage rose and fell. His arms encircled her, his chin wedging into the side of her head.

"Didn't we almost have it all?" she said, trying to laugh when her eyes were blurring.

"Enough with the eighties songs," he murmured against her hair. "But don't you forget about me."

"I think we can agree on one thing," she said, striving desperately for levity.

"Can we?"

"All of this is Nate's fault."

He huffed in agreement. "It really is."

"No regrets, right?" But she knew that was a lie.

Why wasn't love enough?

CHAPTER TWENTY-EIGHT

THE QUIET HAD BEEN AN ADJUSTMENT, keeping him awake on his first nights at the farm, when he usually slept like a rock with the white noise of suburbia at home no matter what was bothering him. He'd become accustomed to the subtle country sounds; crickets and frog song. Last night though, he lay awake for hours, staring at the ceiling. It wasn't until he heard Nate and Liv leaving that he finally fell asleep.

When his alarm woke him he thought about ignoring it. She probably wouldn't question it if he didn't show. Maybe she'd even forgotten, or didn't want to see him, after last night. Or maybe this was one, small thing he could do for her, when she'd done so much for him.

The sun was up, and he thought about Liv and Nate at the racetrack, training the horses. He got why they loved it. It was a hard life, but a rewarding one. Equine athletes had the same struggles as human ones — mindset, injury, fitness — and it made his own journey seem simple in comparison. Lots of hockey players owned racehorses, so maybe one day he would own one. When he earned a spot on the Flames. When he got a contract. When he had some job security. He had the right connections, that was for sure.

He still couldn't believe Emilie didn't have her own horse. When he had all of that — the salary, the security — he'd buy her a horse, too. One of her very own. *If I had a million dollars...*

But maybe she didn't want that, just like she didn't want him.

Last night was a blow. It hadn't gone the way he'd hoped, though if he were honest, he wasn't sure how that would be. She was right, of course. And he felt he had to prove to himself he could have these feelings for her and still play the way he needed to. He was good at hockey, when his head was in the game. But maybe there wasn't room in there for anything else. And maybe there wasn't time. How did you make time for the things that were important when thousands of miles separated you? What if they both ended up hating each other when it wasn't enough? It might be better to accept defeat.

He was going to make sure she didn't forget about him though, in the little time he had left. Her camera bag was in the kitchen, on the table. After finding some breakfast, he slung the bag over his shoulder and started walking.

The horses in the pasture next to the office barn stopped him, the way the light backlit them as they grazed. He pulled the camera out, the telephoto already in place, and composed the shot — *snap* — then carried on, the strap around his neck. It was heavy, so he still held it, but he wanted the security of the strap in case something happened. All he needed was to break her camera. His position was precarious enough as it was.

Sunlight glinted off the chrome on Jodi's motorcycle, parked outside the training barn, and he snapped a few photos of it. Then he waited, far enough away to frame the doorway so when Emilie and Jodi appeared with Curtis he got some candid shots before they saw him, the light capturing them against the dark of the barn's interior.

"Yes!" Emilie said, though her smile was lumens below what it would have been before last night. Appreciative, but with a layer of sorrow he couldn't ignore — because he shared it, a cannonball wedged behind his ribs.

Taking photos that were supposed to help her sell Curtis felt like a betrayal, but he was glad to have something to do; something to think about. *Frame, focus, fire.* There was plenty of room on the memory card so he showed no restraint, not checking the images as he went. He didn't know enough about riding to know if his shots were good or bad, so he only would have been looking at her, and tried to keep himself from doing just that, taking into consideration the horse too. Because he was starting to see they had expressions. They had moods. They had big personalities. All of it without verbalizing a thing.

When they took a rest and just walked, he still found interesting things to shoot: zooming into Curtis's head, to Emilie's face, her hands, her leg. Sometimes he pulled out his phone, the tele taking him too close, and captured a broader sense of the scene — the atmosphere, horse, rider, coach — until they started trotting again.

It probably should have been boring, but watching Emilie would never bore him. And Curtis was cool to observe, the way his ears swivelled, like he was trying to tune in her thoughts and desires because whatever physical signals she gave him were invisible to Tim. They did circles and serpentines and some sideways stuff at Jodi's bidding. Sometimes Jodi's commands came with a description of what Emilie's hand should do, what her leg should do, what her seatbone or her weight should do. Tim tried to watch her, to see if he could see. The obvious stuff he could — the turn of her head and shoulders, the lift of a hand — but most of it was a mystery to him.

"All right, take a break," Jodi said, Emilie's sigh of relief visible as she dragged the arm of her sunshirt across her face, pink with exertion.

Jodi began setting up something complex using uprights and poles: some poles spaced on the ground; some crossed, braced against the uprights to make an x-shaped jump so low he could have walked over it. Then she dropped the rails to the ground so everything was flat.

"When was the last time you jumped?" Jodi asked, brushing her hands together to remove the dust she'd picked up with the rails.

"Um," Emilie said, looking embarrassed. "When I was eleven?"

"Did you ever do gymnastics?"

Didn't everyone have to in gym class? Tim almost interjected, but the whole lesson thing seemed sacred, so he kept his wisecracks to himself. He didn't think she meant that.

Emilie's chin dipped in a quick nod. "Yep. On the push-button ponies my sister schooled ad nauseam so they were point and shoot. Never a green-bean like this guy."

"That's okay. Your lower leg is solid from galloping those racehorses. We'll let him go over the poles first, though."

Tim was so engrossed in the progression he almost forgot he was supposed to be taking photos. First, they made sure Curtis would walk over a single pole on its own; then two, then three. Next Jodi adjusted the distance between them and asked Emilie to trot, Curtis looking comical as he exaggerated the lift of his feet to negotiate the poles. Jodi made them turn around and come in the opposite direction, and as Emilie was circling back for the next pass, the coach made adjustments.

"Come ahead." Jodi waved her on.

Curtis navigated the spaced poles with confidence, but his

ears flew forward at the little x jump at the end of the line, slowing noticeably as they neared it.

"Leg!" Jodi ordered, and Emilie must've responded, because Curtis clambered over — not with particular grace.

"Again," Jodi said, and this time it was smoother.

Then she made the last jump straight across, and set up one before it in an x, still with poles on the ground leading up to it. Curtis bounced through it like a pro, Emilie's grin huge.

"He wants to jump higher," Jodi said.

"Okay." Emilie dragged the word out, not sounding convinced as Jodi put the last jump up.

"Just remember to commit to the fence and don't get ahead of him."

Curtis was happy to play, his focus matching Emilie's as they approached once more.

"Ho-oh," Emilie said, pulling back enough Tim noticed it, her jaw clenched.

"Let him go," Jodi said. "Trust him. He wants to do this."

Even Tim could see Curtis wanted it. *I got this,* he was saying, powering over the poles, though he didn't touch a single one. But Emilie said *ho* again. He leapt over the first, smaller jump awkwardly, then slammed on the brakes, Emilie swearing as he tossed her forward onto his neck with enough force to leave her hanging off the side. She swore again, then let go, tumbling to the ground.

Curtis stood, head dropped; snorting at her like he couldn't figure out what she was doing down there. Emilie rose slowly, reaching for the reins, and stroked him.

"Sorry, buddy." She led him away from the jump and checked over her saddle.

"That wasn't my fault, was it?" Tim asked. He didn't think so, but he remembered her toppling off of Twizzle because of him. She was never going to want him to watch her ride again.

"No," Jodi said, walking over to Curtis to help Emilie back on. "That was all Emilie. I hope you got some pictures of that!"

He shook his head.

"Never stop shooting!' she said, grinning. "Fail photos are a requirement for being an eventer. Come on, Emilie. I thought exercise riders were brave! Go again."

The goading seemed to do the trick because she nailed it this time, her face set in determination. Tim let the motor drive do its thing, following her all the way through the line, Curtis soaring over the last jump.

"Once more to prove that wasn't a fluke, then we're done," Jodi said. "Next time we'll let him do a little course."

After Curtis bounced through the exercise like he was skipping through the park, cantering off after it with a big snort like he was all proud of himself, Emilie brought him to a walk and dropped her reins, holding them at the end where they buckled together. She scrubbed his neck furiously under his mane.

"Such a clever boy. Isn't he great?" She beamed, their parting of ways forgotten. "I can't wait to see the photos!"

She hopped off, loosening the girth, then wrapped her arms around Curtis's head, pressing her cheek to his forehead.

Snap.

The image made him sad again, but at least it was something he could take with him. He'd make her a deal: he'd send her the video he'd shot of their second time through the jumping exercise, if she sent him some of these photos of her. Some guys wanted naked photos of a girl, but the way she smiled when she was with that horse? That would do just fine.

He fed Curtis a peppermint as Emilie picked his feet out. *Solidarity, dude. She doesn't want either of us. I'd buy you for myself if that were in any way practical.* Except, what would he do with a horse?

"I should get going," he said, with a final pat for Curtis and a broken smile for Emilie.

"Thanks for the photos, Tim," she said, but she didn't meet his eyes.

He eased himself into the deck chair next to Nate after a swim. Doing easy laps was good low-impact cardio and a great upper body workout. It had been a bonding thing too, to swim alongside Nate. The pool was only a few lanes wide, so they'd pulled through the water, side by side, like they were doing a marathon swim. This pain he was feeling might be Nate's fault, but would he trade it? Go back in time and refuse to come? No.

Liv came from the house and handed them water bottles, the plastic sweating and cool to the touch. They were no doubt BPA-free; he couldn't imagine Emilie allowing anything else in this house. He nodded his thanks and took a long drink. It seemed counterintuitive that swimming made you thirsty, but it did.

"Emilie needs some jumps for that charity horse show thing. How do I make that happen?" he asked, now that he had both Nate and Liv here without Emilie. It was another thing he could do. He knew how important that show was to her.

Nate reacted first with a raised eyebrow, then looked thoughtful. "Talk to Will and Dean. Dean's pretty handy. Maybe Kerrie can give us someone for a few hours?" He glanced up at Liv.

"Kerrie would probably help too," Liv said, twisting her hair into a bun not quite on top of her head before slipping on a swim cap. "If they're not overly busy, you can have the whole farm crew. You should be able to find lots of ideas and plans online. I'll text you the heights they need to be."

"And I'll help," Nate said, "if it happens when I'm not riding."

"Monday afternoon, then. Be there," Tim said.

"Got it." Nate grinned as he pushed himself out of the chair.

Tim stayed for a while, watching Liv swim as he air-dried. She went at it with more intensity than he and Nate had, her neat stroke coming with the practiced, punched revolutions of hours spent in the water. This pool was here because of her, according to Nate. Meant for what she was doing, not for merely splashing around to beat the heat on a hot summer day. He recognized it for what it was. More than just exercise. A coping mechanism.

He wondered if that was why Nate had thought Emilie was right for him. Like Liv and Nate, not quite opposites attracting, just a sensible personality fit. And Liv and Nate had found their balance. He didn't want to be afraid for them, thinking of Mom and Dad in a similar arrangement. They must be aware of that, and maybe that would help them navigate, if not avoid, the hurdles they might face down the road.

What did compatibility matter, though, when he and Emilie were in different time zones? But he couldn't bring himself to give up because of that, even if she had. He would do this. Get settled. Establish himself once and for all as a valued member of the team — then figure out how to get her back once and for all.

He retreated into the cool of the house. He had homework to do, so he parked himself in the kitchen with his laptop to see if the Wi-Fi was going to play nice today. When it did, he researched cross-country jumps and started making plans.

CHAPTER TWENTY-NINE

"GIRLS VERSUS GUYS? ARE YOU SURE?" Nate said, leaning on his stick.

"Absolutely," Emilie said.

"But —"

"Nope. We're good, Miller," Liv said, wandering to the spot on the house's asphalt driveway that approximated centre ice. "Get over here. Let's go."

It was hilarious to see Nate and Liv line up, sticks poised, staring each other down. They weren't competitive; not at all.

This had been Kerrie's idea for Tim's going-away party: a good, old-fashioned game of street hockey. They were on the driveway perpendicular to the lane that led to the office barn so it wasn't technically a street, but it was paved smooth, and the overhead trees provided shade. Afterward they'd have a barbecue.

And the day after tomorrow, Tim would leave.

Don't make me drive you to the airport, she'd pleaded. So Nate was taking him. Tim would go into the track, and after training was done for the morning, Nate would drop him off at nearby Pearson International while Emilie stayed at home, hoping the horses she rode kept her from dwelling on her wounded heart.

This would help, too. She hadn't told Tim she'd played hockey when she'd lived in Montreal. She'd been young, and had no aspirations beyond having fun, but she loved to play, more than she liked to watch, actually. Except, now — if watching meant watching Tim.

She tossed and caught the bright orange ball in the air, then dropped it to Holly, sitting next to her in between Nate and Liv. Holly claimed it with a snap.

"Now let the ball hit the ground before you attack it, please? If either of you hits my dog, there will be consequences." Emilie left Holly holding the ball and backed up to her position. The Black Lab's thick tail swept the asphalt in anticipation.

"Toss it!" Emilie called from right wing.

With a flip of her nose, Holly sent the ball between the two centres and dashed to the sidelines, clear of the fray.

Liv won the faceoff, sending the ball immediately to Emilie. Tim kept his eyes locked on her, but hockey meant war; she would not be distracted playing opposite him. Liv ducked past Nate, her feet light and swift, and Emilie passed the ball to her — but Nate intercepted and took off toward their net. Liv spun and charged after him, Emilie rushing to help defend.

Their girls' team was weak on defence; Jillian, who worked on the farm, volunteered to play with the disclaimer that she was that person no one wanted on their team in middle school. It didn't matter; Kerrie in goal more than made up for any deficit.

"Don't feel you need to do anything heroic. I don't want you to get run down if things get intense. We just need you as a number," she'd explained.

Jillian had nodded, looking mildly terrified rather than insulted. Maybe Emilie shouldn't have phrased it that way, but warnings needed to be given.

Nate was being all fancy with his feet, like he was pretending they had as many players as a full football team instead of three-on-three hockey. Liv was on him like a sweaty shirt and when Liv poke-checked him, he stumbled, falling. Emilie cackled, racing past to get control of the ball.

"Don't hurt yourself, Miller!" Liv called over her shoulder, tracking Emilie. "You've got to ride tomorrow." Then she took Emilie's pass and popped the ball in the net under Will's elbow on the stick side.

"Woo-hoo!" Emilie said, hopping over to Liv and throwing her arms around her sister.

Will scooped the ball from the net and fired it toward the other end, scowling. "What was that, Miller?"

"I caught an edge!" Nate complained.

"You're wearing running shoes."

"Details," Nate cracked.

"If you weren't so busy showing off, maybe you'd have stayed on your feet," Will growled. "And Dean! Were you sleeping? A little support, man."

"I'm not warmed up yet," Dean grumbled.

"Excuses, excuses," Liv said.

"Get the ball, Holly!" Emilie trilled, and the Lab bounded down the driveway, skittering to a halt to grab the round orange thing. "Faceoff!"

The Lab knew the command. She barrelled back with her prize and lined herself up at the centre point, waiting.

Tim had been playing cool up until now, probably underestimating the women, but his vision narrowed. "Try and win this one, will you, Nate?"

"Pressure's not gonna help, kid," Nate shot back. But this

time when the ball dropped, Holly scurrying away, he gained control and popped it to Tim before Liv hip-checked him. "I thought this was no contact? Weren't you the one who said don't get hurt?"

Liv gave him a shove for good measure then grabbed the back of his shirt as he tried to get away from her, both of them grinning the whole time.

Meanwhile, Tim stood in place, stickhandling. Emilie wasn't going to fall for the trance, so she rushed him, only for him to duck around her with ease. His head was up, and he was looking for Dean — but Dean was out of position and Liv still had Nate too covered for him to break free. Finding no one to pass to, Tim evaded Emilie again, easily bypassed Jillian and all Emilie could do was watch, sure it was going in, even with Kerrie in net. But with some miracle feat of flexibility, Kerrie stretched, getting her arm there in time, the ball deflecting out of play.

"Yes! Great save, Kerrie!" Jillian yelled, her stick clattering to the ground as she bounced up and down, clapping.

"Yeah. Nice save," Tim said, respect dawning on his features. "Are you okay? That was a hard shot."

Kerrie pulled up her long-sleeved shirt to show the welt forming. "It stung a bit. I'm sure I'll have a nice bruise, but I'll live."

"Wait —" Dean wandered up, something coming over his face. "Now I know why you look so familiar. You're Kerrie-Lynn Evans!"

"What?" Nate snapped, and Emilie and Liv started laughing.

Will pushed up between Nate and Dean. "The Kerrie-Lynn Evans? Goalie for the gold-medal winning Canadian women's hockey team?"

"How did we not know that? Did you know that?" Nate stared at Liv.

"Of course I did. Emilie told me after she first talked to Kerrie, before she agreed to take the manager job."

"How could you keep that from me?" Emilie almost believed he felt hurt by the discovery that Liv had failed to share this particular piece of information with him.

Liv shrugged unapologetically. "I guess with everything happening at the time, I just forgot. It wasn't relevant to the position."

Tim grinned, the first to offer his hand. "It's an honour."

"You don't feel so sorry for us now, do you boys?" Emilie quipped as they each exchanged handshakes.

"Nope," Nate said. "But now it's game on."

The final score was 3-1, Tim finally getting one past Kerrie late in the game. After they lined up for the traditional handshakes like they'd just finished the Olympic gold-medal final, the guys joked around with post-game interview clichés.

"Y'know, we played our best. We gave it a hundred and ten percent, but they had a lot of energy."

"We needed to get more pucks to the net."

"It was do or die. We died."

"You're going off-script, Nate."

"Sorry, buddy."

"Are you taking notes, Tim?"

"Sure."

"I'm starving," Faye said, picking her way from the sidelines where she'd been safe from getting mixed up in the rivalry. "Let's eat."

"You didn't even play," Dean said, throwing an arm around her.

"Ew. Get away from me. You're sweaty." She pushed him aside.

"Will's not. He didn't play hard enough to sweat," Nate quipped.

Faye had outdone herself as usual with the meal prep and Dean started up the grill.

"I hope Will made those black bean burgers again," Emilie said.

"Those are for Tim," Will said. "And he's the guest of honour."

"With all this food, I'll share," Tim said, those delicious eyes settling on her.

The timbre of his voice stirred a longing in her. She covered it up with a brief smile and grabbed a plate. "I'm going to get started on the salads. They look amazing."

She was afraid if she remained near him she'd do something ridiculous, like launch into a soliloquy about the tragedy of their love, but they fell together anyway, because it seemed unnatural not to. He followed her as she made her selections, choosing his own; loading up on the beans and vegetables, instinctively going for the healthy options. If he hadn't taken her for ice cream, she would have had serious doubts about their compatibility. Except she would give up sugar for him if he asked her to, if it meant they could have a life together.

Eventually Tim got pulled away. She was surprised how much he'd changed from the guy at the wedding. But again, maybe it wasn't so much that he'd changed as how the different context allowed him to be more himself. Nate sauntered up next to her with a beer and a non-bean burger.

"How are you doing, Em?"

Nate always had a way of pushing past the veneer and getting to the heart of the matter. She curled in her lower lip and bit on it, hard, because she wasn't going to cry.

"Great. I'm wonderful. You okay? You went down pretty hard."

"I can't believe you brought in a ringer to play goal."

"I'm pretty proud of that, actually. I never knew how handy Kerrie's unique skill would be." She found a grin.

"I guess none of us put it together, always seeing her in street clothes."

She elbowed him. "Sorry, not sorry."

"Nice deflection, by the way."

He wasn't talking about a play in the game. She sighed, looking at her plate of food, losing her appetite. She needed it back. There was dessert. "How much do you know?"

"I know he's leaving in two days, and you're staying here."

"You thought I'd go with him?"

"No. I guess not. You are a Lachance, after all. But at least Liv didn't completely write me off when she pushed me to put my career first."

Well. That was a slap in the face.

"I can't take it, Nate," she said. "I can't take letting go again. I'm not as resilient as you."

"And by resilient, you mean stupid."

"No, obviously not. It all worked out for you. But that doesn't mean the same thing is going to happen for me. There has to be a time when I cut my losses." And go live in a remote northern community.

"Maybe," he said. "Maybe not."

"You're so helpful." She glared at him.

"Anything for you, Em." He kissed her on the cheek and wandered away again.

She set aside her plate of food, feeling guilty it might go to waste, but she either needed alcohol or chocolate. As Faye had whipped up some decadent salted caramel brownies with chocolate chunks that were right in front of her, she went with that.

Stuffing half the brownie unceremoniously in her mouth,

she looked around the group that had gathered for this farewell. Tim was standing with Dean and Kerrie — he'd be happy there because he could talk hockey like Emilie talked horses. Jillian had excused herself before they'd gathered for food. Emilie made a mental note to collect a tin of sweets for the farm staff to have at coffee time in the morning. Nate and Liv were with Faye and Will; happy couples united.

She had become her sister; they had officially changed futures. She was by herself, making herself one with the brownies. It felt like her destiny, so she enjoyed every bite, but it left her with a craving she couldn't deny.

CHAPTER THIRTY

He shifted from foot to foot on his skates, scanning the semi-circle of little kids in helmets and oversized jerseys who stared up at him in awe. Just say the words "NHL player" to a Canadian child and their eyes lit up, even if the title wasn't totally accurate.

Last night at the barbecue Dean had asked him, "What are you doing tomorrow?"

"I don't know. Packing. Working out. Until we start building those fences," he'd replied.

"I'm helping out with a local hockey camp," Dean said. "It would thrill the kids to bits if you'd come. What do you think?"

"Dean Taylor." Nate put an arm around the neighbour. "You are such a good guy."

Dean peered down at him. "Careful, or I'll rope you in too, Nate."

"I'll come for sure. Not that I have the same allure as Tim."

Tim had smirked. "I'm a nobody."

Nate, always quick to call him on his insecurity, said, "But you're going to be a somebody."

It sounded like fun, especially once Nate volunteered, so he'd agreed. Besides, he wouldn't feel as much like he owed Dean for helping with the cross-country fences if he did something in return. It would be an effective diversion; eat up some time until they gathered at the farm for Project Make Emilie Jumps. And Tim liked little kids; they were easy to impress. It reminded him of Emilie saying he'd make a good teacher — except if he was giving up Emilie it was to play hockey. He was making the team, not going back to school.

Being on the ice again felt good, even if it was just this. It boosted his confidence; reminded him how at home he was at the rink — any rink. He felt ready to face the powers that be in Calgary. They'd assess where he was and give him the help he needed to return to top form so he could be that promising rookie they'd thought they had on their hands back in December.

A long time ago he'd been one of these kids, scrambling and falling more than skating. He barely remembered it. Helping them with basic skills fed his determination to become the hero they mistakenly thought he was. Maybe one of them would make it big one day. He was almost sad when it was over — but there were jumps to be made.

He dumped the borrowed skates behind the seat of Dean's pickup and climbed in, waiting impatiently for Dean to finish talking to one of the parents so they could get to the lumber store. After handing over the list of things they'd need once they got there, it was Tim's turn to pull out Nate's credit card to pay for it all; Nate had said something about Dubai making a donation to New Chapter to pay for the jumps. Emilie would be good with some of the money they'd made from that big race going to her cause.

"Thanks for the help," Tim said as he stuffed the card safely back in his wallet.

Dean shrugged. "It's Emilie. We all love Em. Wouldn't miss a chance to help her out. But good for you, for organizing it."

Dean slapped him on the bruise Nate had left a few days ago. Tim rubbed it briefly as they returned to the truck to head to the loading dock.

Driving back to the farm, Tim picked up the papers he'd left rolled and jammed in a cupholder in the door. "I printed the plans and made some sketches. Think we can do this?"

"Of course we can. Just don't ask me to get on a horse and jump any of them." Dean grinned and Tim was afraid he was going to get smacked again.

They drove to the field that had been designated — behind the training barn and indoor arena; an area that was isolated from where the mommas and babies lived. Liv had agreed to all this, but she'd been adamant it had to be separate. Horses carried stuff like flu, just like humans did, and the babies were as susceptible as kids, so the horses coming to the farm for the show wouldn't be anywhere near the ones who lived here.

Will showed up as he and Dean were unloading the wood and helped them finish stacking it.

"This is supposed to be one of the easiest," Tim said, smoothing the paper out on the tailgate of Dean's Chevy once the bed was empty. "It's called a ramp. We'll start with that. We're making three sizes of each."

"Three!" Will exclaimed.

"Yeah. They want one for the beginner people, and one for the more experienced people, and one size in between."

"Are the riders all jockeys or former jockeys? I think they all know how to ride," Will said.

"That doesn't mean they all know how to jump," Nate said.

"Which one are you?" Will said, eyebrows raised.

Nate laughed. "I don't know yet. I haven't jumped

anything intentionally since I was a kid at your grandfather's farm and we used to go over downed logs. Think I should get someone to give me a lesson before I try it at the show?"

Kerrie stood with hands on hips, grinning. "It's going to be entertaining, either way. They have to have paramedics on site, right?"

"Logs," Tim said, determined to stay on task amid the joshing. "Where can we get some logs?"

"Where can we get some beer, is what I want to know," Will said.

"Don't you have more stress baking to do, Will?" Tim snapped. They only had so much daylight to work with, and tomorrow, he was gone. "Grab a hammer. Maybe the beer will show up once you've done some work."

"Slave driver," Will grumbled, backing away.

"Way to crack the whip, kid." Nate laughed.

It was hot work, the sun doing them no favours by cheerily keeping an eye on their progress with no respite. Faye showed up midway with sandwiches and cold drinks, though not a beer to be found among them. No Emilie, either. Faye had promised she'd find a way of getting her here without spoiling the surprise.

"Wow," she said after she spread everything out on the tailgate of the truck. "Those look... solid. Good work, though."

Tim accepted the bottle of water she offered and stared at her pointedly.

"Relax. Liv's on it," Faye assured him. "It made more sense for her to drag Emilie out into the middle of a field than me."

Maybe it did, but it didn't keep him from being anxious.

Once the sun set, they had no choice but to stop and pack up. They restacked the remaining wood and took stock of what still needed to be done: things to secure the fences to the ground, the flags which told the riders which direction to jump them, and numbers to indicate the order — but that would have to happen without him.

Finally, in the fading light, two figures approached the group of workers, but he only had eyes for one of them. He knew her shape, the way she moved, saw the white of her smile as she drew closer, her ponytail swinging as her head turned from one side to the other to take in the obstacles.

"This is amazing!" Emilie said, "You're all amazing. Thank you so much. I love you all."

When the sweep she made of all their faces ended on his, he didn't look away. A few days ago, after the cottage and before the words, she might have skipped over to him, pressed her lips to his. And he would have grabbed her, picked her up, and kissed her back. Instead, they stood apart. He didn't know exactly what he was expecting; only what he'd hoped, and it wasn't this.

They were both being so accepting, so compliant; letting go as if, because they'd spent so much time fighting it, they didn't know how to fight for it.

He had to learn how to fight for it. This wasn't over.

There was only one remedy for what she was feeling. Wine.

When was the last time she'd had a drink? Plate Day, maybe? Before the cottage, for sure. It was odd they'd taken no alcohol with them, but no one seemed to miss it. She hadn't, around Tim. Tonight, though, it wasn't enough. She swallowed a generous amount and set the glass on the counter, closing her eyes.

She'd known the end of this story before it had started. Tim would come. Tim would leave. It wasn't his fault she'd failed to follow her own advice and avoid him, though she hadn't expected things to go the way they had.

How had he organized a jump-building party — for her — and kept it under the radar? And she'd thought him bringing her coffee and pastries the other night was sweet. He kept surprising her. After all the disappointment, he'd made up for it a hundred times over.

The guy who wrote "Feelings" had it right. Another glass or two of wine and she'd be singing it out loud instead of just in her head. She'd indulge herself; let herself wallow in self-pity, then get up early to say goodbye. She had to do that much — but tonight, wine and sad songs in her head it would be. Closing her eyes, she started humming.

When she opened them, slowly, she pictured him standing in the kitchen's doorway. He still wore the faded jeans and dusty t-shirt with the hockey team's logo he'd had on to build jumps, his tawny hair windblown, his eyes more espresso than macchiato in the dim light. But when she tried to blink him away — because he had to be a projection — he was still there.

All she could do was meet his gaze thinking, *what did we expect, really?* His expression said something different; there was a curious sense of purpose in it.

"Regressing to the seventies?" The humour was all in his words, none in his tone or face.

She wished she could smile, but right now the proper muscles in her face didn't appear to be working. She wasn't even embarrassed having been caught drowning her sorrows and humming a really bad song. The appropriate thing to do was to take another sip of wine.

When she drew her eyes from its empty consolation he was gone — back to his comfort zone, no doubt. Her image probably served as a warning: she was not, in fact, the girl for him. Sad

girl working on drunk, sad girl was not attractive. Except...
there was music.

It reached her, beyond the realization he'd plugged his
phone into the speakers in the living room. The opening notes
built to an arrangement she recognized, the familiarity of it like
a finger being traced to the centre of her chest.

I love this song.

But she'd never heard it like this before, with him hovering
in the doorway again, playing it for her.

Gorgeous.

It made her more self-aware than she wanted to be; took
her back to that moment on the rock he'd said she was beautiful, and she'd wanted to respond, *no, you are.* She couldn't
afford those emotions now, when in twelve hours he would
board a plane back to Calgary and his future there.

When he walked toward her, she pressed her eyes shut
again and turned away, reaching for the wine bottle like a blind
person. Had Nate tossed those muscle relaxants? One of those
to knock her out would be good right about now, so she could
avoid whatever this was. Sleep, then wake in the morning, reso-
lute she would give him a polite send-off.

The pull of him was strong, standing so close behind her,
and she kept her lids pinned, clutching the stem of the glass.
Could she tell him to go away? But he was going away.

"Would you dance with me?"

His voice touched her instead of his hands, his breath like
smoke in her ear; numbness spreading from the base of her
skull to her neck.

"Why now?" When this was the end? Maybe it was his
way of saying goodbye. Best of luck in your future endeavours.
You should have just sent a card.

She had every intention of telling him exactly that as she
finally faced him, but he smelled like sunshine and hard work

259

and she inhaled like it was her last breath. In a way, it was. Fire danced to her nerve endings, taking over her entire body as she counted the inches between her body and his, staring at his chest, hands tingling as she remembered how it felt against her palms. Knowing how much better it would feel against her own. Then her eyes dropped to the hand that waited, palm up, for her answer.

"I already told you I'm sorry about the wedding. And my whole reason for going to the Plate Ball was because of you and then everything got out of control. But please. Dance with me now. Let this be my do-over."

The finger he placed under her chin was unexpected and he used it to lift her face to his. His eyes entreated, like he wanted to make amends for things she'd already forgiven.

"You'll have to teach me," she managed, the syllables tripping out as if the wine had failed to lubricate her vocal chords.

He nodded, taking her hand. "It's not an easy one."

"You're a good teacher," she murmured.

When he held her, his stance was formal without being stiff; comfortable and confident while she was unsure of herself. The touch of his fingers lit her up, her pulse disregarding the tempo of the music. Was his right hand really supposed to be *there?*

"Shoulders back. Chest open. Head up. Just like Jodi keeps telling you when you're riding Curtis."

Except Jodi wasn't face-to-face; not to mention oh-so-male and hands-on. His focus commanded her attention, but he'd disrupted her sense of rhythm and she struggled to rediscover it, sure she wouldn't be able to keep up as the music took off from its lazy beginning. She nodded, her head heavy.

He tipped her face to his again and reset his hand. "I'll count. Think of it like your jumping lessons," he said. "When you count down to the jump."

"You mean the strides? It's not like that." Her frown of concentration quickly reversed.

"Not really. But it made you smile."

"It did." And it helped, at least temporarily, to reduce this to instruction, like how Jodi would tell her where to put her leg or her hand.

"Ready?" and he set off. "One, two, three and four, five and six."

Enough tension drained away that it became easier to let him move her as he quietly talked her through. Each beat meant something: the placement of a foot, the turn of bodies, the adjustment of a hand.

Though he kept their steps economical, because there was only so much room in the kitchen, it felt like they were travelling — with none of the awkward bumbling she and Chad had suffered through at the ball. It was as if Tim loaned her a portion of his grace; carried her with him, made her feel as if she was, like the song said, gorgeous... just like him.

It wasn't just physical. That this man lived inside the same body as the one who had scowled at her on a beach in Florida, abandoned their online chat, hidden behind a book in the airport, panicked at the café — it baffled her. Was there a switch he flipped? Did it take an out-of-body effort? And did he need to do the same to play hockey? Consciously set aside one version of Tim and dress up another, in skates or a suit as the situation demanded? Which one was real, and which one was an act?

If he could do it, so could she. She forced herself to stop thinking, to just feel the rhythm of the music, concentrating on his gaze, steady and self-possessed. He sent her away and drew her in again; unravelled her, and reeled her right back, her spine tight to his chest, his breath warm in her ear. She was sure he kept her there longer than he should have before he segued to something else, but that might have just been her wishing he had. Each time he reminded *look at me* it sent a whisper trickling over her skin, the tiny hairs all on end. Then *breathe* — like that was an option.

"Now the dip," he said.

Further cues were lost in the rush of blood to her ears as she tightened her core and tried to let go, the brace of his thigh at her back the only thing that stopped her from hitting the floor as she clutched him. This wasn't how it was supposed to be; she was off balance, not graceful or sexy. He could drop her any second — like she'd dropped him.

"Trust me."

Did she? She nodded, sucking in a breath, keeping her eyes locked to his.

His hands shifted to reposition her, so she was more stable, but she used that steadiness to grasp the front of his shirt, tugging him toward her. The shirt had too much give, and he remained rooted, keeping her suspended.

"I don't want to dance anymore," she whispered, and maybe it was wrong to make herself heavy; unfair to let herself collapse, testing his strength. But it wasn't altogether fair of him, doing this, was it?

A raised eyebrow, a pursing of his lips; then he gave in, lowering her, his face finally close enough she could lace her fingers through his hair and eliminate the gap. One of his hands slid to the floor to brace his weight, and she didn't care if she should or shouldn't, she was going to do it either way: reset the straight-line press of his lips by interrupting it with her own.

He eased her the rest of the way down, the slate tile cool against her back, his mouth warm and accommodating on hers, and she held on to her complete denial for as long as she could, drinking him in until she couldn't take it anymore.

She thrust him away and scrambled out from under him,

propping herself against the cupboards, panting. After braining their way through this, coming to such a grown-up decision, she couldn't let herself cave to attraction alone. Good to know it was there, though. Or maybe not.

"Sorry," she said. "But I hate this."

He mirrored her, slumping into the fridge, and reached for her hand; a dangerous move. But she let him pull her into him, no longer anything formal about the way he encircled her with his arms.

"My mother always said you have to really hate something to change it," he murmured into her hair.

But there was another saying about accepting what you couldn't change, and that was where they needed to be.

CHAPTER THIRTY-ONE

HE DIDN'T MIND RISING LONG before dawn. He even insisted on cramming himself into the back seat of the Porsche — if it could be called a back seat — Liv and Nate riding in front, not even dozing as he listened to them discussing the morning to come. It meant one last visit to this fascinating place where horses lived in the midst of the country's largest city.

As the grooms prepared the first set to train, he cleaned their feed tubs and water buckets, then followed Nate and Liv when they headed to the main track. Nate rode Jay, the big chestnut superstar. Now that Tim knew that's what the orange colour was called, he paid attention to the variations. Some of them were burnt orange; some, like Reba, were brighter; others, more faded. Liv was on Paz, the pony. He didn't question the strange vocabulary of this place anymore, like why they called the horses who didn't race, ponies. Even he knew a pony was a small version of a horse — except on the backstretch. Here it wasn't about height. It was about occupation.

Jay was breezing, which meant he got to go fast today. Not racing fast, but a sprint to sharpen his speed, while the daily longer, slower work built stamina. Conditioning was something Tim had no trouble understanding. He parked himself on the rail, weathering greetings from others present who he may or may not have met before, listening to their stories as he watched. Horses being good. Horses being bad. All of them beautiful.

In a few minutes Jay flashed by, vibrant coat glinting in the rising sun with Nate curled, impossibly still, on his back. Then he was gone, disappearing down the training surface until he reappeared minutes later, travelling much slower, Nate standing in the short, short stirrups holding the reins relaxed in front of the saddle. When Jay came off the track he looked pumped and ready for whatever they asked of him next. Tim had overheard the plan about England; somewhere called Ascot that made everyone's eyes large and sparkly when they talked about it. He kept meaning to look it up and wondered how crazy it was that they put horses on airplanes and flew them all over the world.

Nate left once he got off Jay, promising to be back in time to take Tim to the airport. Part of him wished something would happen to make him miss his flight — except it would only delay the inevitable. At least he knew what he was leaving behind, just not what he was returning to.

When he followed Reba out to the training track, Marie riding her, he couldn't help thinking of Emilie — as if she ever left his mind. He'd hoped she'd reconsider taking him to the airport. She hadn't.

He missed Emilie's camera, too; the filly silhouetted against the rising sun as she came around the turn, layers of orange and yellow and brown like a postcard. The ones he took with his phone would have to do. Once Reba galloped past he flipped through the images, selecting the best one; cropped it, tweaked it, opened up the messaging app. Then he scrolled all the way back to March, and Emilie's name, hesitating with the memory of it before pressing his finger to the screen, their last conversation popping up.

That lonely "?" in the bubble on her side lingered, the previous one asking, *Are you okay?* stirring his old guilt. He liked to think he'd overcome that in person and made a conscious decision to step past it. Messaging the photo to Emilie was an unspoken plea to keep communicating with the one who'd put a stop to their exchanges in the first place. He kept checking on the walk back to the barn, hoping she'd respond with something, anything. She didn't.

Sue gave him Reba to walk after her bath and he and the placid filly toured the shedrow together, Tim not bothering to watch the clock posted in the tack room. They went round and round until Sue asked him to come outside onto the apron in front of the barn where she hosed the sand from Reba's feet, carefully dried her legs, then sent him to the lawn to let the filly graze.

He'd never thought, when he'd come here that first day, he'd become attached to the place. In just a few weeks he'd learned to love it. The more he found out about the horses, the more he wanted to get to know them. The crew in and around the Triple Stripe barn had adopted him as one of their own — Nate's little brother was their little brother. He wasn't naïve; he knew there were plenty of sketchy types on the backstretch, and not everyone treated their horses the way they were treated here, but the overall impression was a positive one. They worked hard, all of them, but horses and humans were both part of the family.

Even Faye showed up later in the morning with coffees and pastries, including a care package for Tim to take on the plane. No Emilie with her, though. Nate appeared, grabbing one of the cups but resisted the pastry.

"Time to go?" Nate posed it as a question, but it was merely fact, so all Tim could do was nod. He didn't even ask if he could drive the Porsche. He endured the goodbyes from Faye, Liv and the crew when it would have been easier to avoid them.

He was surprised when Nate took the car to the parking garage instead of turfing him out at the curb. It made his departure seem monumental, like even though Nate had gone on about the summer only being halfway over, he didn't actually believe Tim would return any time soon. The closer Tim got to getting on the plane, the more he resigned himself to that being the case.

It seemed stupid to be here so early when he'd checked in online and didn't have to board for an hour, but he was glad of the chance to spend just a little more time with his brother.

"How are you feeling?" Nate asked once they'd found a place to sit.

He surprised himself with his own honesty. "I'm scared."

Nate nodded. "I get that. I was the same way last fall, coming back after my injury. I didn't know if I'd be able to be competitive anymore. Thought I might be done."

"Obviously you weren't."

"You're not, either. I didn't have enough time to really whip you into shape, but you don't have to be embarrassed about your condition. You know you're not going to fall over when you step on the ice." Nate grinned.

A hint of a smile lifted his lips. "It was fun, with the kids. I'm glad we got to do that."

"Me too," Nate said. "Sorry we never managed any sightseeing."

"That's okay." It wasn't as if he felt he'd been deprived. He shifted in his seat, sliding his eyes to Nate. "So what do I do now?"

Nate still nursed his coffee, rotating the cup in his hands

"About Emilie? I wish I had that answer for you, other than, wait it out. Talk to Mom, maybe. That's the best advice I can give."

Another thing he'd pushed to the background crept to the forefront. "I'm worried about Mom and Dad, Nate."

He felt a stillness, like there was a bubble around them the air had been sucked from, Nate's voice losing its resonance when he said, "What do you mean?"

"Something's just not right. It's like they've been avoiding each other."

"That's not really unusual, is it? They're always done their own thing," Nate insisted. "They're fine. Mom would have said something."

"Don't be so sure."

Nate sat up, twisting toward him. "You should have told me, Tim. That's not something to carry all by yourself."

"I should have told you," he agreed. "I'm sorry. But now you know."

Nate leaned back, sinking into the chair. "Guess I'll have to ask some direct questions next time I call her. Not that there's anything either of us can really do about it."

Tim watched him crush the empty coffee cup. Now Nate could feel helpless too, though it wasn't a burden Tim felt better about sharing.

"Well — I guess I can't put this off any longer," Tim said, glancing at the time, standing slowly. "Thank you. I didn't know how much I needed this."

Nate was smiling as he broke off their hug. "When I asked if you'd come, I was just being selfish, so I'm glad it worked out that way. Keep us posted on how things go, okay" The way their eyes connected, Tim could tell Nate was talking about their parents as much as his career. "I'm sure you'll do great, but I'm going to miss you."

"Yeah. I'll miss you too." *I'll miss all of it.*

He was still looking for Emilie when he waved goodbye to Nate, vainly hoping she'd show at the last minute. She didn't.

She heard the ping just as she stuffed her phone into her pocket before leading Excursion out and paused. Who could ignore a Messenger notification? Not her. Maybe it was someone who would cheer her up with a stupid meme or video.

Instead, it was Tim. An attachment; not words she could preview without opening it. The last time she'd had a message from him it had been something seemingly insignificant — the one before she learned he'd been sent to the minors. The one before he'd ghosted her. This was not something that would cheer her up, so as it turned out, she could ignore a Messenger notification.

She didn't do it to be mean, or to pay him back for that time, but she wasn't ready to return to that easy thing they'd had before. How could it ever be the same? Part of her wished he'd texted her instead, because she could look at what he'd sent without him knowing. If she opened this attachment, he'd know she'd seen it, and right now, she didn't want him to know. Maybe she did want to be mean, just a little. Just for a time, so he could understand how it had felt, having a message hanging in cyberspace, unacknowledged.

"It's up to you to cheer me up, Curtis," she said, giving the gelding a light smack on the neck and pulling the reins over his head to lead him to the outdoor ring. Except she was worried even that wouldn't happen, because it was Tim who had started calling him Curtis, so she couldn't think of one without the other.

It was time to start advertising the gelding so she could find his forever person — before she became any more attached. No keeping Tim. No keeping Curtis. To do so in either case would be selfish.

"Change of plans, buddy," she said, leaving the gate open when she walked toward the mounting block. Going on a hack was the thing to do at times like this.

Today was day one. Day one of moving on. No more feeling sorry for herself.

They meandered around the farm, stopping and standing near the pasture with this year's filly-foals and their mothers, easily picking out the flashy dark bay from the group that cantered over and clustered at the fence. Léa was Liv's next great hope, daughter of the mare she'd dropped out of vet school for, Claire.

Claire hadn't bothered to follow her precocious daughter, grazing lazily a distance away, secure in the bond she shared with her firstborn. Léa's personality was emerging; more like her sensible mother than her saucy father, Just Lucky, which was a relief for all concerned — because Just Lucky's foals had earned a reputation of being spicy, the most famous of them Chique, who'd been quirkiness defined as a racehorse. They awaited Chique's first baby, due the end of January, with a complex combination of excitement and trepidation because the stallion she'd been bred to had a reputation of his own.

She did a little conditioning set on the perimeter of the hay field: *trot, walk, trot, walk, trot, gallop, trot, walk.* Curtis ticked all the boxes for a good event prospect. He loved to hack; he was a great mover, and was proving to be a careful but keen jumper. When she sold him, he would fetch a decent price. Thanks to the resurgence in popularity of Thoroughbreds because of the big retired racehorse makeover in Kentucky, getting a sound horse for a dollar off the track was mostly unheard of these days.

She'd miss him, but there would always be another project horse.

She'd miss Tim, but would there be another guy like him?

Walking home she waved to the barn staff and Kerrie as they finished up the broodmare barn, the tractor chugging along, pulling the manure spreader. Curtis acknowledged with pricked ears, then returned his attention to the path before him, setting an example she should follow: looking ahead, not back.

She gave him a proper bath with soap instead of merely a hose-off, and after schooling the New Chapter horses, did a little training with Holly before sitting down in front of the computer to check some more tasks off her show prep list. On a break, she ended up on a job website after absently viewing her socials, out of curiosity typing in "physiotherapist." Location: Calgary. She hadn't thought she was considering it, but how could she not? It wasn't as if it was Australia. If she went out there, and it didn't work out, she could easily come back. The search returned several jobs.

He would be in the air still. If she were a nice person, she would look at his message; see what he'd sent. At least give him that, if not a response. On the other hand, would it help either of them right now?

So she resisted. She wouldn't look; ask how he was doing. Because if it was anything like her, she didn't want to know.

<hr>

On the surface, nothing seemed different back at the house in Calgary. Mom hugged him and fussed over him when she picked him up at the airport, a massive veggie lasagne with cheesy garlic bread waiting for him at home. Comfort food. Did she know?

Dad was working late, Mom saying he'd understand if he

didn't see Tim till tomorrow, because he was jetlagged and wanted to get to bed. Nothing unusual there. As he ate, he told Mom all about the horses and Holly; about Nate and Liv and the races — but he couldn't talk about Emilie, so he left her out, which felt terribly wrong because she was such a massive part of all of it.

"I think I will go to bed now," he said, after helping her clean up. "I was up pretty early."

She held him tight. "It's good to have you home."

He swallowed hard, and just nodded, because he wasn't sure it was good to be home, but he couldn't say it to her. At least he hadn't come home to find Dad had moved out. Somehow between him and Nate, they'd learn what was going on, even if, as Nate had pointed out, it was out of their control.

There was no reason to sleep in the guest room — he'd left the crutches to collect dust in Nate and Liv's garage in Ontario. The basement was cool and too quiet and he didn't unpack, leaving his bags by the bed and opening his laptop, already knowing there was no response from Emilie. It wasn't as if the website would tell him a different story from his phone but he checked it anyway. Nothing.

He stalked her profile for updates, but there were none, and nothing on Instagram, either. Maybe that was good, because it meant she was sad, and missing him like he was missing her. Or maybe her life had just reabsorbed her, the busyness taking her back, leaving no room for pining.

One thing he'd decided on the flight — he needed to move out. Staying here, obsessing over Mom and Dad, did neither him nor them any favours, so he spent a few minutes scrolling through apartment rentals. Whether he played for the farm team or the NHL franchise, he'd be based in Calgary, so at least he'd be close to home. He was meeting his agent for coffee — or not-coffee, in his case — because Erik had texted he had something he wanted to talk to Tim about, and it needed to be in person.

Coffee made him think of Emilie.

He set the laptop aside and pulled his novel and notebook from his bag. He could rely on the novel for a happy ending, at least — it wasn't his first time through that story. The abandoned lyrics, badly written, hadn't been reworked and staring at them now didn't seem to help. Instead, he copied them, word for word, into the response box under his unnoticed photo from early this morning. If Emilie decided to look, maybe she would laugh.

CHAPTER THIRTY-TWO

THE SKY WAS BLUE; the footing was dry, and a cooling breeze drifted from the northwest. She couldn't have asked for a more perfect day for the New Chapter Charity Horse Show.

Except for one thing.

She hadn't really expected him to appear; she'd only hoped. Eventually she'd looked at his message — she wasn't any good at ghosting. The photo from the morning he'd left was pretty, and the poem had made her snort. Then they'd kind of fallen back into their old rhythm after all, when she'd responded, *What was that?* And he'd said, *I don't know.* Feelings were best left out of their communication right now, so they didn't go there. He was busy; she was busy. That was enough to know.

This charity show was the culmination of her dreams, her passion, and she was already planning for the future. It just would have been a bonus if it could have included that little something extra that his presence — here, and in her life — would have brought.

Her mile-long checklist was mostly a series of lines drawn

through items at this point. The sand ring was perfectly harrowed with a freshly painted dressage ring perimeter and letters in place. The show jumping course was set in the paddock next to it with the fence line temporarily altered so the riders would jump into a larger field with half a dozen cross-country jumps. Jumps Tim had designed and made. She missed him. So much.

The New Chapter board of directors had agreed to the expanded concept for the show, so there were two divisions: the celebrity riders, and the graduates. The celebrity group was small, but they'd come out of the woodwork for the graduate division and a stream of spectators begged her to do another show open to all retired racehorses, not just New Chapter grads — so as soon as this event was under her belt, she'd plan the next one; for the fall, maybe. She had to keep her mind from racing off, thinking of the classes they could add. Line classes for conformation. Maybe a trick class to inspire those whose horses couldn't be ridden. They could hold it around Halloween and offer a costume class. Down the road, she envisioned a Canadian version of the American Thoroughbred makeover challenge.

Once she stopped laughing at Nate and the other male jockeys in traditional English riding habits, she thought they did really well. Their dressage test was a simple walk-trot, then they did a mini jump course and a couple of small cross-country fences — nothing that would tax either them or their horses but still entertaining for the crowd. Braveness was not an issue for the jockeys; equitation was another story. Liv and Cory kicked their butts in that department — they'd both shown as teenagers — but the men were good sports.

The graduates all seemed to be having a good time, and Emilie watched with undeniable envy. One day, maybe she'd be out there herself. She and Curtis probably could have handled the lowest level — but someone was coming to see him tomorrow, thanks to Tim's wonderful photos. She didn't expect to have him for much longer.

"Here, Em."

She glanced over her shoulder to see Liv, still dressed in tall boots and breeches from her earlier ride, holding out a bag.

Emilie peeked in. White breeches, a show shirt and black jacket. "What's this?"

"Go change. You're up," Liv said.

Emilie's brow furrowed in confusion. "What are you talking about?"

"Everything's under control with the show. It's your turn. Go!"

She backed away a few steps, still staring at Liv until Liv made a shooing gesture, sending her scurrying into the training barn.

A horse stood cross-tied in the aisle and she stopped dead. Not because Excursion was there, tacked up with one hind leg cocked — but because Tim was next to him. As a kid she might've had it drilled in that you don't run around horses, but that went out the window. She ran. Curtis was an ex-racehorse. He could take it.

"You came!" she cried, her voice muffled by his shirt as she buried her face into his chest.

"I came," he said, his laugh a rumble to her ear. "We'll talk later. Go get ready."

Outfitted in the gear Liv had provided — and her own tall boots and helmet — she met him outside and checked the tack.

"Did you put this on?" She raised an eyebrow at Tim, and he nodded. It was perfect. It was true; he paid attention. She grinned, tugging on gloves. "You're hired." After he gave her a leg up, she added, "Nice job, groom."

It didn't matter that she hadn't slept much last night — all the caffeine in the world wouldn't make up for that — the surge inside her thanks to Tim and his co-conspirators wiped away all of it. There were no ribbons in this for her — she was the show organizer, after all, and announced as exhibition only — but it wasn't about that. After a too-brief warmup she trotted down the centre line, just like in her dream. *X, halt, salute.*

Liv read her test for her because there was no way she was going to remember, and Curtis did a valiant job trying to make her look good. It wasn't his fault her circles weren't quite round and her transitions were far from perfect. Everyone applauded good-naturedly when she was done.

"Quick outfit switch," Liv said as Curtis sauntered out of the ring. "Tim's got him. Take off your jacket. And your shirt."

"What?" Once again she found her jaw hanging, but she shrugged out of her jacket and passed it to her sister.

Liv dangled a long-sleeved navy sunshirt with red and white stripes down one arm and their last name on the other. "Shirt. Off."

She had a sports bra on, so she figured it wasn't that bad, but she blushed when she glanced at Tim anyway before she slipped it over her head.

"I love it." She beamed, smoothing the shirt and picking up her reins.

"Come on," Liv said. "I'll warm you up."

It was all happening so quickly, the easiest thing to do was follow her sister's direction. The way Liv methodically prepared her for the jumping portion of the short course event calmed the nerves she'd barely had time to acknowledge.

"You know the course, right?" Liv asked.

"I'd better. Jodi designed it and I did the diagrams for it." She looked down at Liv with a rush of emotion. "Thanks, Liv."

"Go have fun!"

She jogged Excursion into the ring, going over the course in her head. The surge of adrenaline from the dressage test ambush had dissipated, and her lack of sleep was catching up, but she could get around this, at least. If she found she was too exhausted to do the cross-country, there was no shame in retiring.

Curtis didn't set a foot wrong, making up for her inadequacies, taking her to the fences like he'd been doing it his whole life. These little jumps were child's play to him and he didn't touch a single rail. When she pointed him to the gap in the fence line with the low log, his ears pricked and she felt the racehorse in him come back out. *Uh-oh.* But she let him go and he hopped over the log easily, galloping into the field, ready for the next one.

He loved this, and his enthusiasm wore off on her; there was no way she was pulling him up. She pointed him to a cute ramp which he leapt with room to spare and she laughed, reaching forward to rub his neck with her reins in a fist.

"Good boy!" she sang, turning her head to see the next fence as he bounded across the grass. He popped over it like this was the best thing in the world, and at the moment, she agreed with him.

The endorphins were back, a grin on her lips as the wind rushed past her ears. Curtis carried her up a slight slope in the field with one fence to go. Three heights met them and he zeroed in on the biggest one. Why not? He took her there, and they soared.

"Woo-hoo!" She slapped his neck when they landed and eased him bit by bit; rocking back to a bouncy canter, then a trot and finally slowing to a walk. Her cheeks burned pink and her arms ached from his pulling but her heart felt so big it was going to burst. What a star this horse was. He'd make someone a fabulous partner.

"So much fun," she gushed as they met her — Tim, and Liv and Nate.

Barely feeling the jar as she dropped to the ground, she didn't know who to hug first. Tim handed her a bottle of water, her camera slung around his neck, and she guzzled it gratefully before kissing Curtis on the muzzle.

Then she kissed Tim quickly. "Let's cool this guy out."

He didn't seem to mind she'd kissed the horse first. She might just have to keep him.

As if that was an option. Here she was, making plans, when nothing had actually changed.

Once bathed, Curtis tore at the grass outside the training barn. Emilie didn't know where Tim had gone, just that everything seemed to be going smoothly with the show wrap-up without her supervision. Trailers drove out, Ava cleaned up the registration desk. Sylvie put away what was left of the baked goods — which wasn't much. Faye helped Will at the food truck. The café's previous owner, Lucy, had agreed to look after it for the afternoon so Faye could be here.

"I'd say that was a success," Liv said as she and Nate wandered over.

"Thank you both so much." Her smile was permanently sculpted into her face. "I couldn't have done it without you."

"It was fun," Nate said. "Except for that part where I almost lost my front teeth on a rail."

"That would have been a shame," Emilie said, grinning. "You have such nice teeth."

She aborted the conversation with her brother-in-law and sister, but how could she help it? Tim approached behind them and she let herself soak him up. She had to stop the pretending, though. The hoping. It was just nice he was here.

A dark-haired man was with him, a few inches taller and heavier than Tim. He was older, and if he wasn't a hockey player too, he probably had been one in his younger days, if his build was any indication. Tim shoved his hands in his pockets as he came up, stopping next to Emilie, the man standing between him and Nate.

"This is my agent, Erik," Tim said, then made the introductions one by one, Erik going around the circle exchanging handshakes.

Emilie tried hard not to frown, but she didn't want to like this man. She held him responsible for taking Tim away, back to Calgary, even if her sentiment was ridiculous. It wasn't the agent's fault. It wasn't anyone's fault, really.

"I have some news," Tim said.

The words made Emilie go cold; backward on such a warm, sunny day. She and Liv and Nate all stood in stoned silence, Erik looking infuriatingly cool as Tim's eyes shifted from one person to the next.

"I've been traded," he said. His eyes went to Nate instead of her. She was imagining him moving to Tennessee or Los Angeles, and he was concerned with Nate's reaction?

Tim blew out a breath. "To Toronto."

Emilie screeched and threw her arms around his torso, only vaguely aware of Liv picking up the lead rope attached to Curtis. *Oops*. Not that Curtis was going anywhere when there was a lawn to trim.

"You approve?" Tim grinned as Emilie tipped her face up to his.

She laughed. "Go Leafs go?"

"Don't say that out loud, please, Em," Liv pleaded, but she was laughing. "You're going to give Papa a heart attack if you ever say that in his presence."

"Speaking of which, I'm assuming Dad knows?" Nate's original look of shock had softened to a wry grin. "What hospital is he in?"

Tim pulled one of his arms from Emilie and swung it at Nate as if he was going to hit him, but it turned into some kind of hand-clasp fist-bump shake. "He's going to live, they think."

"Congratulations." Emilie snaked her hands to his neck and pulled him down, meeting his lips.

When they came up for air, he brushed away the hair that had fallen onto her face. "One more bit of news."

She tilted her head as he slipped a hand around hers, then turned her like one of those dance moves that night in the kitchen. He wrapped an arm loosely around her abdomen and Liv held out the rope attached to Curtis's halter. Tim took it, and placed it in Emilie's hand.

"Congratulations yourself," he said, his lips against her ear.

She tried to look over her shoulder at him. Was this some kind of joke? "What are you talking about?"

"He's yours."

She gaped, staring at Liv. "Really? But —"

Liv nodded. "Tim bought him for you."

Curtis reached the edge of the patch of grass and lifted his head, smearing his mouth against her white breeches. She laughed, breaking away from Tim to enfold the gelding's neck in a hug, then turned, lacing her fingers over the bridge of his nose and pressing her lips to his muzzle.

"I don't know what to say." Warm tears pricked her eyes, and she blinked them away, meeting Tim's gaze. "Except I guess you can afford fancy off-track Thoroughbreds on your new salary." She grinned.

His lips crimped enough to show his dimple. "Your sister gave me a pretty good deal. That reminds me. I still have to pay for him." He reached into his pocket and flipped a coin toward Liv. She grabbed it from the air and tucked the one-dollar piece into her pocket with a nod and a grin.

"That is a deal," Emilie said, sliding her eyes to Liv.

Liv shrugged. "Family rate."

Curtis shoved her rudely with his head, but he knocked Emilie into Tim, so she forgave him. She kissed Tim again and whispered, "You're the best."

EPILOGUE

THE WINTERS' cottage was as wonderful as she remembered it from last summer, only better. Holly was here this time. Chad had all but slapped himself in the forehead when he'd learned she had a dog.

"Of course she would've been welcome. I wish you'd asked."

But maybe things wouldn't have happened as they had, then. Emilie wasn't looking back anymore. Only ahead.

Tim had impressed the Toronto coach and management enough in training camp last summer and continued to do so in the pre-season, earning himself a spot in the Leaf's starting lineup. He wasn't their leading scorer — not yet — but he'd secured a spot on the team. He was still away a lot — Emilie rarely travelled with him because she had her responsibilities on the farm and at work and with New Chapter — but such was the life of a hockey girlfriend.

Excursion was progressing so well most of the time Emilie felt she was holding him back, and wondered some days if he'd have been better off with an advanced rider, but Liv assured her Curtis was always going to be happiest staying with the people on the farm where he'd been born. Athletic pursuits were secondary. Last weekend they'd done their first official event and even taken home a ribbon. So it had been green, and they'd only been competing at pre-entry but she didn't care. She'd had a blast. But when she returned from this cottage trip, she was starting dressage boot camp with Jodi because dressage was their weakness and she was determined to improve their score in the sandbox.

From the beach Tim threw the orange street hockey ball into the water, Holly bounding after it, pushing off the sandy bottom, her tail balancing her as she swam. She snatched it expertly, carrying it back to him in her mouth, releasing it to his hand.

Chad puttered about the boat, putting the ski rope on while Sylvie tossed the life vests onto the dock. Tim was determined this year he was going to try one ski, and Emilie thought she might give those short fat trick skis a go. Two of them, though. Sylvie was content to maintain her position as designated lookout.

Sylvie's plan for a summer fling last year hadn't worked out. Instead, she'd gradually accepted a steady blooming of affection for the veterinarian who proved he really was seeking something more permanent. She'd moved from Montreal, transferring her studies to the University of Toronto.

After dinner it was Chad and Sylvie's turn to wash up so Emilie took Holly for a stroll to the point and back again, ending up on the big rock. She parked herself on a ledge, looking out at the lake as the sun began its spectacular descent. Soon Tim joined her, and they watched the colours become more brilliantly saturated as the giant orb sank to the horizon, a dazzling orange strip reflecting across the water.

He found her fingers and laced his through them, the

gesture still melting her because he wasn't big on physical exhibitions, enduring her public displays of affection. They were alone here, though, except for Holly. Emilie dropped her head to his shoulder and settled into his arms.

"You know I love you, right?" he said.

She tilted her head just enough to catch his eyes and smiled. "That doesn't mean I get tired of hearing it."

He bumped her off his shoulder and grinned. "I have another question for you. Holly, go find it!"

Emilie laughed as her Lab tore off to find whatever toy she'd abandoned. One or the other of them was always breaking off to cater to Holly. "What's your question?"

Her Lab's return distracted her before he said anything more. Holly did have something in her mouth, but it wasn't a toy. It wasn't a pinecone. It wasn't a branch.

Emilie couldn't breathe. Her heart stopped. Her brain threatened to follow suit.

Holly wriggled in front of her, sitting squarely, tipping her muzzle up with a blue velvet box clenched carefully between her teeth.

"Ask her for it," Tim murmured.

Emilie made the request, her voice trembling as shaking hands clasped the box. She was barely aware of Tim slipping the dog a treat as he said, "Open it."

He was sliding down next to Holly as he said it and Emilie closed her eyes tight. She was going to cry. At least it was the cottage; she didn't have makeup on. She wouldn't end up looking like a raccoon. Maybe she should just accept all the emotion and give in.

She cracked the box open slowly, afraid and thrilled all at once. The ring was a modest-sized diamond in a beautiful setting of white gold, because he had good taste, didn't he? Just like his brother. He would have known she'd have berated him if he'd spent the percentage of his salary he was supposed to on a precious stone. It would have been huge, and she led a practical life. She couldn't be weighted down by something like that. This was perfect.

"What's your question?" she whispered, blinking away her tears as she met his eyes, resting on one knee before her with a hand reaching for hers, his other arm pulling Holly against him. The Lab licked him and he had to regain his composure before speaking.

"Emilie. Will you marry me?"

Yep, she was bawling. She slipped off the rock ledge and threw her arms around his neck, kissing it, then his cheek, then finally his lips, saying over and over, "Yes, yes, yes, yes. Forever and ever, yes."

In the middle of it all, she'd failed to hang onto the box. Holly picked it up dutifully and shoved her nose between them.

"I think you need to put it on," Tim said.

He accepted the box from the Lab this time, and removed the ring, easing it onto Emilie's finger. All Emilie could do was stare at it in wonder until she had to kiss him again.

"The pressure's really on Faye now," she said, laughing.

The sun had dipped below the horizon leaving a brilliant splash of colour on the dappled clouds above the treeline; yellows and pinks and purples blending into the deepening blue of the sky. The first stars were visible overhead, and there were meteor showers expected later. If they didn't wait right here — which was entirely possible — they'd be back.

The novelist writing the story of her life had gone back and done revisions, giving her even more than she'd thought she'd ever wanted. She still had the perfect job, and the perfect friends and family — and of course the perfect dog. But now she had the perfect horse, and the perfect man, and the happily ever after to go with it.

All the best things.

I hope you enjoyed All The Best Things. Reviews on your favourite retailer, as well as on BookBub, are always appreciated! They feed authors, which lets us keep writing more books for you. It doesn't have to be long — pick some stars and write a few words!

For news on latest releases, free books, sample chapters and a peek into my life be sure to sign up for my newsletter at

https://www.lindashantz.com/writes

Join my Patreon to read as I write!

https://www.patreon.com/lindashantz

THE END

ACKNOWLEDGMENTS

Thanks first of all to Adeline Halvorson, who agreed to read and offer feedback chapter-by-chapter as I wrote the second draft. Her insight into ballroom dancing was integral, and errors are my own. In addition to being an amazing artist, Adeline has also published a cookbook for those wishing to consume more plant-based meals. The recipes are also gluten and dairy-free, so it's a useful add to your library for when you might need to cook for someone with those restrictions! ***What Do I Cook? Quick and Easy Plant-Based Recipes that are Gluten-free, Dairy-Free and Budget-Friendly*** is available in paperback, hardcover and e-book.

Jackie Bellamy-Zions loaned me her persona as the motor-cycle-riding event coach and checked my riding scenes. While it hasn't been as long since I've had a lesson with Jackie as it has been for Emilie in the book, I appreciated her updated thoughts on what I'd written. In addition to being a certified Level 2 Eventing coach in Canada, Jackie has her judges card for dressage. Sometimes the resemblance in a book to real-life people is not a coincidence!

Once again I'm grateful to my beta readers, who take time out of their own busy schedules to provide invaluable help. They keep me on track with details and readability and help catch stray typos (though some inevitably make it through, so if you see one, don't be shy about emailing me). Thank you,

Allison Litfin, Nathalie Drolet, Ingrid Shantz and Kristen Frederick DVM (who also makes sure my veterinary details are right).

And thanks go out once again to my early readers, June Monteleone, Ariana Feldberg, Sharrell Kline and Mary Hatheway.

If you're reading this, thank you, too! I hope you'll consider leaving a review to share your thoughts with other readers. You can also email me at the address below.

If you're interested in joining my review team for future books, email me at linda@lindashantz.com

ABOUT THE AUTHOR

I began working at the racetrack before I finished high school, and after graduating the following January, took a hotwalking job at Payson Park in Florida. Once back at Woodbine, I started grooming and galloping. While the backstretch is exciting, I found I was more at home on the farm — prepping and breaking yearlings, nightwatching and foaling mares. Eventually I started my own small layup/broodmare facility, and in the last few years I've transitioned into retraining and rehoming. Somewhere along the way I did go back to school and get a degree. I should probably dust it off and frame it one day!

I live on a small farm in Ontario, Canada, with my adopted off-track Thoroughbreds and a young Border Collie, and I'm probably better known for painting horses than writing about them — if you like my covers, check out my artwork at www.lindashantz.com

Made in the USA
Coppell, TX
21 October 2023

23158101R00164